THE
LAST STAGE
TO BOSQUE
REDONDO

[signature] 8/7/2017

GARY L. STUART

BOOK THREE IN THE ANGUS SERIES

For information about this title or to order other books and/or electronic media, contact the publisher:
Gleason & Wall Publishers
7000 N. 16th Street, Suite 120, PBM 470, Phoenix, AZ 85020
www.garylstuart.com
gary.stuart@garylstuart.com

ISBN: 978-0-9863441-4-5 (Print)
       978-0-9863441-5-2 (eBook)

Printed in the United States of America

Cover and Interior design: 1106 Design, Phoenix, AZ

Other Books by Gary L. Stuart

The Ethical Trial Lawyer

The Gallup 14

Miranda—The Story Of America's Right To Remain Silent

*Innocent Until Interrogated—The True Story of the
Buddhist Temple Massacre and The Tucson Four*

AIM For The Mayor—Echoes From Wounded Knee

Anatomy of a Confession—The Debra Milke Case

Ten Shoes Up

The Valles Caldera

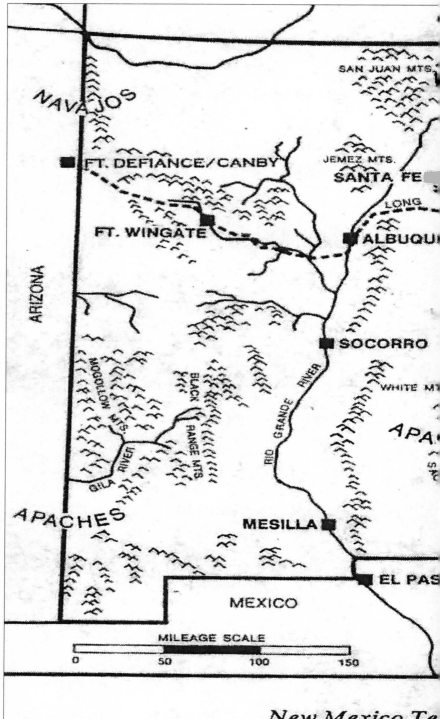

New Mexico Te

RADO

KANSAS

^^^^ OS

SANTA FE TRAIL

KIOWAS

FT. UNION

LAS VEGAS

OF NAVAJOS

CANADIAN RIVER

FT. BASCOM

FT. SUMNER

LLANO

BOSQUE REDONDO RESERVATION

PECOS

ESTACADO

COMANCHES

T. STANTON

PECOS RIVER

VALLEY

GUADALUPE MTS.

N

TEXAS

c. c

ry in the 1860s

CHAPTER 1

Chama, New Mexico–1888– Angus Gets a Telegram

I WAS OUT BACK, TALKING TO my horses, ignoring the mules, and speculating on the sunrise when Jill called from the porch, "Angus, there's a boy here with a telegram for you. Try not to break a leg jumpin' over the corral rail when you come get it."

"Is he out front?"

"Yes, darlin', just don't startle him, he looks still half asleep."

The sun had just peeked at us over the notch in Ten Shoes Up twenty-five miles east of the Rio Chama on a crisp Friday morning. I'd planned on spending the day repairing tack and studying a new map the by-god U.S. government survey boys sent to me. They said it showed "precise detail" of the Toltec Gorge. I was hoping to ride the gorge next week, but the telegram cast a shadow on that. It was from Sheriff Ramsey. I knew that because he's the only man that'd ever sent me a telegram.

"Morning, Bernie," I said to the pink-cheeked boy sitting on the hitching rail in front of Jill's barn.

"Morning, Marshal," he breezed back at me through a gap in his front teeth. "It's from Denver, Colorado and Sheriff Bo String said you'd be grinning just to see the envelope. What's he mean by that, Marshal?"

"Never mind, Bernie, just you hand it over and trot back up to the sheriff's office. I expect he's about ready to go for breakfast, and he'll take you with him if you hurry."

He handed it over and then stood back waiting to hear the news so he could tell Bo, so Bo could tell the whole damn town. But I dashed that plan by sticking the telegram in my vest pocket and giving him a good bye over my shoulder as I went into the big cavern of a barn.

Sliding my finger under the flap, I was pleased to see that Jill's speculation was right.

MAY 15, 1888 TO: US DEPUTY MARSHAL ANGUS ESPERRAZA—CHAMA NEW MEXICO—STOP—FROM US MARSHAL GEORGE RAMSEY—DENVER COLORADO—STOP—ATTENTION—NEW ASSIGNMENT—MARCH 1, 1888—STOP—YOU ARE TO REPAIR TO FORT MARCY, SANTA FE NEW MEXICO—LEAD AND ESCORT GOVERNMENT PARTY FROM FORT DEFIANCE ARIZONA TO FORT SUMNER NEW MEXICO—350 MILES—STAGE COACH ESCORT—OFFICIAL BUSINESS— STOP—MORE DETAILS IN LETTER ON WAY TO YOU STOP —TWO MONTHS' SALARY PLUS EXPENSES—PROVIDE PRIVATE STOCK—STOP REPLY YOUR SOONEST STOP

Trying to suppress a grin, I handed the telegram to Jill and stood more or less at attention while she read it.

"Why does he always say that?" she asked.

"Say what?"

"Your soonest. It's so old fashioned and formal. From what little I know of your sometimes benefactor, he's a lawman, not a fussy bureaucrat."

"Well, I don't expect he writes the damn things himself. He'd assign that to Mrs. Kittering, the bureaucrat who guards his front door from the likes of people like me. That sounds like her—bossing everyone around, including Marshal Ramsey himself. What do you think of the assignment?"

"It sounds like he knows you spent most of the winter in the barn, except for two short hunting trips, plus you took one three-day ride to see the spring run-off last week, and that you're itching to mount up and ride again. It's in your nature and in his best interest. I do hope you won't have to shoot anyone."

Jill and I got married three years ago, following the gun-fight up in the Valles Caldera. She was a gunsmith and a much better shot than I was. Since then, we loved one another and nobody got shot. I'd been deputized three times to gather up suspects on federal arrest warrants, but none of them took me into new territory. I'd ridden down the Rio Colorado eight or nine years back. A trip that took me across the upper part of Arizona, but not close to Fort Defiance. And I'd ridden the Rio Cimarron and the Rio Pecos, but not as far south as Fort Sumner. So, I was real happy to get the chance. Setting my hat down tight against the morning frost, I walked up to the Western Union office at the train station to send a reply to Marshal Ramsey.

MARCH 1, 1888 STOP To US MARSHAL GEORGE RAMSEY
STOP FROM US DEPUTY MARSHAL ANGUS ESPERRAZA STOP GOT
YOUR TELEGRAM STOP ASSIGNMENT ACCEPTED STOP WILL AWAIT
YOUR LETTER STOP

A week later, I was surprised to find Marshal Ramsey himself knocking on the front door to the barn just after dark. He looked tuckered out, in need of food and drink, and excited about something. Picking up his valise, I asked him where he'd come from and why he was here. He gave me the straight of it in three sentences.

"I rode the train, like anyone with good sense. Who except you would ride a horse from Denver to Chama? I'm here to talk to you about that telegram I sent."

Once inside, I introduced him to Jill, who spun some of her magic on him right off.

"Marshal Ramsey, I cannot tell you how wonderful it is to meet the man who lets Angus stay home most of the time, but makes sure he gets out once in a while to chase felons running away from federal judges. Angus showed me your telegram about a 350-mile horse ride across most of New Mexico. Are you riding with him?"

"No ma'am, sorry to say I'm not. But I got a letter from the people in Washington, DC, and took it as an opportunity for a short trip myself. My idea of a fine excursion out of the office is the train ride from Denver to here through the Toltec Gorge. It's a mighty fine way to enjoy some of the best country on God's green earth. And it presented a chance to meet you, a woman I think gets credit for stabilizing this young man of yours."

We'd already had what Jill called an early supper, but George was awful hungry, so he and I went up the street to the only saloon in town to get him a steak and me a little something to sip on while it was cooking. I told him right off that I was happy to get the chance to take a long ride through new country, even if it didn't involve high mountain ridges.

"Thought you'd jump on this like a horse fly on a fat mule's behind. But I have to tell you right off, this is an odd damn thing."

"Sounded odd to me, too. An escort? You want me to escort a stage coach 350 miles? What's the U.S. Marshal's office in Colorado got to do with that?"

"First off, the assignment is coming from my office only as a courtesy to the U.S. Treasury Department in Washington. I got a little packet in the mail giving me a sketch, and I do mean only a sketch, as to what they're up to. Washington is always up to something, don't you know? And it rarely makes any sense to me. Here's all I know. My boss at the Justice Department is coordinating this with the U.S. Treasury Department. Both are lending a hand to the Smithsonian Institution back there, and they asked for help on what they said was a writing and research project covering some unpleasant business that happened twenty years ago."

"Unpleasant? That's what they said? I know you got a U.S. mint in Denver. Is that why the Treasury Department called your office? What's that have to do with New Mexico? And why me?"

"First off, they didn't pick you. I did. They asked me to recommend a good man that could ride a horse a long way across the whole damn New Mexico territory. They wanted a sworn deputy to give safe passage for the people in the stage-coach. Hell, I don't know. I asked what kind of research and they said mostly it's just a report after-the-fact. Twenty years after, to be exact. I'd never heard of it, but it involved putting Indians in a camp they called Bosque Redondo, over at Fort Sumner. You ever heard about that?"

"Indians in a camp? No, can't say as I did. What kind of Indians?"

"They said it started out with Apaches from New Mexico and then the U.S. Army added Navajos from Arizona. Here's the crazy part—they said the Army marched those Navajos 350 miles across the desert from Fort Defiance west of you, to Fort Sumner east of you. And there was a whole bunch of 'em. You ever been to either fort?"

"No, I mostly avoid military forts and other places where somebody is always in charge. I rode the San Juan River once from the New Mexico border west through Utah land over to where it empties into the Rio Colorado. Just one trip, scouting with some Utes and a troop of soldiers out of Fort Garland. But we didn't get to Fort Defiance. Never heard of it before your telegram. I heard of Fort Sumner a few years ago. Seems like it was about a rancher down there who bought the land when the Army closed the fort. Coulda been fifteen years ago."

"Angus, you're close on your dates. I had Mrs. Kittering look it up. She talked to a woman who was married to an officer at Fort Marcy in Santa Fe, where the U.S. Army general that runs things in New Mexico lives. The woman was visiting kin in Denver and knew about the research project the Smithsonian was planning. Said her husband was not keen on it. Said Fort

Sumner was decommissioned in eighteen and sixty-nine, and Fort Marcy was happy to see it go. Her husband ain't going on the ride, but told a little about it. This stagecoach you're escorting will stop at where Fort Sumner used to be twenty years ago. I think he said there's a nice little ranch there now. Don't know the particulars, except that you'll have to figure out the same track the Army used to herd those Navajos all the damn way across New Mexico twenty years ago; they want to see the same country, only twenty years later."

"How many Navajos?"

"I asked that but they seemed a mite confused on the number. It was eight-thousand or maybe ten-thousand men, women, and children. All of 'em on foot. The soldiers were mounted cavalry. Not all of the Navajos survived the trip. Put me in mind of you—never walk when you can ride—and never ride short. Right?"

"George, it's perfect. Horseback for 350 miles, following an Indian track and a bunch of soldiers. But I don't have a sense of why this is happening, or why the Army can't retrace its own tracks."

"You got the nub of it, right there, Angus. The Army is not running this show and is probably suspicious of it. The short version I got involves Kit Carson—you heard of him, right?"

"Yeah, old Indian fighter—some say Indian killer—but it's not a history I know very well."

"The Smithsonian Institution knows history—about the Army, the Indian Wars, Kit Carson, and something else, too. The man on the phone asked me if I knew much about what he called "Manifest Destiny.""

"Manifest what?"

"Destiny, that's what he called it. I allowed as how I'd never heard of it so he spun it out for me. Apparently as the West was opening up to Eastern settlers before the Civil War, the U.S. government got the notion that it had the God-given right to spread all the way across the entire country, from the Atlantic Ocean to the Pacific. That meant, so the man said, the government had the right to ignore laws, traditions, or cultures of folks who claimed otherwise. So the Indians, who thought the land was theirs, would have to be dealt with, one way or another. The Mescalero Apaches and the Navajos were downright stubborn about it. So they conjured up this experiment to deal with them."

"Experiment? What's that mean?"

I heard a loud noise from the kitchen and the German cook cussing about spilling something all the hell over the floor. A minute later, he brought George a well-burnt steak and said he'd be right back with another baked potato.

"This so-called experiment was thought up by a big man in New Mexico near the end of the Civil War—name of James Carleton—a general who came to Santa Fe to head off the Confederate invasion of New Mexico. Once that was done, he was named military commander of New Mexico. First thing he did was to get President Lincoln to let him establish a new fort to protect settlers in the Pecos River Valley from marauding Mescalero Apaches, Kiowa, and even some Comanche from over Oklahoma way. But soon's they let him do that, he turned it into a place to keep Indians under Army guard—called it *Bosque Redondo*. It was supposed to be a reservation, the first one in the West."

"A reservation? If they marched Indians 350 miles under armed guard, I'd say the Indians thought it was a prison, not a reservation."

"Coulda been—you know the Army ain't always straight-forward about their plans. Anyhow that's about all I know about the assignment. I figured it would be a peaceful ride for you, on government salary, and no risk to worry that pretty new wife of yours."

"She will be pleased about that, and probably won't mind getting me out of our house and out of her barn for a few weeks. Her livery and gunsmithing business is a full-time job, so she never minds when I go off and ride a mountain ridge by myself, as long as I come home after a couple weeks and don't get myself into any more shootouts with men of a hostile nature, like Mendoza Mendoza."

"Well, God knows I remember that one. It still stands as one of the most talked about gunfights any deputy of mine ever had. Still amazes me you never lost a man while managing to kill three of those bastards that tried to ambush you and Jill. Still rankles me."

"It's done, George. And this new assignment comes at a good time for me. What's the next step?"

"Well, that's another strange twist. They aim to have a pow-wow in Santa Fe soon. That's why I decided to come on down and pow-wow with you and them, in Santa Fe. Besides, I got some funding issues with the U.S. Marshal there."

"Hoowee! You're going to ride down to Santa Fe with me? We've got a little mare in the barn that . . ."

"Hell, no. I ain't riding a horse all that way. I'm taking the Overland stage down there tomorrow. You'll be getting a letter any day now from Washington about the pow-wow. I'll sit in on it with you, but then I'll take the train back up to Denver by way of Trinidad. As I get it, the meeting will be with the commanding general at Fort Marcy just north of Santa Fe. His office is helping out because the Smithsonian people are looking into Army business. But I'm told a man from the Smithsonian is in charge of the trip. He's gonna take the train from Washington to Santa Fe and get organized there, with your help. Don't let them fool you, Angus. I think there's more to this than just a report and a look-back at something the Army did, but ain't proud of anymore."

"What makes you think that?"

"Because it was not the Smithsonian that asked me to identify a lawman who could guide a wagon train. They want someone who could undertake an arrest if need be. That alone tells me there's more to this than some history professor writing a report that will make the Army look bad. It was a U.S. Treasury official who exchanged a half-dozen telegrams with me."

"Yeah, I remember you said that first off. But you never said why the Treasury was involved."

"Angus, I expect you don't know much about the other things the Treasury does besides make and keep track of money. They also are in charge of a law enforcement agency called the Secret Service Division. You heard of those boys, right?"

"A little, but I'm not sure what they do."

"They were created in 1865 to suppress counterfeit currency. Two years later, so the man on the phone said, their job was expanded to chase after scalawags who cheated the government. I asked the man what he meant. He said they go after Ku Klux Klan bastards down south, whiskey smugglers up north, and men out west involved in land or government-agency fraud. I guess they do other crimes, too; not sure about that. I think he mentioned all that so I would recommend someone like you to lend a hand—not just a horseman who could escort a stagecoach across unsettled land, but a man who can handle a gun."

"I won't be telling Jill about that last part."

"Of course. I expect it'll be a fine horse ride across some interesting country. I'll see you in Santa Fe next week."

I told George he was welcome to sleep in the barn since we did not have a spare bed in the house. He allowed as how he had not slept in a barn for twenty years and the hotel here in Chama already had a room for him.

The next morning, I had coffee with him and walked him over to the stagecoach depot. "Have Marshal Knop find me in Santa Fe when you get there. It's only a four-mile ride to Fort Marcy. We'll ride out there together."

"Is there a stage to there?" I asked with a grin.

"Don't get sassy on me, Angus. I can still ride a horse a few miles. Anything further than that is for young deputies like you. See you at the La Fonda in Santa Fe."

CHAPTER 2

"A Letter from the Smithsonian"

TWO DAYS LATER, I got a thick, brown envelope from the Smithsonian Institution in Washington. Inside the envelope, I found a grainy photograph, a copy of a three-page handwritten letter from the "Smithsonian Institution, Washington, DC," a printed circular, and a five-page typed letter to me. The circular was about the Smithsonian's research mission—documenting historical events in America. The five-page typed letter was to me and four others: Mr. Teddy Bridger, Mr. Jay Leonard, Mrs. Luci Atsidi, and Sgt. Mather Bell. Never heard of any of them. The letter said copies were being "circulated to other interested parties: United States Marshal George C. Ramsey, United States Marshal Dave Knop, Judge A. Craig Blakey II, Smithsonian Inspector General Stone Lucawziter, Deputy United States Attorney General Oreal K. Rotherberg, Undersecretary of the United States Treasury Heye Cass Gilbert, and Fort Marcy

Commanding Officer Major Nathaniel Ortiz." I knew Ramsey, Knop, and Judge Blakey. Jill was outside in back of the barn, so I took it there.

"Jill, would you look at this! The biggest envelope I've ever seen, all brown and official looking. It's stamped postage free—Official United States Government Business. Take ahold of this; it weighs more than the song book you use at church."

"Is it about the happy 350-mile horse ride you're going to take for Marshal Ramsey?"

"It is. But the letter, which I'm about to read, once I pour myself a glass of buttermilk, is five pages long! That's the longest letter I've ever seen and two pages longer than any report I've ever filed in a federal court case. You know how brief and to-the-damn-point Marshal Ramsey likes his deputies to be. Mrs. Kittering calls him 'three-page-George' to his back."

"Well, I see he got a copy. Do you suppose he will read it all or leave that task up to you? By the way, I'm not Mrs. Kittering and I'm on my way to the workshop. I have to adjust the trigger pull on Mel Thatcher's Burnside carbine. Would you minding reading it alone and then telling me about it over lunch, say in two hours? I'll get this trigger rebalanced; you get your work done for the Smithsonian Institution. Or is it the Marshal's office? I'm not clear on exactly who's hiring you for this ride."

I left Jill to her work and walked back into the kitchen. Spreading the contents of the envelope out on the kitchen table, I wondered what Marshal Ramsey would make of all this. We'd talked about a long horse ride but this seemed more government than fun. I glanced at the grainy photo, the crisp circulars, undid the string around the letter, and pressed the pages flat. Before reading it, I took a long look at the grainy photo—an odd one, I thought. It was maybe four or five inches long and three wide. It showed a bunch of Indians; at least I took 'em for Indians. There was a soldier in uniform with a long rifle folded across his arms, wearing a blue tunic, light colored pants, and an infantry man's billed cap. It was taken from behind everyone. You could not see faces, just backsides of people sitting cross-legged on the ground. They were all looking away into the distance. Guess it was the first photograph I'd ever seen from the back. The soldier was probably guarding them, but he was standing casual like, with his foot up on a dirt beam between him and the Indians. Couldn't tell what time of day it was taken. There was a low mud wall of some kind between the Indians and the soldier. The photo had the number 97967 marked in ink in the lower left corner. A tag attached to it said, U.S. Army Signal Corps. Rations under guard—Fort Sumner NM—1865.

The three-page handwritten letter was a photographic copy, on small paper, like women use for notes to one another. It was dated May 22, 1873, and signed, "I have the honor to be very truly yours, Joseph Henry." It was addressed to "Dear Sir." The last page had a small handwritten note at the bottom, "Ltr to Mr. W. T. Sherman, U.S. Army." It didn't register when I first read it, but I learned from one of the circulars that John Henry was the founding Secretary of the Smithsonian. Everyone in America knew the name of the man he was writing to. He was the commanding general of the whole United States Army, William Tecumseh Sherman. I felt a little guilty reading it before I read the one to me, but a handwritten letter to a four-star general ought not to be put off in favor of a typed letter to me.

> Dear Sir,
>
> In view of the occurrence at the present time of Indian hostilities in different parts of the country under which liability to such outbreaks involves military movements, I beg leave to inquire whether some general order might not be issued to commanders of departments and detachments instructing them to embrace any opportunity as may be pursued in the course of the service to secure items sent to Washington including specimens illustrating Indian life and warfare. You are aware of the importance of having in the national museum a complete appropriation of the manners and customs of our Indian tribes and of the difficulty of obtaining such illustrations. We are desirous of procuring large numbers of complete accruements in the way of dress, and weapons of war, applications of travel and harness and horse trappings. It would include such domestic items bearing on the character of the Indians.
>
> I have the honor to be very truly yours,
> Joseph Henry.

Is this what the 350-mile horse trip is about? Getting Indian clothes and horse trappings for a museum? I put off reading the circulars and read the typed letter to me. Right at the start, just like Marshal Ramsey said, there was more afoot here than just riding from one Army fort to another.

> Dear Gentlemen, and Mrs. Atsidi,
>
> It is with pronounced pleasure that the Smithsonian Institution congratulates each of you and expresses our sincere appreciation for your able assistance in the important research and writing project pertinent to the unfortunate circumstances that necessitated the transfer of certain individuals of Navaho heritage from ancestral grounds near Fort Defiance, in the Arizona Territory, to Fort Sumner in the New Mexico Territory from 1864 to 1868.

Now I don't claim to be well-educated and can't say I'd read very many official letters from government institutions, but this one deserved a second reading. It helped a little. It was signed, "Most Respectfully Yours, Morgan Pierpoint Roaster, III." Three names; no wonder he lives in Washington. The first page of the letter was not anything like you read in newspapers, or on wanted posters. The main point was to tell me that the Smithsonian was dedicated to the "increase and diffusion of knowledge." They said they'd been increasing and diffusing since President James K. Polk signed an act of the United States Congress on August 10, 1846, making them official, "*to wit,* an establishment for the increase and diffusion of knowledge among men." They could have said it plain—to go get it and spread it all over—but I was getting my first glimpse of how different people talked in Washington. They went on to make sure I understood that this "Institution relies on congressmen, educators, researchers, social reformers, as well as the general public." That got me to thinking why in the world they needed a deputy marshal like me? Reading the rest of the letter didn't shed much light on that question.

They recounted the fighting between the U.S. Army and Navajo warriors in a place called Canyon de Chelly, describing that as part of the "Navajo Wars of the 1860s." The language was fancy, but the plain of it told me a story that made me blanch a little. The letter called it "forced removal." By 1864, the U.S. Army had captured or killed what they thought was damn near every Navajo in the territory. To get them to give up their warlike ways, they marched 'em at gunpoint more than 350 miles to a place called Bosque Redondo. It was confusing because Marshal Ramsey had talked about taking them to Fort Sumner. Turns out it's one and the same; just depends on who's doing the talking. This happened after Col. Kit Carson killed the ones that wouldn't surrender. Best guess was the removal took eighteen days. They speculated about nine-thousand Navajos made it all the way. 'Course, they said, "hundreds died along the way." 'Spect so—it was winter time. On the last page of the letter, they called it the "1864 deportation of the Navajo people." I'd eventually learn that it was not just that one march. There were dozens more forced marches between 1864 and 1866, but that's getting ahead of my story, and their letter.

The middle page in the letter got down to business. Since the Navajo people did not have written records, and the Army only wrote down things like official orders and what they called "procurement and deployment plans," the Smithsonian would take up the slack in the rope. Leastways, that's how I read it. The job was to record, for the sake of history, "the details of place, time, participation, cultural perspective, and individual responsibility associated with transporting and maintaining Indian peoples at the Bosque Redondo." The confusing part was not what they were trying to do; it was how they planned on doing it.

The Smithsonian recognized that there was no clear record "regarding the consequences or the ultimate advisability" of this forced march. So, best as I can decipher Washington language, they wanted to figure out who was to blame, and whether transporting a whole Indian tribe was the right thing to do. That's not exactly what they said, but it's my sense of the deal. To do this, they needed two particular individuals—a Navajo lady named Luci Atsidi and a military man named Mather Bell. She was one of the Navajo women who walked all the way from Fort Defiance to Fort Sumner. He was one of the men pointing his gun at her all the way.

I could hardly believe my eyes. The plan was to put these two people in a stagecoach, get them talking to one another, and write a record that would help folks understand what happened and whose fault it was? Apparently, they knew how unlikely that was. That was where Mr. J. Leonard came in. He was, they said, "a respected researcher and noted anthropology lecturer." His work at the Smithsonian involved "many studies and documentation on Indian culture and habitat." He would "facilitate" discussion between the Indian and the Army sergeant, for the "purpose of arriving at mutual consensus." No wonder they needed me. This might be another Navajo war.

The fourth man's name was Teddy Bridger. They described him as an experienced teamster who would "attend to all aspects of travel by stage, including selecting and handling a suitable team of horses, equipping the stagecoach with essentials, and providing meals and sleeping accommodations, as necessary." I liked this part—I was not all that good at harnessing a four-up team, driving any kind of wagon, or cooking grub for others. I figured he was a man I could talk to. The other two were already giving me indigestion. Thought I'd ask Jill to pack me a bottle of Dr. Flint's Quaker Bitters. That always helped my stomach.

They described me in the letter as a "scout, sworn U.S. Deputy Marshal, and intermediary with other law enforcement entities, as needed throughout the trip." My duties, they said, "would be to identify the proper roads and trails, consistent with the original U.S. Army route, maintain proper security *en route*, and provide adequate guidance about the weather, trails to follow, rivers to cross, as well as secure approval for transit between Fort Defiance and Fort Sumner." That's a mouthful. Intermediary was something I had to look up in Jill's *Merriam-Webster*. They defined it as "a person who works with opposing sides in an argument or dispute in order to bring about an agreement." Me? I was going to settle the hash between the Army and the Indians? That's not how Marshal Ramsey described the job to me. He said something like, "You need to get the Army boys and the stiff-collar man from Washington DC all lined out."

They closed the letter by asking me to make contact with the adjutant at Fort Marcy in Santa Fe "your soonest." There it was again—that government way of telling you to tighten your cinch and throw your leg over the saddle.

CHAPTER 3

"Marathon"

THE PLAN OUTLINED IN THE letter from Mr. Leonard had
me going first to Fort Marcy, near Santa Fe. Then, I was
to head west to Fort Defiance, where the trip back across to
Fort Sumner would start. So, for me, the trip would be one-
hundred miles from Chama to Fort Marcy, then west for one-
hundred-fifty miles to Fort Defiance. From there, we'd retrace
the original Navajo long walk—three-hundred-fifty miles east
to Fort Sumner. Then, about a month after we started, I'd ride
back, hopefully on my own, from Fort Sumner to Chama, a
distance of about two-hundred miles. Altogether, I figured
to cover close to eight-hundred miles in a month. That'd take
a lot of the sand out my boots, and I'd need a young, sturdy,
long-walking horse to do it.

Fort Marcy was one-thousand yards from the Governor's
Palace in Santa Fe. Before and during the Civil War, it was

an important military encampment. It's ancient history now. Now the talk's all about Santa Fe, which predates Fort Marcy by a hundred years. It was the boss town for the north part of the Republic of Mexico. In 1846, the United States declared war on Mexico over a border dispute between the new State of Texas and Old Mexico. The Army of the West, commanded by General Kearney, marched into Santa Fe and claimed it, and calle everything around it the "Territory New Mexico." He built the fort within cannon range of Santa Fe's plaza, thinking it might quell any thought the local Spanish-speaking population might have about rising up and taking their town back. Truth was, he conquered New Mexico without firing a shot. He picked a mesa with a good view of the plaza to the south and the Rio Grande to the west.

Telegraphs from official law offices were done at county expense, the new sheriff, Bo String, reminded me. The U.S. Army ought to cover the cost both ways, he said, but they won't. Still, he authorized mine with a smile on his face—this is important law business, he suggested. I suggested it may be a fool's errand. My telegram was under ten words, which made him feel good. I asked when I was supposed to report to Fort Marcy. The reply came back within an hour. It was five words long. Report Wednesday, June 13, 1888. That gave me five days to settle on horse, mule, tack, and gear for what I thought would be at least four weeks riding in open country.

The stagecoach road from Chama followed the Rio Chama southeast, then forded the Los Brazos just shy of Tierra Amarilla. It ambled south by east for seventy odd miles to the confluence of the Rio Grande and the Rio Chama, a place locked deep into my heart. Some bad hombres tracked me and Jill there a few years back. They tried to kill her and she shot one of them. That's another story. From there, the road is mostly flat as it drizzles south down into Santa Fe. A government surveyor told me once that the Chama-Santa Fe stage route was not quite a hundred mile pull. A long-trotting horse in good shape can do that downhill at about seven miles an hour. While it can be done in one long day in the saddle, I almost always split it into a two-day ride and enjoyed a good night camp on the way.

Finding the right horse for this trip was not going to be easy. My two best horses, Tucson and No Mas, were no longer fit for a ride that far, in a month. Tucson was lame from a torn fetlock, and No Mas had some age on him. So I decided to buy or borrow a new horse. I wanted one that would cover a lot of ground at the trot, eat whatever we could find along the way, and mind his manners around the four-up team hauling the government stagecoach. Also, since I figured on ponying a stout mule for my provisions, the horse would have to be one that didn't mind tugging Snow, all eight-hundred-pounds of him, on a fifteen-foot lead rope. Last, the horse would have to be as fit as a race horse, but not near so easily spooked as they were. He'd have to have what cowboys call a gentle mouth and an easy head. Turns out, I didn't have far to look.

Over dinner that evening, I told Jill all the particulars of the horse I had in mind and asked if she'd seen the kind of horse I was looking for anywhere close to Chama.

"Not since breakfast, darlin'. You've been busy, so you might not have noticed that big chestnut gelding that Smoker brought in this morning. You remember Smoker, right?"

"Smoker? Is he the banjo player or the mill rider?"

"Yes, you do remember. He tends all the windmills for fifty miles in any direction. And he carries his banjo on his back between ranches. Folks say they can hear him coming two miles off if the morning air is still enough. He's in Chama today working on four windmills—two for the railroad, one for the town, and the last one for that sheep ranch just south of us. Smoker said his big chestnut is the longest-walking horse he's ever owned. Eats up roads like they were sugar cane, he said."

"Sounds like the right kind of horse but he's unlikely to part with him."

"Well, that's what made me think of him. Smoker said he wants to leave the horse here in my barn for three months. He's taking the train north to Denver, where he's switching to another line to Minnesota. His folks are there and are not well. So he's going to spend the summer working on their farm and catching up on family things. I expect you can broker a loan that will be good for both of you. His horse won't be in a stall for three months, and you don't have to buy another horse, which we don't need for the long run."

I couldn't wait for morning to get a look. That's all it took—one look, by lamp light, and a rising half-moon. But even in dim light, a Tennessee Walking Horse is something to behold. New Mexico probably did not have a dozen of these horses. I only knew about the breed because a man I met at the La Fonda Hotel in Santa Fe last winter had one. He said his was the first to come this far west; hauled it out here by railroad. He rattled on and on about its gait, which he said was exaggerated. Made no sense, but he explained it as a "running-walk." I tried to get his meaning, but he was not good at describing horse traits. Turned out he bought the horse for his son, who was not much of a horseman. It had a calm disposition, was smooth in the saddle, and sure-footed. "What did you name it?" I asked. He couldn't remember. I paid him no further mind.

The next morning, I found Smoker, working on the windmill near the railroad yard. Not wanting to interrupt his work, I leaned on the fence and watched him. He interrupted his work, walked over, and stuck out a big callused hand.

"You interested in windmills?" he asked.

"Nope, just as long as they turn and produce water for my horse, that's as far as I go with 'em."

"My name's Smoker. Two things I like most on this earth are smooth-running windmills and long-legged horses."

"Well, we have horses in common, Smoker. I'm Angus. Jill's husband. She told me about your horse and that you're looking to board him for the summer in her barn. I just gave him a carrot in his stall. He's a horse any man would take a second look at—got that long distance look about him."

"Name's Marathon," he said.

"Marathon?" I asked. "That's your horse's name?"

"You bet. Perfect name for him. Marathon is Greek. A Jesuit priest who knows about such things told me about a battle there a thousand years ago. One Greek soldier near ran himself to death to tell the king about the battle. He never stopped running. That's my horse. He just won't stop as long as you're in the saddle. Never had a better horse. Why you asking about him?"

I explained my situation.

He studied me for a moment, then asked, "So you're Jill's new husband?"

"Only one, far as I know," I answered.

"And you'd take proper care of Marathon this summer?"

"I would, but I'd take him on what might turn out to be an eight-hundred-mile round trip from here—all over New Mexico. What might you be asking as rent for that kind of a ride? I expect it might take a month or so."

"Well, here's my thinking on it. I'd be willing to let you take Marathon on that long haul you're talking about because I hate the thought of him being in a barn for three months. Hell, I might even pay you to ride him to keep him from getting barn sour. You suppose Jill would not charge me the daily stall and feed rate while you're riding him across the territory? That'd be all I ask."

So, we traded favors. I got his horse and guaranteed Smoker that Marathon would not be barn sour in September.

Back at the barn, I went into his stall, tied a horsehair halter on Marathon's neck, and led him out to the big corral on the lee side of the barn. Careful to walk directly in front of him, but at least ten feet away, I let the fifteen-foot lead rope hang loose between us. I listened to his breathing as we walked. Slow and easy. Once inside the corral, with three other horses on the far end, I let the rope drop to the ground and walked twenty feet away from him. He stood quiet, inspecting me and the other horses. He had funnel-shaped ears that twisted my way, collecting all the sounds around him. His eyes were high up on his head, about the same height off the ground as mine. Horses don't have binocular vision and don't judge distance well. But he could not sense any danger within his range so he felt comfortable standing with one hip slant.

I walked back to him, mumbling my easy-son-easy mantra. He had a long neck, and like all horses, a huge jugular vein collecting brain blood, which was protected by his long red mane. I could feel his pulse, slow and regular, by touching the mandibular artery under his jaw. Stooping down, I picked up his foot, checking the trim and pressing down gently on the frog. He had dark red socks on three feet and white on one. The fastest-moving part of a horse's leg is his foot. The lighter the foot, the less energy he needs to move it. That's why cowboys don't ride plow horses. This big boy had a small foot—and a mighty stout cannon-bone. Like the best of long-riding cow horses, Marathon had powerful muscles concentrated high up on his legs so the weight on the moving part of his leg was as small as possible. I could tell from feeling the bone structure at the top of his legs he'd have huge extension and a long running stride.

For me, the most important thing about any horse is how well he senses danger. With eyes on the side of his head, he can see almost all round himself. But he has a blind zone directly behind him and a little way in front. That's why all good hands approach horses from an angle. They want to keep you in view. Horses move their heads up and down to focus. They see through slit-like pupils. Marathon had no trouble tracking me as I moved toward him. When I got close, maybe five feet from him, I suddenly jumped into his blind zone. He reacted immediately, tossing his head up and bolting away. Then, regaining sight of me, he stood his ground, but his breath sound increased. I gave him a high whistle, which he picked up immediately. This was a young boy, I thought. His ears were perked, telling me he both heard my boot sounds approaching and the high pitch of my whistle. Ears always signal a horse's emotional state. Submissive horses turn their ears back toward the rider. Angry horses lay their ears flat back. Marathon's ears were neither. I suppose he was cautious, but not afraid. A good horse can smell water from a good distance away, although they aren't as good at this as a dang mule. They choose food mostly by smell. For Marathon, that test would have to wait.

Rubbing a horse's chest and belly can be tricky. But doing that to Marathon was a pleasure for both of us. Some horses bolt with the softest touch. Others seem asleep when you poke 'em with a stick. The difference is always how dangerous you seem to them. For sure, Marathon wasn't afraid of me. He watched me stroll back toward him and didn't flinch when I started rubbing his head and nose, smoothing his mane, and lifting his feet; then, easy and slow, I slid up on him, bareback. Sitting a horse bareback is something most cowboys never do. I can't tell you why—it just seems unnatural. That was never true for Indian horsemen, who rode most of the time without a saddle. Once I was up on him, with the lead rope looped around his neck, he started to jig a little, unsure of my intentions.

When you're sitting on a horse's back, the relationship changes. It's no longer one way. Riders need the horse's attention, but some don't know the language. Horses give signals back at us, but some riders can't read them. Marathon was at the ready but didn't move. All he needed was a cue, something I knew Smoker would have gotten him used to. The thing about climbing aboard a new horse is to remember a basic rule.

Every horse, in any situation, will do what he did the last time he was in that situation. I nudged him forward with a slight pressure from my knees. He started walking straight ahead. I laid the rope on the left side of his neck and he turned to the right. I gave a low whoa sound, tugged back on the rope, and quickly released the tension; he stopped. And I felt every step he took, coming up through his shoulder blades to the bend in his spinal column. He never flattened his ears or twisted his neck back to see me. He knew exactly where I was, and I knew I'd found my eight-hundred-mile horse.

An hour later, after brushing him down, I snugged my saddle blanket up on him, threw the saddle over, and cinched him up. I thought he had an easy mouth, so I used a short snaffle bit. I didn't bother with a tie-down, thinking he wouldn't throw his head at me, and swung a leg over the cantle. I walked him as slow as he seemed to want to go around the barn to the pasture out back. Then I gave him a little knee pressure to move him up into a trot. Didn't take a minute for him to teach me a thing or two. That fella in the bar at the La Fonda was right! Marathon did not know how to trot; but he, for damn sure, had a "running-walk."

I have to say I'd never ridden a horse that ran while he was walking before; it took a little getting used to. It's smooth as velvet and seems effortless when you're in the saddle. I tugged him back into a normal walk many times. And then moved him up into that running walk he seemed to prefer. He would step out smart enough on the regular walk, but by ignoring the trot cow horses use, this Tennessee Walking Horse glided over the terrain like he was on wheels rather than horseshoes. I didn't know it that first day, but a horse seller in Santa Fe told me later that this horse would give me ten to fifteen miles an hour in this gait, without breaking a sweat. And, he claimed, the longer the stride the horse has, the better walker he'll be. He was right.

That afternoon, I began putting my riding kit together. Jill was, as usual, happy for me to ride out, but showed her concern by fussing over my tack, ticking off things I'd missed, and giving me that upper lip attitude that made me eager to get back home. Already. I focused on what kind of gear I'd need for riding, sleeping, and bad weather. I didn't have to figure out what to eat—the government was going to take care of all the grub. Jill offered to take charge of the weapons. She was much better at that than I was.

"Angus, there's no reason to think about gunfights, hostiles of any kind, or arresting a horse thief, is there?"

"No, I'm not sure what all we'll be doing, but from what they said in the brown package they sent, this is a research and writing trip. No real need for law enforcement, which makes it curious why they needed me."

"All right, then. I don't think you ought to pack your Buntline Special on your holster belt. My favorite Navy colt is the one they call the Peacemaker. It's a Colt .45, serviceable, accurate, and powerful. It doesn't lock up, fail to spin the revolver, or misfire. And it's easy to clean and not too heavy. You ought to take a reliable carbine, but not the Winchester 73 you've been packing for years. I just acquired a nearly new carbine from a customer in exchange for gun work and training. It's a Winchester, Springfield model 1884. He didn't like the carbine model because its best feature is a new sight. It's wonderful—a rack-and-pinion-style windage adjustment. You know the base on most rifle sights isn't used for any position other than point blank. But this new one has a raised leaf with graduations from two-hundred to fourteen-hundred yards."

"Why didn't the fellow like it?"

"Because he isn't really a marksman, he's a foreman on a working ranch west of us. Marksmen really like this new sight, but maybe it isn't the best choice for working cowboys. They think it's an annoyance."

"How come?"

"I guess because in the carbine version, which is shorter than the rifle version, the rear sight could be easily damaged when removing the rifle from the carbine boot. But I've fixed that. I modified the rear barrel band to include a rear sight protector. You won't have any trouble sliding it out of the scabbard on your saddle."

"Don't expect I'll ever need to slide it out on this ride, 'cept for an occasional rattlesnake sunning himself in the middle of the stage road."

"That's good to hear, but," she said with a grin, "you have a way of attracting more blood-curdling situations. I'll feel better with this one in your scabbard. The 84 model is a solid redesign—they came out with it because they needed a full-power gun since centerfire cartridges are available most everywhere now. It has a squared receiver to take those new cartridges, a new loading gate set on the right side, and a very smooth ejection port along the top. I've fired three boxes of ammo from it. It has a fifteen-round ammunition tube. You'll never need that many, will you?"

"Doubtful," I said.

"Fine. That's settled. Let's do some test firing tomorrow. You won't be leaving too early, will you?"

"No, tomorrow morning any time will work for me. I don't want to load up until early afternoon."

"Angus, darling, I have some promises you need to make. You want to hear them now, or in the morning?"

"Now, I suppose."

"Do you promise you won't try fording any of the cataracts in the Rio Chama on that borrowed horse?"

"No, I learned my lesson on No Mas. Besides, Marathon probably can't swim."

"You also learned how hard it was to ride a horse, shoot a gun, and apprehend a criminal with a broken arm, too, didn't you? Do you also promise not to try to rescue any young girls in Bernalillo? You will be riding through there, won't you?"

"Yes, ma'am, but I won't be there till about noon day after tomorrow. The girls will still be sleeping at the Silva Saloon."

"OK, then. I have one more promise to ask of you. Can I ask one more?"

I said sure, but it made my stomach a little queasy. Since we'd been married, I'd made a half-dozen trips alone, riding high ridges and giving the world an up-close look. This sounded a little ominous.

"I'd like you to write me a little note along the way. You'll be going through towns from time to time. I've made up a little package for you. This leather pouch has two good pencils, five envelopes, ten cut pieces of paper, and a good luck charm. Just write me a note on the trail and tell me what you're seeing. I want you to enjoy yourself, but you do that best when you're communing with eagles and cooking your own breakfast alongside a mountain stream. This trip with other people inside a stagecoach sounds awful to me. Awful strange, I mean. Whatever will they be doing, and why do they need you? Please promise you'll write and tell me the straight-out truth. Once a week is all I need. You'll find ten quarters and five U.S. postage stamps in there. You do know our address, don't you?"

I spent the next day squaring away enough gear to last me a month in high country, even though I figured most of the trip would be over mostly flat ground. I gave Jill a mighty strong good-bye kiss, patted the coat pocket on my duster to show her I had that little leather pouch, and we lit out. Me, Marathon, and Snow, the mule I'd used on the last two trips. He brayed as I tugged him out of town.

CHAPTER 4

"Fort Marcy"

FORT MARCY WASN'T MUCH. I rode in about two hours before sundown after a long push down the east bank of the Rio Grande. No one seemed to notice me; expect that's because the Army decommissioned this fort in 1868, twenty years ago. There were no troops garrisoned here anymore, no wars to fight, no Indians to subdue. The buildings were abandoned, except for one with a sign on it—United States Army—Fort Marcy New Mexico—Commanding Officer's HQ. It was in the middle of what probably was a parade ground back when it really was a fort. The adobe buildings were all a shamble, fences down, barns and corrals mostly empty. But they still had a flagpole and Old Glory was snugged on top, blowing in the twenty-mile wind that faced me, Marathon, and Snow all the way up the long slope from the Rio Grande.

Santa Fe had grown around the fort. I intended to stop in here first before going down the road a half mile to the plaza and the La Fonda Hotel. There was a hitching rail out front of the only building still inhabited. It was sizeable, looking to be more 'n fifty feet wide. A good-sized double door centered the building, with small windows flanking it on both sides. The door was closed; it had a cut piñon knocker hinged on the left door. I banged it once.

"Enter," someone with a voice that sounded like a big Indian drum.

When I swung the door open, I got my first surprise at Fort Marcy. I'd expected an office with desks and such, but this was a huge room, maybe thirty by thirty. It was airy, freshly painted, and filled from wall to wall with tables, chairs, book cases, maps, photos, papers tacked to the walls, and three men looking at me from the rear half of the room. I could see doors on all three sides of the room. They were closed but some had plaques with names stenciled on in white paint. Later I noticed they were for officers that no longer occupied the fort, like commanding general, adjutant, post supply officer, and captain of cavalry. One of the men, sporting a dark brown suit, black string tie, and odd-looking shoes came to the door with his hand out.

"Good afternoon, I'm Jay Leonard from the Smithsonian Institution. I hope you are Marshal Angus, am I right?"

"Right," I said taking his grip. It wasn't much. City man, I thought. He was of middling size, pale complexion, and just a little bent over, even though he was maybe ten years older than me. Bespectacled to boot. Working behind a desk too long, I thought. But he was well-scrubbed, clean shaven, with a set jaw and an honest smile. Liked him right off.

"You are the second of our collective to arrive. I got off the train day before yesterday. Sgt. Bell joined us last evening. We won't meet Mr. Bridger until he brings the stagecoach from somewhere in Texas to Albuquerque early next week. And then, of course, we won't meet Mrs. Atsidi until we arrive in Fort Defiance to officially begin our trip in one week's time. Would you like some coffee? It's late-in-the-day coffee. The man who made it called it Army coffee. I think he meant that it was angry at us. Or would you like to see to your animals and settle in a bedroom? Actually, it's a bunkhouse, we will share it with Sgt. Bell tonight and tomorrow night. There is a small kitchen, but I thought we'd take the wagon down to the La Fonda for dinner. Will that be suitable for you . . ."

"Nice to meet you, too," I interrupted. Right off, I could tell the man would always have something to say. "But I won't need an inside bunk. I always like to sleep outside, unless it's raining. No rain in sight, is there?"

"No, sir. No rain here in March. Mr. Strudy, I'll introduce you to him shortly, says it never rains until early summer. I don't know why; those mountains to the north of us look perfectly capable of capturing rain clouds. But please, let me take you back and meet the other fellows. We have much to talk about before dinner."

The bearded, barrel-chested man turned out to be Sgt. Bell. He had dark black eyes that seemed to be in a torment, like he'd just been in a fist fight. He was unkempt, for a military man, and breathed out loud, kind of a wheeze, probably from the cigar he was puffing. It would turn out he was rarely without one. He had a web of purple lines running up his cheeks from the speckled salt and pepper undergrowth. He didn't get up, but stretched a hambone-sized hand across the table. I took it and felt him give me that test big men often do. Tried to squeeze hard before my hand was all the way in his. I pushed back with my forearm, and gave him a look.

"Marshal," he said, as though it were a condition rather than a greeting.

"Sergeant," I said, intending to be respectful, but not inviting.

Placing his hand gently on my elbow, Mr. Leonard turned me toward the two other men at the table, and pointed at them in right-to-left order. "This is Mr. Strudy, whom I mentioned at the door. He's in charge of facilities here at what's left of Fort Marcy. And this is Captain Ortiz, who, like Sgt. Bell was once stationed here full time. Captain Ortiz travels quite a bit for the Army coordinating maneuvers and operations with the more active forts in Colorado, Utah, and Arizona. He's our official host." I shook their hands. Ortiz was the oldest man, early forties I guessed. He looked curious about me and Mr. Leonard. Strudy was one of those men who you thought you already knew because he looked so ordinary. There was nothing about his features or his manner of speaking that would distinguish him from any other man his age in the territory. I got the feeling they had been biding their time as hosts, waiting for me to arrive. Now that I was here, Mr. Strudy and Captain Ortiz got up and walked briskly to a set of office doors at the back of the room. Mr. Leonard motioned me to a chair opposite Sgt. Bell. There was a small stack of documents there, a notepad, and a fountain pen. The middle of the table featured an ink well, blotter, and a metal pan for Sgt. Bell's cigar ashes.

Mr. Leonard began.

"So, my new friends, shall we dispense with titles? I'm Jay. It is Angus, right? Can we call you that? And Sgt. Bell, is Mather acceptable?"

"Why not? I ain't been a sergeant for nine years," he said in a raspy but clear voice.

"Sure," I said.

"Fine, then let me just start with logistical details, none of which were all that clear when I first wrote to you from my office in the Smithsonian. Now, as to the mode of travel, I think I mentioned it would be by stagecoach for myself, Mather, and Mrs. Atsidi as inside passengers. Mr. Teddy Bridger, our teamster and cook, will drive the stage. He is also bringing along, I think, a man or perhaps a boy to assist with the horses that will pull our Concord stage, and to be the wash-up after meals. Either Mr. Bridger or his man will attend to tenting and bedrolls, when we need them, although I believe there will be hotels at several stops on our reconstructed journey. Angus will lead us on his fine horse, a Tennessee Walking Horse, I think. Is that right, Angus? Additionally . . ."

A man who asks a question without wanting an answer begs for an interruption.

"A Tennessee Walking Horse, it is, Jay. Name's Marathon. My mule's name is Snow. But if you don't mind my interrupting, could you maybe give me a rerun on why I'm here? Why does the Smithsonian Institution need a federal marshal for this— what was it you just called it?—our reconstructed journey?"

"Certainly, Angus. Interrupt any time. I have been told by my wife I blather on and by my departmental supervisor that I tend to stray from the essence of things. To be frank, I do not know why you, a sworn United States deputy marshal, were chosen to lead us. We have maps, of course, which I will give to you first thing in the morning, but reading the map and knowing the best way to navigate might turn out to be two very different things, at the very least. We have Mather here, who was on the original ride, and Mrs. Atsidi, who walked it, but our thinking—that is, the Smithsonian's committee to advance this research effort—was that we would need a local guide, or scout I think they call it. I should also say that the Department of the Treasury is funding part of this excursion. Indeed, it was one of their officers who selected you. I don't know why they thought a peace officer was necessary."

"So, there's no federal criminals involved, nobody in need of arresting, have I got that right?"

"Dear me, no. This is a research and writing project. Our mission—that is, the Smithsonian's mission—is one of discovery and retention. We believe the forced march of the Navajo people and the continued holding against their will of the Apache people was a dark time. By study and introspection, we might cast light on the whys, wherefores, and consequences. But as for criminal activity, no, that is not our understanding."

Mather had been looking a little uncomfortable; he chimed in.

"Mr. Leonard, that same thing's been rubbing on me. So, you're telling us the government is not out to blame the Army for doing its job, which was to make this part of the country safe for settlers and peace-loving white folks. Angus, as a federal marshal, ain't here to investigate us, right?"

"Gentlemen, let me be as instructive as I can be. The Smithsonian is not a government institution. We were created by an act of Congress to carry out the wishes of our original financial benefactor, James Smithson, but our 1846 charter established us as a charitable trust. We are not under the control of any government agency. We answer to a board of regents of prominent, private citizens, and to a general secretary, whom they appoint. We have no law enforcement function. Our only mission is to advance history by creating reports and storing important physical and documentary items in a museum setting in accordance with Mr. Smithson's wishes—which was the increase and diffusion of knowledge. Our mission here in the New Mexico territory is not one of investigation or blame. It is one of acquiring a better understanding of the march of several thousand Indians from their homeland to a government reserve hundreds of miles distant. Understanding and reporting are at the core of acquisition and diffusion of knowledge. I don't know how else to say it."

That seemed to satisfy Sgt. Bell. While it rang true the way he said it, there was a knot on the log. Damn near every federal warrant I ever served started out by somebody doing something others thought was wrong. I couldn't shake the feeling that finding out the particulars of the 1864 march from Fort Defiance to Fort Sumner would ruffle somebody's feathers somewhere. And one of them might be this man sitting across the table from me—Sgt. Mather Bell. Who, I wondered, picked him?

J. Leonard spent another hour talking about what books had already told him. He'd read the Army documents. He'd researched the Navajo Wars. He'd read several books that didn't mention the forced march of either Navajos or Apaches. He made the point several times about how useful it would be to make this trip in the company of two people—a man who rode carrying a rifle—and a woman walking. He seemed hopeful, confident even, that as we traveled back over that same trail, his interviews would produce a consensus as to what really happened. Maybe, he said, that would give him, a researcher and writer, a thesis which the American people could assess. It was all about knowledge, he insisted. Not about blame.

CHAPTER 5

"Albuquerque"

THE NEXT DAY, WE WOKE UP to another pot of Army coffee, a platter of hard-boiled eggs, fried bacon, and biscuits.
Turns out, the cook house was just behind the bunk house
and the smell of an early morning breakfast made me hungry. J. Leonard announced that our departure time would be
"nine o'clock this very morning." I wondered whether Marshal
Ramsey would be joining us. Mr. Leonard had said earlier that
Teddy Bridger might already be in Albuquerque.

"Or might not," he said. "He's bringing a special stagecoach
from Texas or somewhere."

The plan was for all of us to ride down to Albuquerque—
J. Leonard and Sgt. Bell on the Overland & Humboldt Stage
from Santa Fe to Albuquerque. He said, I would "be following
along." I allowed as how I might lead out and break trail for the
coach. That didn't seem odd to Mr. Leonard, but Sgt. Bell gave

me a little guffaw. The ride, almost all downhill, would cover sixty-five miles in about eight hours. That would put them in New Mexico's biggest town by "five o'clock this very afternoon."

The flat stage road would be my first test of how fast Marathon could get there with his running walk. If he made the ten miles per hour, like Smoker said he could, we'd be there not much after three o'clock. That's what I meant by "breaking trail." Turns out, we got there ten minutes to three. I was mighty pleased with Marathon's exaggerated gait. But Snow, my mule, was not. Even though he was under a light load, he looked to be worn down to the nub.

As I rode into Albuquerque down Central Avenue, I could see the livery stable ahead. It brought to mind the city jail yard just up the street. That's where Sheriff Perfecto Armijo hung Milton J. Yarberry back in 1885. He was Albuquerque's first city marshal. A poor one at that since he became first lawman to be hung here for murder of another Albuquerque citizen. I watched that miserable event, along with a hundred of Albuquerque's finest citizens. Soured me on the town.

The livery barn, one of the biggest in the territory, was set back about fifty feet off Coal Street. Albuquerque had a good many streets with names on little corner posts in 1888. Stopped dead center in front of the barn was a sight to see: a gleaming red and gold Concord Stagecoach with a team of four matched horses in harness. A big man wearing heavy gloves and a dusty, black, wide-brimmed hat was just climbing down from the driver's box. I'd ridden in three or four stagecoaches, but none looked like this one. It looked to be about seven or eight feet tall, with a large iron-bar box on top, a five-foot rear box, called the rear boot, with long leather flaps tied down, and a front boot that might have been four feet deep below the padded leather seat for the driver and whoever would ride shotgun. The rear wheel measurement was hard to guess at from horseback, but I'd call it at least four feet in diameter. The front wheels were probably just shy of three feet. The seven-foot long brake handle was unpainted, highly varnished hickory. It had a foot-long leather grip.

I swung around the coach and tugged Marathon to a smooth stop at the hitching rail. Dismounting, I led Snow into the barn and put him in a stall. Before unleashing the diamond hitch over the canvas tarp, I took a closer look at that grand stagecoach outside. I figured it might be the one Mr. Leonard had said would be used for our trip. It was already gathering a crowd of gawkers. It was dusty but the bright red and yellow lacquered paint showed through. The big man up top climbed down, took off his gloves, and said something to the livery man who had hold of the lead horse's big halter. I didn't make out the words but the sense of it was for the liveryman to tie off the lead horse and let all four of 'em stand awhile. The man turned toward me, walked over, and pointed to the badge on my vest.

"Howdy, Marshal. Your name's Angus, and you're here to meet with Mr. J. Leonard, right?"

"I am. Curious as to how you know that, friend."

"This is your coach—the one you're going to lead. I'm the up-top driver. Name's Teddy Bridger."

We shook hands—strong grip of a teamster, or an iron worker. He wondered if I'd mind giving him a hand unharnessing the matched team.

"You know, these horses are steamed up on account of that long haul we just made from Lincoln."

"Lincoln? You drove this team up here from Lincoln? That's a haul for sure."

"Where'd you come from?"

"Santa Fe. I bunked last night at Fort Marcy; can't say much for it as a fort but it's lee of a pretty mountain and windward of the Rio Grande. From my way of thinking when you're between a river and a tall mountain, you got two mighty fine ways to go."

"Lee and windward? Angus, you don't have the look of a nautical man, but you use seafaring terms. I'm from Virginia Beach myself. I favor long coastlines and horses that don't mind slogging through salt water. Once we get these team horses settled in, I'd like to hear what you think of this Smithsonian adventure we've signed up for."

He did the unharnessing and stacking the long leather reins, breast collars, and such. I led the big blacks to the water trough, two by two. Teddy said to loop the lead ropes from one horse to the other as they stood pulling long slurps of water and playing some with their noses deep in the tanks. I asked him if he wanted me to take them into the big barn but he said no, the boy will be back out here shortly.

"He'll lead 'em in and commence to brushing 'em. He knows this team better than I do."

That made no sense at the moment, but I had Marathon and Snow to take care of so I didn't give it any thought. I led Marathon into the barn to join Snow. There were two dozen stalls, twelve on each side. The ones on the south side had double doors—one entering the stall from inside the barn and one going outside to a big corral for all the stock on the south side of the barn. I put Snow in a north side stall, figuring

he'd best be left alone to bray and sleep. He liked his sleep, old
Snow did. And he was tuckered out. So I spent the next hour
rubbing Snow's legs with water and Laddlow's dressing. Once
I got him fed and brushed down, and a grain sack snugged up
over his nose, he'd likely lean over against the wall and clamp
his eyelids down for as long as he could. He'll sleep standing
up once it gets full on dark. I put Marathon directly across
from him on the barn's south side and opened his back door
out into the big corral. I wanted to see how he'd do with a half
dozen strange horses in the big corral. I figured Teddy would
have his four-horse team settled in. It was past sundown but
not full night yet.

"Angus," Teddy hollered at me from the north side of the
stable, "come on over here! I'd like you to meet the boy I was
telling you about."

They were about forty feet away. Teddy was standing
on a wood shelf that supported the rear boot of the coach. It
looked like they were rearranging the boxes and sacks inside
the boot. I could see them clear, now that the big canvas tarp
was rolled up and strapped to the top of the stage. The man
helping him up top had coal black hair under what looked to
be a drummer's bowler hat. His back was to me. As I walked to
them, the man turned to face me. From a distance, I thought
he was a kid.

"Meet Chinorero. He's the boy I hired to help me take care
of the team and give us some assistance on the road from Fort
Defiance to Fort Sumner. Hell, he might even be helpful with
directions once we get to the Pecos River. I call him Chin for
short, but I don't think he's taken to nicknames. Chinorero,
this is United States Deputy Marshal Angus Esperraza."

Chinorero nodded down at me from his knee position on top of the coach then turned back to adjusting the top strap on the canvas tarp. Once it suited him, he stuck one foot down onto the big iron-rimmed wheel and sprang to the ground like a gazelle leaping over a four-foot fence. Plainly, he was a man of few words. He picked up a McClellan saddle and a worn dusty saddle pad, flung both over his shoulder, and turned toward the barn door.

"Chinorero. That's a fine name, mister. Where you from?" I asked.

He looked back at me through slanted eyes. He was dark as piñon bark, maybe a foot taller than a fence post, wearing leather leggings over heavy standard-issue cavalry boots with those short, blunt steel spurs favored by the Army. Right off, I didn't think he'd appreciate my Mexican vaquero spurs with two-inch rowels. He wore a faded denim shirt, which might have once been blue. Looked like a hand-me-down from a much bigger man. It drooped down over his thin shoulders and cuffed up over his wrists with a leather thong. He had it all tucked inside the waistline of his well-worn leather pants. He had a wide, dirty, cotton sash wrapped around his waist and wore a leather belt over that. It holstered a small pistol, with two ammo pouches on one side. A deer-handled skinning knife was sheathed on the other side. I couldn't see much skin because he had a red calico scarf wrapped around his neck, with a long string of beaded coral hanging below his Adam's apple. He could not have weighed much over a hundred pounds, counting the pistol and knife.

"Fort Union," he said turning his back as he climbed down from the rear boot and turned to a saddle, bags, and a pad on the side of the Concord.

I turned to Teddy. "That your McClellan?" I asked.

"No, that's Chin's. We ponied his little horse half way here from Fort Union. His horse ain't much bigger than he is but he's got some run in him, I can attest to that. I think Mr. Leonard might have mentioned in his letter to you, same one he sent me, that I'd probably bring a boy along to help me with the stock, camp set up, pot and skillet cleaning, and for company up top, once in a while. The Concord was at Fort Union, up on the Canadian River, where it had been used as part of the stage line for mail and Army supplies from Texas. I got there on the Santa Fe railway, which reached Fort Union in 1879. They have all kinds of wagons and teams there, including long tandem freight wagons, pulled by twelve-yoke teams. They supply forts all over the Southwest from goods delivered by the Santa Fe. Chin more or less came along with the Concord. Suppose he knows more about harnessing and keeping the coach greased than any of the soldiers there."

I watched him stride to the barn door with the McClellan covering most of his back. His short legs moved effortlessly and he seemed not to notice the twenty-five pounds of saddle, blanket, and bags on his back.

"He live on the fort?"

"Not sure. The Mescalero reservation is way south of there—not sure how he got from the reservation to Fort Union, but it had to do with an old horse soldier. Way I heard it, that Irish horse soldier took a liking to him when he was about twelve. I got that from the soldier, not Chin. The soldier's name was Feeney. He started looking after Chinorero when his Indian father took off for Mexico eight years ago. That's what he told me, anyhow. Don't know any more than that. Chin is friendly and handy, but he ain't one for jawboning. He's a flash rider and knows how to follow orders. Been around the Army most of his life, I guess. So, Angus, I expect you know this town. Where we can find a good steak and a cold beer?"

Walking together, we hauled our kit and bags to the La Posada Hotel. I asked him why Chin was not joining us.

"'Cause he sleeps in the stage. Has for years, when the Army's not using it. One of the soldiers, probably Sgt. Feeney, built a box with a padded leather top. It fits snug between the two coach seats on the brake side of the coach. Chin's an inch over five feet and the distance between the two facing seats in the coach, from back to back, is exactly five feet. Makes a damn fine bed for him. You might have noticed the coach has a glazed window in the door on each side, but the four openings are covered only by canvas down flaps. It's a tidy and comfy place to sleep if you're only five feet tall. You'd be corkscrewed in if you tried it."

"Is that what you think he'll do, once we get fully loaded in Fort Defiance?"

"No, I doubt it. He's pleasant enough, speaks good English, but he's still an Apache. He told me on the way up here, he'd be pitching his own camp some distance off from the Concord. I've brought tents for you, Mr. Leonard, Sgt. Bell, and the Navajo lady, Luci Atsidi. But now that I see how Sgt. Feeney rigged the passenger cabin on the coach, I expect she may prefer to sleep in there. But mostly, we'll be staying in stagecoach inns and little hotels. But that depends on where you lead us. Have you got that figured out?"

"Where we'll be stopping? No, sir, I have not. I just got copies of maps last evening and haven't studied them yet. And I expect Mr. Leonard will want a say in that, too."

We got to the hotel. Since the stage was not here yet, even though the sun was set, I asked the desk clerk whether a Mr. J. Leonard had booked rooms for us.

"Mr. Leonard? Would he be with the Smithsonian group?"

"Yes," Teddy said, "and so are we. This here is Marshal Angus. I'm Teddy Bridger."

"Just so," said the desk clerk in a crisp tone from behind a razor-thin mustache barely visible on his nutcracker face.

He gave us each a brass key, said a boy would take our kits up. We both said no, we'd carry what we brought. The rooms were on opposite ends of the second floor. Teddy suggested we wash up, meet in the bar, and wait for the Smithsonian man to join us for dinner.

"Tab's on him, right, Angus?"

"'Spect so," I said.

A half hour later, in the bar at a table for four, Teddy and I drained two beers each before turning to the job at hand. There was no sight yet of Mr. Leonard and Sgt. Bell.

"Angus, what's your take on this fella, J. Leonard? About all I know is what's in his letter."

"We talked a bit last night. He's a talker and uses words like you and me use air. We have to breathe to stay alive. He lives to talk. Upfront, he told us last night, this is a research and writing effort. He wants to interview Sgt. Bell and Mrs. Atsidi while they are inside your coach traveling the long trail between Fort Defiance and Fort Sumner. I ain't got any notion of exactly why he thinks they are going to tell him what really happened. I mean, goddamn, it was thousands of Navajos and probably a hundred soldiers. The Indians were prisoners. The soldiers were armed with their blood up. Lots of Indians got shot, or froze to death, or starved." Bridger downed his beer and called out to barman for a fresh one. Then he gave me his take on things.

"So, getting the man pointing his rifle together with the lady shuffling in the dirt, inside a coach, even one as fancy as yours seems foolish to me. Sgt. Bell will be armed inside the coach. Mrs. Atsidi may have a skinning knife in one of those medicine bags Indians always carry. Mr. Leonard's fine college education may not serve him well inside the coach."

"Maybe that's why you, a well-armed U.S. marshal, are on the trip. Maybe you ought to be inside the coach with them, keeping the peace. You bring a peace pipe with you, by any chance?"

I laughed but he was asking a question I still had no answer for.

"Teddy, I have no plans to ride inside your coach, comfy as it might be. And my job is not to guard anyone. Everyone's here as a free person. Free to talk, or ride off anytime they want. I wish I knew exactly why 'n hell I'm here. Once when I was about fifteen, working on a cattle ranch, the foreman had a saying about useless things. He thought talking was mostly useless. Like barkin' at a knot, he said. Don't you know that knots never listen to anyone?"

We talked about the quality of the beer, and the good smell of burnt beef coming from the kitchen behind the bar. We agreed that since Mr. Leonard and Sgt. Bell were delayed, probably by a poorly equipped and broke-down stagecoach, we'd order dinner, and put it on the Smithsonian tab. We ordered burnt steaks, a pile of fresh vegetables, whatever they had, and apple pie for dessert. I asked for chili on mine. Teddy shook his head. When the steaks were cut down to the bone and before coffee and apple pie was served, I returned the question to Teddy.

"Just because I don't know why I'm here, doesn't mean you have the same problem. What's a teamster and cook from Virginia doing out here, hauling and cooking for the Smithsonian?"

"Long story, but we got time, right? I'll tell you my story tonight. Tomorrow night, you can indulge me with yours. My family's from Maryland. My father was a VMI graduate—the Virginia Military Institute. He was an engineer and built roads and bridges for the Army. He was one of only a handful of VMI grads to serve in the Union Army. The rest became generals for the Confederates. I graduated from VMI in 1877, served two years in the Army Corps of Engineers, building bridges like my father had. But the part I liked best was working with teams of workhorses in all kinds of rigs. I wasn't cut out to be an Army officer so I only did one tour. I'd always liked being in the kitchen at home with my mother. Once I joined the Army I had to put up with bad food coming out of Army kitchens. Since I left the Army, I've been cooking the way my mother did."

The waiter interrupted to bring coffee and pie. I said the coffee was better than what I was used to on high mountain slopes where I loved riding. He said the pie was acceptable, but not flakey enough by Chesapeake Bay standards.

"You make a living with horse teams and cooking?" I asked.

"No, that was more what I loved than what I did. I hired on for six months as a civilian with the Corps of Engineers, then moved to another government agency, the U.S. Treasury Department. You'd be surprised what they haul around the country, what with mints, railroad facilities, and checking up on other government agencies that spend Treasury money. Government work is attractive because no one's actually in charge. There's always bosses, but in the right agency, you can work on your own."

"So, you're doing government work here? I'm not sure I understand."

"The U.S. Treasury supports some nonprofit entities. The Smithsonian is one of those. I was available and heard about this job out west. They said it would take a month in the summer. I said, hell, send me. They did. I've got seven years' seniority now. And time-in-grade counts in government work."

We talked over coffee, with whiskey for sweetener for another hour. Finally, about ten o'clock, Mr. Leonard and Sgt. Bell walked in the bar, looking some the worse for wear. Mr. Leonard blamed it on a wheel condition that "should have been avoided by better maintenance."

Sgt. Bell said, "Busted goddamned spoke."

They ordered eggs, pie, and coffee. All of us went to our rooms by ten-thirty with instructions from Mr. Leonard "to repair at eight to the dining room for further orientation and breakfast."

CHAPTER 6
"Shots Fired"

I WOKE UP AT DAWN, pulled my boots on, splashed water on my face, used the facilities down the hall, and walked to the livery barn to check on Marathon and Snow. No surprise that Teddy and Chinorero were ahead of me, looking after the wagon team. The surprise was a little Morgan gelding—the Apache boy's horse.

"That's a fine-looking Morgan you got there, Chin. How's he ride?"

"Ride? He's the wind in the morning and a storm at night. I am Shis-Inday."

"Shis-Inday? I thought you were Apache."

"Yes. Mescalero Apache. Father says our name for ourselves is 'People close to the mountains.' He bought this horse for me; you call him a Morgan horse. I don't. We don't name our horses like the white man. But we ride in the wind and the storm—that is how he rides."

"Teddy calls you 'Chin.' Alright if I use your full name, 'Chinorero'? I haven't been around too many Apache. Mostly Utes and Navajos up around Chama."

"I am my father's son. His name is Chinorero, too. He was at Bosque Redondo. That's why I'm going there, with you."

"Happy to have you. Do you know what an outrider is?"

"Outrider? Some days I ride out early in the morning. I learned English from the padre at the church school Davis Mountain. What does outrider mean?"

"Well, the coach that Teddy is driving will be behind me. Two men and a woman will be inside the coach. I'll be riding lead. Any man who rides with the wind and into the storm would make a mighty fine outrider. The outrider watches our back trail and warns us about trouble. You up to that?"

"I can do that. Does Teddy want me to be the outrider?"

"We'll ask his opinion."

He turned back to his job—working the leather on the big horse collars.

"What's that you're rubbing on the leather?" I asked.

"Cactus oil and something else I can't smell. But it makes old leather soft. Feels good on the horse's neck; it makes the horses calm. Teddy says that."

Teddy came out of the barn carrying a long leather box with straps and brass hinges.

"Morning, Angus. Knew you'd be down here before the sun got up over that big mountain range. What do they call it?"

"The Sandias. It means watermelon in Spanish. When the western sun sets in the evening, the mountain looks like a giant slice of fresh-cut watermelon, all green down low and red across the top."

"Any sign of life in the dining room at the hotel?"

"Don't know. Didn't look."

"Well, there's coffee on the pot at the back of the barn. You tend to your stock and I'll tend to mine. Then, we'll breakfast up before Mr. Leonard comes downstairs with another lecture on what he calls the finer points of Western frontier culture."

"Gentlemen," Mr. Leonard said after breakfast, "this is our first day of travel. My map says Fort Wingate is due west of here but we have to first travel south along the Rio Grande to Los Lunas. A soldier at Fort Marcy said it was about 150 miles to Fort Wingate from Albuquerque. Figure three days? Angus, have you been to Fort Wingate?"

"No, but I rode to Los Lunas, on a hunting trip. I figure if we leave here before noon, we'll be there by sundown. I spent some time last night after dinner on your maps. That'd be my recommendation for today's run."

"Teddy," Mr. Leonard said, "what is your estimate of travel time in that splendid coach of yours to Los Lunas?"

"Yes, sir. It's due south of here, could be thirty miles. We'd cross the Rio Grande there—good heavy wagon bridge, I'm told. Lots of freight wagons with big six-horse teams using that bridge. Then we'd ride another thirty miles and camp for the night."

"What rate of travel might we expect? There is a good stage road alongside the rail track, isn't there? When I looked at the Army map, I think Los Lunas is on one of the routes from Fort Wingate to Fort Sumner. Right?"

"Right. I agree with Angus. We can make fifty or sixty miles today, and then a long full-day ride to Fort Wingate. After that, we go through Gallup where we leave the railroad track, which stays on a true west trajectory, and turn north on the stagecoach road. Gallup's got some history, you know. Never been that far west, but a railroad friend from Chama told me how they named Gallup. Want to hear that story?"

"Sure."

"The AT&SF paymaster rode the tracks twice a week, all across New Mexico. His name was David Gallup. The crews followed him from one stop to the next—they said they were 'going to Gallup.' Meaning they would get paid. So, seven years ago, when a little railroad boom town sprung up, they called it Gallup. It's surrounded in every direction by Indian tribes."

Teddy studied the map on the table in front of him. "Suppose the four-up team can manage an easy nine-mile-per-hour run on mostly flat ground. We'd need an hour stop for water and to give the team a breather. So, say seven hours. There's a water tower the AT&SF uses near a Pueblo called Laguna. There's no hotel there, so you'll be wanting me and Chin to set up sleeping tents and a cook fire?"

"No, there's a barn and a rooming house with a small kitchen at the water stop the Santa Fe Railway uses. That's what the manager of the La Posada told me this morning. Teddy, I have several bags and trip provisions stacked up behind the front desk. Should I have them taken to the barn, or will you bring the coach up here?"

"Whichever way you want. I've got the front boot full. But the rear boot's empty—it has lots of room and we've got space up top—not much up there yet. Angus is hauling his kit on that gray mule; don't know why somebody'd name a gray mule, Snow. We ought to save room for the Navajo woman's bags on top. Why don't I just drive the rig up here and load passengers and gear at the same time? Then, we just ride the east bank of the Rio Grande, and we're in business—Smithsonian business."

Once everything was loaded on the Concord, I looped Snow's lead rope around my saddle horn. I'd oiled and cleaned my guns, tied my slicker behind the saddle, strapped on the Colt to my waist, slid the Winchester into its scabbard, checked Marathon's cinch, and we moved out.

Teddy was up top. Mr. Leonard chose the forward-looking seat inside the coach. Sgt. Bell sat alongside him. Plenty of room to prop their feet on the opposing padded seats. Chinorero wheeled his little Morgan around and took a position about fifty feet off to the north side of us. The livery man had warned me about the Bosque all the way from Albuquerque to Los Lunas. If you get too far off the stage road, you'll risk bogging down in the Bosque. Said it always took the sass out of long-stepping horses, like mine. He was right. I tried to stay a quarter mile in front of the Concord. I made two turns looking back and noticed Chinorero dropping back. He was now a half-mile behind us, and I kept losing sight of him as the stage road twisted in long looping turns following the big river south.

We'd traveled maybe six miles when I gave Marathon a little breather. We were a quarter mile ahead of the Concord. I was just sitting my saddle watching the Concord's team struggle some when I heard the sharp crack of a rifle. Two shots in quick succession, then a minute lag, then two more. Couldn't see Chinorero. I had wheeled Marathon back toward the Concord when I heard the popping sound of a small caliber weapon. Had to be Chinorero's little .25. He fired five shots. I'd ridden a hundred yards when I heard the last rifle fire. Gunfight, I thought. I dropped Snow's lead rope and spurred Marathon into a full gallop. It took me five minutes to get back to him.

He was off the Morgan, nestled in between two rocks. His horse was fifty feet north, standing stock still up against a huge juniper. Chin was on his side in the dirt with both hands holding tight against his belly. His hands, long shirt, and the top of his canvas were covered with black blood. "Chin, hold on, partner!" I hollered down to him as I swung off Marathon. There was no one else in sight.

He mumbled something but I couldn't understand him. His face was rigid with pain. He tried to talk but his breath was shallow.

"Knew they were out of range but fired all five shots. My gut is on fire. Don't want to die here. Take me home, to my people."

"What happened?"

"Not sure. Walking my horse behind the coach. Heard rifle fire over there."

He nodded toward a sandstone bluff east of us.

"One man, or two?" I asked.

"One. Shot my direction but not right at me."

"What?"

"I saw the bullets hit. First two hit a tree limb on a rock right over there to the south of me. Then two more shots hit the rock shale to the other side. I jumped off my horse and ducked down behind this big rock, right here. I saw a man, white man, climbing back up onto his horse with his rifle slung across his back. As he was wheeling away from me, I pulled my pistol and emptied it at him. He was too far away."

"I heard one more rifle shot, Chin. So the man must have stopped to take one more shot at you."

"Wasn't him. There was another man, never saw him. He fired right at me from up ahead of us. Between me and the Concord. He got me in the gut."

I pulled my knife from the belt sheath and was cutting a strip of cloth from the back of his shirt when Teddy's big Concord rounded the bend down toward us as he hauled back on his reins hollering "whoa!". I could see his big right arm pulling the brake handle back as the stage skidded to a shudder stop. Teddy looped the reins around the hook on the stop rail at the front of the driver's cabin and jumped down.

"Chin, you alright? What 'n hell . . ."

"Teddy, you stay with Chin. Get Sgt. Bell to help you bandage his wound. He's gut shot. Get him in the stage. I'm going to see if I can find tracks. There were two of 'em. One up front and one down toward the river. They both fired on your man."

I rode slow and easy backtracking to the north, where Chinorero'd said the first shots came from. It was a good two hundred yards away. The man had dismounted; there was a fresh pile of horseshit on the ground. He'd laid a dead tree branch across a big rock for a rifle stand. Boot marks showed he'd spread his legs to steady his aim. Two brass casings were laying in the soft sand. He must've lit out in a hurry, just like Chin said he'd done.

As I was fingering the cartridges, Teddy rode up on Chinorero's horse. He had a gun rig tied down on his left side for a cross draw. He swung down like a cavalry officer hitting the ground an instant before the horse slid to a stop. I remembered he was a VMI graduate.

"What'd you find, Marshal?"

"One man. Off his horse. Made him a little stand for a long bore rifle. Here's two spent cartridges. But, Teddy, I told you to get Chin back to Albuquerque."

"Sgt. Bell is tending to him. He thinks he's got the wound packed. J. Leonard's a mess—came completely apart. The shooter didn't police his brass. Tells us he either was not military, or in a hell of a hurry. Looks like an ambush to me. That your take on it?"

"'Spect so, Teddy. But there's something wrong here. The man had a clear shot at Chin. Long bore rifle. A fairly short shoot. There's a cigar butt over there, and it looks like he was sitting down in the sand for a while. You can see boot marks there where he stood up. Probably to get his shot lined up. Chinorero's hurt bad. You sure the bleeding's stopped?"

"No, I just hollered at Mr. Leonard to stay inside the coach. Sgt. Bell jumped out right away, gun drawn. I told him tend to Chin. My gun rig was up under the driver's seat. I strapped it on, and ran to where Chin was. Then I jumped his little Morgan and came looking for you. What'd he say happened?"

I told him Chin's theory—one man firing his direction but not trying to hit him—another up between him and the stagecoach. By the time I got here, I added, I thought I saw a man on horseback, way down the hill. Just a speck moving toward the river and too far away to catch.

Teddy studied the ground carefully.

"Marshal, let's spread out and see if we can triangulate the other man. I'll take the north track. You ride south about a hundred yards that way and then turn up toward where you were when the firing started. One of us will spot his back trail."

So we did. Teddy was right. The second shooter had not dismounted but had been sitting his horse about fifty yards ahead and a hundred yards off the stage road. He was in a perfect place to bushwhack us, or Chin. The track showed he stopped, turned the horse a couple times, but never got off. Then the tracks headed south and looped back around.

"He's headed for the river, too. Can't figure this," I puzzled.

We rode back to the Concord. Chin was inside the cabin laying down on the forward-facing double seat. J. Leonard was in the other seat, leaning forward to hold the packing on Chin's belly. Bell was up top, scanning the horizon in four directions with a pair of Army-issue binoculars. He'd holstered his gun but wasn't asking questions. We told them what we'd found.

"We've got to run this team flat out to Albuquerque. We'll get that doc across the street from the La Posada to fix Chin. If he makes it that far."

We headed back.

CHAPTER 7

"Dismount & Confab"

IT TOOK A LITTLE OVER TWO HOURS to reach Albuquerque. Teddy switched back and forth from a fast trot to a slow lope with his big team. He didn't stop at the livery barn. Drove straight to the hotel so we could get the doc quick. I peeled off a block away toward the livery barn to stable Marathon and Snow. I'd finished brushing Snow and was working on Marathon when Teddy came back with the four-up team. I helped him unhitch and move the draft horses into the rear corral.

"How's Chin?" I asked.

"Not good. One bullet in the gut. Bleeding's stopped, but there's no exit wound. You know that's often one bullet too many. Goddamn! Can't figure why someone would shoot an innocent boy like Chin. You got any idea on it?" he asked me.

"Well, wouldn't call it an idea exactly. Wild ass hunch would be more like it. I think the first shooter was trying to scare Chin. Or us. Don't know which. He did his job and lit out to the east. Long gone before I got to Chin. But Chin emptied his little pistol at the other man, on the opposite side of the road and between him and your coach. That man, with five bullets coming at him but falling short, took aim and fired a long-barrel rifle. Got Chin in the gut. No idea who they were or why they are on our back trail. But I'll tell you this. Wasn't no damn robbery. It was something else."

I helped Teddy with his team. Just as we finished, a boy from the hotel showed up and said J. Leonard told him to tell me Chin was unconscious but alive. We did a fast walk back to the hotel where the doctor was just coming out the front door. He was a man short on words.

"Your man, Chinorero, is unconscious but alive. He has a mortal wound. Believe he'll be dead by morning."

"Angus, this changes what my plan was. Let's walk down the road a bit. Got something to tell you."

We got to the river and turned upstream to a sizeable clump of cottonwoods. We hadn't talked along the way. Suppose neither of us wanted to start the conversation. But now that we were there at the east bank of the Rio Grande, things needed saying. I started.

"You got a nice hand for driving a four-up team, Teddy, but you're not a teamster, are you?"

"No. I'm not. How'd you know?"

"You got a teamster's handshake, but no callouses. And you sit a horse better than you do a wagon seat. When your Apache boy came under fire, you jumped that little horse like you'd done it before. So are you still in the Army? Is that what you're really doing here—making sure Mr. Leonard doesn't find something the Army don't want him to find?"

"No, I'm not. He asked as he took a seat on a log.

He stretched his legs out in front and layered one black boot over the other. Reaching inside his vest, he fished out a leather wallet folded in half, and tossed it to me.

"We are in the same business, Angus. I'd planned on telling you once we were out on the mesa and away from Albuquerque. Out of earshot."

Just from the feel of it, I could tell it was a badge. Inside the flap was a shiny piece of brass plate—five pointed stars with rounded tips—United States Secret Service—Division of the U.S. Treasury.

"Secret Service? Mr. Leonard said he had a grant from the U.S. Treasury, but he didn't say anything to me about you or any other law officer being part of this trip. What am I missing here?"

"Mr. Leonard doesn't know I'm an agent. He also does not know why the Treasury Department gave him such a generous grant. But my orders were to tell you everything first chance we got, with the understanding you wouldn't talk about my job here—being as we're both law enforcement officers and all."

"Teddy, I don't know why I'm here, much less why the U.S. Secret Service has its own agent along for the ride. I was told somebody in Washington thought this man, J. Leonard, ought to be escorted by a man with a badge. Just in case."

"In case of what?" Teddy asked, with a squint in his eyes.

"Not sure I know. The Indian Wars are over, but not everyone in New Mexico is comfortable around men we were at war with just twenty years ago. Some white citizens fear the red devil. Others hate Indians because some kin got scalped decades ago. Some are just ignorant and hate everyone that ain't the same color as them. But that's not why you're here, is it? The U.S. Treasury has no stake in healing old war wounds, or in preserving history for the Smithsonian. Am I right?"

"Right. Our mission, since 1865, has been to deal with counterfeiting bank notes and federal currency. Did you know that, during the Civil War, more than half the currency in circulation was counterfeit?"

"No, but nothing about the Civil War surprises me. With the exception of one battle, some say it was a scuffle, at Glorieta Pass, in eighteen and sixty-two, New Mexico shucked the entire war. I guess I remember some confabulation about mustering out of the Army with nowhere to go—least for the officers. The high commanders, some said, needed another war; so they made war on the Navajo. Feller named Kit Carson got right famous for killing Navajos. And not just Navajo warriors. He killed horses, sheep, dogs, and most anything that was in front of him during a full-on charge with bugles blowing. He shot men by the hundreds. But that's another thing. Tell me, do you think the soldiers were counterfeiting money, or was it the Navajos?"

"We have some evidence of Navajos counterfeiting tokens, but not paper currency. Tokens were used at the Army commissary and the settler's store to get food and blankets. But the Secret Service has no interest in that. Our job today is still to find and arrest counterfeiters whose phony money was and is a danger to the whole economy. The scale of the thing in the South was massive, and out West, well, it was enough to send officers out here after the Civil War. We'll be visiting several decommissioned Army forts and settlers' stores. I'll be looking for signs of counterfeiting. And there was a good deal of cash money spent on Bosque Redondo. Some of the cash may have been counterfeit."

Just then, a pair of good-sized black birds scurried out of a big cottonwood and spun up into the sky. We both studied the birds for a minute. The river was running high, and as close as we were, the noise was pretty loud. Teddy had not said anything about which side of the war he favored.

"You said you were from Virginia, but your family was on the Union side. Am I remembering that correct?"

"Right, Virginia. My father and one uncle sided with the Union because they thought slavery was an abomination. I was too young to have to decide which side to back. But it would have been the Union, not just because the Confederates were slavers, but because we fought for our independence once. Seems like splitting the country into two was going back on the reasons we became the *United* States in the first damn place. Anyhow, I was too young to soldier when the Confederates seceded. I did my two years in the Army in 1876 because my dad did his time earlier. The family sent me to the VMI so I'd have a career. Turns out, they were right. But I'm not an Army man—I'm a lawman, just like you. What I'm looking for on this trip is different than Mr. Leonard's report."

"So, how different?"

"Angus, J. Leonard is a professor. All he cares about is writing history. But he's got a problem. He says the only written records are ones written by soldiers, or by white newspaper people. The Indians have never said, far as I know, what happened to them. He wants to hear their story out of their own mouths. He thinks he can get a better sense of it from just one Navajo—the woman who's gonna be in the stage once we get to Fort Defiance."

"Teddy, suppose you're right. What's he gonna do with the report once it's finished?"

"He intends to store it at the Smithsonian, but he also intends to publish it in every library and school in the country. He wants to write a report about putting Navajos into an open prison out on the prairie. He's got hard evidence of that calamity. And he knows, or he damn well should know, that the Army won't like what he has to say. He's too soft on the Indian problem, they think. The counterfeit money is mostly a cover for my trip. Truth is, both of us are here to protect Mr. J. Leonard from folks who won't take kindly any accusation of misdeeds by them. I'm talking about the Army brass. And there are civilians who profited by selling goods of all sort to the Bosque Redondo commissary. You get my drift?"

"I do. But the law operates on evidence, not on conversations taking place in a stagecoach. Neither one of us will be in that coach. If we're here to protect him, but we don't know who's got it in for him, how do we spot anyone who's a danger to him?"

"We can only protect him by watching his back trail. I can handle things while he's in my coach. I guess it's up to you to spot trouble from a distance."

Teddy offered me a little swig out of a flask he produced from the other side of his vest. It was dark whiskey, but didn't bite back, like the stuff I was used to in New Mexico saloons. He offered me a cigar. Don't smoke, I told him. We let the talk sit for a while. After a good spell, he gave me something else to fester about.

"Angus, all I've got is thin evidence of counterfeiting, mostly opinion, all across the South, including Texas. The Secret Service has no hard evidence of counterfeiting. But we know who did it: educated civilians. We know the Army ignored it. And those doing it at scale were not more than a handful. But the money got spread from Texas to California and up the coast to Oregon."

"Why?" I asked him.

"Why? Well, that's a damn good question. It was my first question, too. Couldn't see any reason my superiors in Washington would look into counterfeiting in New Mexico that took place twenty or thirty years ago."

"What'd they tell you?"

"That the statutes of limitation had long since passed on counterfeiting, but not on buying or selling Indian kids, or murder. There's a connection between using counterfeit money to buy horses and trade goods and holding onto young Indian girls for Mexican slave traders south of the border. They caught a few crooked soldiers, but never could identify any officers or Indian traders in the deal. You ever heard of a group of wealthy businessmen and ranchers called the Santa Fe Ring?"

"Heard of it. But can't say it ever meant much to me. It came up in connection with a case I investigated in Albuquerque a few years ago. Are you saying the Santa Fe Ring dealt in Indian slaves and counterfeit money?"

"No proof of that I know of. But the newspapers accused the Santa Fe Ring of all manner of machination. When J. Leonard asked for a grant to reconstruct the forced march and captivity of seven-thousand Navajos, or however many there were, my superiors at the Secret Service thought it would be worth assigning one agent to make the trip. Maybe I'll discover some evidence—maybe not. Hell, Angus, anytime the United States government can investigate a serious crime by only assigning one agent to the job, it just can't resist the temptation. Since I do a whole lot of camp cooking and love riding atop a big wagon strapped behind big horses, I volunteered for the job."

"Well, Teddy, if there is a piggin string tying the Santa Fe Ring to marching all those Navajos purtin' near all the way across New Mexico it will be old and thin. I just have to say I never did understand what the Santa Fe Ring was, even back when I was looking into the hanging of Milton J. Yarberry just up the road there from we're standing right now. Maybe you, being you're from back east and a government agent and all, can fill me in a little more."

"My boss was in a meeting discussing this grant—the one they gave to the Smithsonian. He told me a little about the Santa Fe Ring, and why I ought to keep my ears open about it on this trip. You could say the name, Santa Fe Ring, was stuck onto most Republican politicians in the state capital in Santa Fe. They had a hand, or maybe a boot, in controlling the legislature and the courts here for the last twenty-thirty years. Some said those powerful men turned a blind eye to corruption. There's no doubt they had a hand in everything that happened here during the 1870s, when ownership of those big Spanish land grants all over the state was being sorted out. Hell, as I heard it, there was land being sold to settlers that nobody owned. Men wearing big hats and suspenders were getting ahold of government contracts to supply beef to Navajos and all manner of tribes through Indian agents, under corrupt political contacts. Thing was, they either supplied less beef than the contract called for, or a poor quality of meat, often spoiled. Some say it was the Army, not high-ranking brass, but younger officers of low moral character who were making more money than their pay grade allowed. They knew about the graft and maybe even got a little side money on the deal."

"So, you investigating that, too, along with counterfeiting and slave trading?"

"No, Angus, I ain't saying that. All I'm saying is that there were misdeeds of all sorts going on at the time the Navajo wars ended. You know, don't you, that we were at war with the Navajo tribe? We killed hundreds and captured thousands more. We hauled them like slaves in wagons and stuck them in an open-prairie prison with Fort Sumner in the middle. The Army and the Indian agents stood to profit from several hundred thousand dollars in U.S. Treasury money. That's the rub of it. *Money.* Always is. I'm not investigating, just keeping my ears and eyes open. They want a report back in Washington, not an arrest. But mostly, they don't want any harm to come to the Smithsonian man. He's likely to ask questions of everyone he comes across on this trip. You know what I mean?"

I didn't, but thought it best to keep that to myself.

"Tell you want, Teddy, it's near dark. Let's walk back to the hotel and talk about how we're going to deal with those two shooters that fired at Chinorero."

CHAPTER 8

"Regroup and Ride On"

WHEN WE GOT BACK to the hotel, the desk clerk, a thin man with a small upper lip who sort of whispered at you when talking, said Mr. Leonard had taken Chinorero to Mr. Sarr's establishment.

"You say a star what?" asked Teddy.

Wispy pretended not to hear so I answered.

"Sarr. Mr. Sarr. He's an old Chinese man who doctors everyone the regular doctor won't take a liking to. Like drunks, half-breeds, Apaches, and Russian miners who cannot speak American English."

The second I finished my rant on the local doctor, Mr. Leonard walked back through the door.

"Good evening Teddy, Angus. I have dreadful news for you. The local doctor here bandaged Chin, but says he won't last the night. Something about a rampant infection in the body cavity. But the effervescent Mr. Sarr has an Oriental approach to medicine and what white doctors say is a mortal wound. He says infection is his biggest danger but some with serious stomach wounds do survive. He's treating our Chinorero with vapors and herbal medicine. He really was the most interesting doctor I've ever met. It was good of the hotel staff to recommend him to us."

We all went into the dining room where we found the chalkboard menu had no rice or corn flats. The feature meal was baked turkey, potatoes, and chili, pork chops with greens, and buttermilk. Everyone ordered something different. Teddy and I ordered beer. J. Leonard ordered tea, hot with milk and sugar.

"Sgt. Bell won't be joining us this evening," he announced.

"Too bad," Teddy said.

"Where'd he go?" I asked.

"He didn't say," J. Leonard answered. "But I do believe I saw him walking down that street where the livery barn is. Perhaps there is another dining establishment that way."

"There is," I offered. "One with better-looking women to serve you. 'Spect we won't see the old horse sergeant before breakfast."

We talked over dinner. I said we needed to visit the Bernalillo County Sheriff, Perfecto Armijo, first thing in the morning to report the shots fired at Chin. Teddy said we ought to consider hiring another man, on a two-week deal, to ride with us from Albuquerque to Fort Defiance

J. Leonard said, "Gentlemen, I have cabled my superiors in Washington, DC. They will take a day or two to get back to me. What I need from you, and Mr. Sarr, of course, is a considered opinion as to Mr. Chinorero's chances. Will he survive this horrendous shooting? And even if he does, won't he be invalidated for quite some time? I must report to Washington on whether this attack is aimed only at Chinorero, or is it aimed at us? Give me your advice on that, if you please."

"Well," I answered, "Teddy and I talked this over. He can speak for himself. But I'd say those boys who shot Chinorero were sending you a message. They probably did not intend to kill the boy—the first shooter missed on purpose. The second shooter was returning fire. He knew by hitting the boy we'd stop to tend to him. By the time we got mounted again they'd be long gone. That's my take on it."

"Agreed," Teddy said.

"My dear, whatever can this mean? A message—what message? Back east you don't shoot people to send messages. Please clarify what you mean by a message."

Teddy gave it a shot. "Mr. Leonard, it may be that somebody here in New Mexico does not want you, or anybody else, dredging up the past. Maybe somebody out here has something to lose if you stir things up about the Army marching nine-thousand Navajos from their homeland over in Arizona to the Bosque Redondo as prisoners. Maybe somebody out here is mad they didn't get all that land. Fear and money are always motivators and there's always gun hands ready to make a few dollars sending lead bullets as messages."

"One week? That's how long it will take for your fine team to haul that big red coach from Albuquerque to Fort Defiance, a week?"

Next morning, I led our little group two blocks over to the sheriff's office. The deputy, a stout man sitting on the front porch, was drinking black coffee out of a white porcelain cup. He said right off Sheriff Armijo was not in town.

"When will he be back?" I asked.

"Depends," he said.

"On what?" Teddy asked.

"You never know with Perfecto," the deputy said, rhyming the words with a grin on his face. "Our sheriff is in charge even when he ain't here. And Deputy Angus, I'm happy to see you back with us. If I'm remembering correct, you were on the invite list to the hanging of Milton J. Yarberry, the first town marshal here. You're riding a different horse now, ain't you?"

"I am. He's a Tennessee walking horse. How'd you know he's mine?"

"My horse," the deputy said, "is that bony, old, white mare in the end stall, just one stall away from your big Chestnut. Mine has seen better days, but my wife is fond of her, so that's the story of how I know you have a new horse. If you think it's important enough, we can send a man on horseback to Perfecto's ranch. It's a three-hour ride east through Tijeras Canyon, but that's your call."

"No," I said, looking at Teddy for his sense of it. He nodded my direction and entered the discussion.

"Sorry," Teddy said, "but I didn't get your name."

"Myers, Shanty Myers. Born in Utah. I'm the oldest deputy now so I get to make decisions when Perfecto's out to his ranch. What sort of matter are you reporting on?"

"Could we go inside?" Teddy asked.

It didn't take more 'n five minutes to tell Deputy Myers what happened to Chin and our suspicions about the two men that shot at him yesterday on the road south toward Los Lunas. He plainly didn't believe that the shooter intended to miss. He squirrelled up his face when we speculated it was intended as a warning to us. J. Leonard tried to summarize the purpose of his federal grant and this reconstructed Long Walk from Fort Defiance to Fort Sumner. But Leonard is not short on words and Shanty Myers kept losing track of the explanation.

Looking at me, but aiming his words at J. Leonard, Deputy Myers said, "I suppose someone with a rifle could of followed you boys out of town, across the river, and up that long pull, but the motive—that's a word Sheriff Armijo uses a lot— escapes me. What would be the motive for doing that? It's a free country, ain't it? You all want to spend a month in a stage coach following a twenty-year-old Army maneuver, no one's stopping you. But who do you think would oppose your trip? If Perfecto were here, he'd ask more questions, but that's the only one I can think of. Who might not want you spending your time on, what did you say it was, a federal grant?"

Mr. Leonard leaned forward in his chair and took in a long breath. "Deputy Myers, what happened here twenty years ago, on this very street, was not merely a *maneuver* by the Army. It was an act of war—the sequel to the surrender by the Navajo tribe of Indians, and the beginning of an internment that lasted four years. The Army documented its actions in official orders. Now the Smithsonian Institution, with generous support by the United States Treasury Department, wishes to reconstruct that trip for research and informational purposes. Yesterday, someone interrupted the first day of our effort by killing a young boy who was a member of our team. That shooting was not a maneuver, either. Will your office investigate this matter for us? We are keenly interested in the safety of everyone in our party."

"No reason to get your dander up, mister. I'm just saying that maybe it was a robbery, or someone who didn't like Apaches—we got lots of people around here who still remember raiding parties and innocent settlers getting scalped. But your men here say it was a warning. Warning of what? I'll say it plain out. Yes, we will ask questions around town. But if it was an attempted robbery, or if it was a warning, I doubt anyone will want to fess up to it. Our jurisdiction is limited to the county line—nine miles south is within Bernalillo County. But wounding an Indian boy, even if turns out to be a mortal wound, is not something that we'll track down except by accident. I'll write a report for the sheriff. I'd advise you to keep a keen eye out. Anything else I can do for you?"

CHAPTER 9

"Ora Gray"

NEXT DAY, WE GATHERED in the lobby of the hotel after breakfast. J. Leonard was solemn.

"Gentlemen, Mr. Sarr knocked on my door at six this morning. Chinorero passed away sometime after midnight last night. I do not know what arrangements must be made, but whatever it costs, the Smithsonian will bear it. Teddy, I will need your direction on this."

Teddy told us Chinorero had no family up at Fort Union but that he might have family on the Mescalero reservation down south below the Bosque Redondo. He'd cable the authorities in Fort Union and get their advice. Teddy said we had to hire someone to take Chin's place on the trip, but he'd understand if J. Leonard wanted to cancel everything given Chin's death.

"But, Teddy," Leonard said, "there can be no thought of scuttling the trip now. Especially not now. A member of our expedition has been murdered. That must be fully investigated. But stop the trip? No, my good man, we will muster on. Mr. Chinorero's memory insists that we do just that. Maybe while we are traveling to Fort Defiance the authorities here will solve this murder. We'll be back here in less than ten days' time. Meanwhile we must find a suitable replacement for our dear departed friend."

Teddy said, "I talked to Angus some last evening about making sure everyone is safe on this trip. I'm fair to middling with a gun and have military experience. So, I think I'll get one of the stable horses and take Chinorero's place riding drag or maybe even lead if Angus wants me to. Will your federal budget stand one more person? We need a man who can handle the coach and help me with the camp routine. This would give us two guns on horseback in case we need them, and one atop the coach. Those men who followed us yesterday weren't scared off. Maybe they're watching the stable to see how many of us pull out tomorrow. If they only see Angus out in front, it might give them an idea about attacking the coach. If they see two of us armed and mounted—I don't know. I'm just saying."

Leonard turned to me. "Angus, security is your expertise, not mine. What do you think of this idea? Money is not a barrier to safety. If you think it's appropriate, then I'd like you to engage whomsoever you can to provide road security. We'll be in open country a good bit of the time."

"Mr. Leonard, thing is, I don't know who was on our back trail yesterday. I don't know why they let loose at Chin. But fact is, they did. Maybe it was a warning, like Teddy thinks. Maybe they shot at him thinking he'd run. Maybe when he fired back, they killed him for that. Don't matter now. This trip is a different damn ride today. If you can afford the extra hand, then that's the easy bet. Why don't I take a ride out to Perfecto Armijo's ranch? He steered me in the right direction once before and he knows everyone packing a six-shooter in this part of the New Mexico territory. That all right with you?"

"Angus, do what you think is best."

"Mighty fine. Teddy, why don't you walk with me down to the stable? We can talk while I saddle up Marathon."

I told Teddy a little about Perfecto Armijo and how much he knew about everything that had ever happened in this part of the country. He thought it was a good idea to talk to him about losing Chinorero but also about the bigger question: What 'n hell are we up against? We talked about that. I told him the sheriff's ranch butts up against the east side of the Sandia Mountains.

"As I recall, it's about fifteen miles from here. Marathon will long walk that in ninety minutes easy. I'll be there before supper time, and back here by midnight."

Teddy frowned.

"Midnight. Isn't that late to be riding? I often read in the evening, but I could not imagine being out in the wilderness at that time of night."

"Maybe you ought to ride more and read less," I said.

Turns out, Marathon was faster than I thought. We hit the front gate of the Armijo spread one hour and twenty minutes before supper time. I found the old sheriff at the blacksmith shop on the side of his big barn. He was banging down hard on a horseshoe that'd just come out of the fire. It was big enough for a small elephant. I could see one of his big draft horses tied up to the hitching rail.

"Hello, Sheriff Armijo, do you remember me?"

"*Buenas tardes*, Marshal. Of course I remember you. You shot my least favorite cousin—the *bandito* of our family— Mendoza Mendoza, up on the Valles Caldera two years ago. *Bienvenidos a mi Rancho.*"

I climbed down off Marathon and stuck out my hand.

"Good afternoon to you, too. I'm mighty happy to ride your ranch. This is a fine spread. And I'm glad to hear you ain't got no machismo grudge over me plugging your cousin. It was a righteous shoot."

"Indeed it was. I read Marshal Knop's report and the longer one written by Frank Chavez. But let us speak no more of that. Can you join us for supper? *Mi esposa* would be pleased if you'd grace our table."

The main building on Perfecto's sprawling ranch was an adobe structure burrowed into the upward slope of the land so deeply that the ground floor, with a double front door, served as public space. It had a big porch, kitchen, and a big open room for dining and talking. The upper two floors had bedrooms and patios. The dark vigas and lighter latias in the ceiling protected a broad inner plaza about fifty feet across. The hardscrabble floor leading to the front door was a path to a building that looked to be more than a hundred years old. You could see how each generation had added a little more adobe to the walls, clay tiles on the floor, and wood shutters on the narrow slits in the outer wall for light and air. Heavy wood planks lined the windows. I'd say it was part fortress and part palace.

Perfecto introduced me to his wife. She nodded and poured me a cup of water from a tall ceramic vase. Then Perfecto took me through the main room to a three-walled space at the far end that he called *mia pensamiento*—"my thinking place."

"Sit, please, Angus. I knew you were in Albuquerque. One of my best cooks was at the medical office of Mr. Sarr yesterday when an Apache boy came in for treatment. My *vaquero* has a broken left arm, and your deputy, if that's what he is, has a gunshot wound in his belly. What, please tell me, is his condition? Not a serious wound, *si*?"

"Sheriff, I'm sorry to say it was damn serious. Chinorero died early this morning. In fact, it's his death that has put me horseback to come up here and talk to you. Oh, and he's not a deputy. He is a Mescalero; just a boy really, but he's got sand. His father was a prisoner down at the Bosque Redondo twenty years ago. I'm here to ask your help on getting another man to make the ride with us, but I'd also appreciate your views on that Long Walk the Navajos took back then. As I hear it, they must have walked through Tijeras Canyon not ten miles from here on the way to Los Pinos."

"I am most grieved, Senor Angus. What was his name, *por favor*?"

"Chinorero."

"Chinorero. A fine name. Named after a Mescalero chief, I think. Perhaps he was the man known as the buffalo finder. Such a man rode to the middle of Texas. Now, Angus, what kind of a man are you looking for? Not a deputy, *si*?"

"Well, *señor,* I'm looking to hire a man who can handle a gun, ride a fast horse, hitch up a team of draft horses to a big ole stagecoach, handle the threads from the driver's box on top, cook a supper for four men and a woman, and smile at an Eastern dude. Anybody come to mind that fits that bill?"

"How long might you employ such a person and at what rate?"

"A month, maybe. But I expect the man I'm escorting on this trip, his name's J. Leonard, would agree to a flat amount of federal currency equal to what a good cowhand would make in, say, three months."

"That would be a generous wage. And when would this person be employed?"

"Now. But I can't do the money handshake. That would have to come from J. Leonard tomorrow. We'd like to recommence our trip day after tomorrow. Sounds like maybe you got a man in mind?"

"Perhaps, if you allow a small deviation in your first requirement."

"My first requirement? You mean a man who's good with a gun? That's number-one on my list."

"No, Marshal. You said you needed a man to do all those things. I do not know such a man. But a woman here fits all your requirements. Would you like to meet her?"

"A woman? Well, I'm married to a woman who can out-shoot most men and is a fine cook, but she could not drive a stagecoach with a four-up team in harness. If she can do what needs doing, sure, we'd be happy to have another woman on board. 'Course, I'd want to make sure the man in charge of this trip agrees. Does this woman work for you?"

"Marshal, this woman, Ora Gray is her name, does work here, but not so much *for* me. Let me explain her presence on this ranch. She is the daughter of my foreman, Marcelles Gray, and a distant cousin of mine, Conchita D'Espinosa. Ora was born on the ranch thirty years ago. She lives in our main ranch house and is very much a part of our family. She draws a salary, but I doubt she's spent much of it. She breaks horses, mends fences, stops stampedes, and leads most of the hunting parties in the fall. The *vaqueros* are afraid of her because she is as tough as they are and gives no quarter when she's mad—either at them, or me."

"Sounds like a top hand."

"That is true. There is one other thing you should know before you consider her. She was only ten when the Army marched a long line of Navajo men, women, and children at gunpoint through the Tijeras Canyon, just a few miles from here. She saw them. Other children at the ranch saw them too. They all cried. But Ora did not cry. She never does. Ora raised her little fist at the soldiers. I can assure you the event is still fresh in her memory. In English, she taunted the soldiers as barbarous. In Spanish, *que los hombres son la escoria de hacer esto.*"

"Sheriff, my Spanish is not much better than my English. But I think she called the soldiers *scum*. Is that right?"

"*Si*, that is the correct translation. She is a strong woman, raised by her father, and the *vaqueros* on this ranch. Her mother died in childbirth. The *vaqueros* taught her many things as a child, including their language and how to fight for things you believe in. She saw those Navajos as slaves and the soldiers as slave traders. She might vex you some. I do not know the details of the job you might have for her. Only that it is temporary, otherwise I would not recommend her to you. This ranch is her home. We would not want to lose her to a permanent job somewhere else, especially one involving a stagecoach."

"Well, that brings up the other thing I wanted to ask you about. I'm curious to know your opinion on the war the Army fought against the Navajo and the way it ended—with the transporting of all those Navajos from Fort Defiance to Fort Sumner. Reason I'm asking is that folks in Washington from the Smithsonian are out here now looking at all that. As I said, I'm escorting a man named J. Leonard; he's a researcher and will write a report. And if your Ora Gray is right for this temporary job, she'll be riding to Fort Defiance with us and then back to Fort Sumner, maybe."

"*Si*, Angus, I do have an opinion, but you might not like to hear it."

"No, sir, I surely do want to hear it."

Before he could start, two young girls came into the *pensamiento*. One carried a tray with a plate of baked cookies—smelled fresh out of the oven—and they had powdered sugar on them. The other girl's tray had a small clay pot and two round mugs. Perfecto introduced them but neither of them looked directly at me. Both smiled nervously, then set their trays down on the tile table between me and the sheriff, and scurried off.

"Beer and sugar-powder-cake cookies are helpful when discussing troublesome issues; do you agree, Angus?"

"Not sure about the beer, but those cookies look mighty fine."

As we ate the cookies and sipped on the strong beer, the sheriff gave me a different take on what Mr. Leonard had explained a few days ago in Fort Marcy.

"The Army. Do you know why the U.S. government sent an army here, the one that made war on the Navajos twenty years ago?"

"I was told by Mr. Leonard it was here to fight the Confederates."

"Yes, that is a common Anglo view. But my people saw that army through New Mexican eyes. We saw them ride through Albuquerque. Long lines of troops from California, led by an Anglo general named Carleton; he wore a long feather in his hat and rode a magnificent white horse. His sword's silver scabbard glistened in the sun. Soon, we knew he asked Kit Carson, from Taos, to form a militia of New Mexican soldiers. Señor Carson was a fierce man, famous for hunting and killing animals and men. Together they raised several hundred local militia men. There was no longer any threat from the Confederates by the time Carleton got here. But still he became the commanding general in Santa Fe. He had an army, and the Texans, the real enemy, were already defeated. The gray-coated soldiers who occupied Albuquerque never lived in the South. All of them were Texans. Texans had always treated the Mexican people unjustly, and these Confederate Texans were no different. The new general, Señor Carleton, could find no one to fight. So he convinced Washington that the settlers and locals were in danger from the Navajo warriors. He was given permission to make war. On the Navajos. That is the opinion you might not want to hear."

I was pondering what Perfecto was saying when his wife came in to tell us that her dinner was on the table. Suppose that was just as well. The thought that Perfecto Armijo might be right was gnawing at me. We got up and went to dinner. That's where I met Ora Gray.

The kitchen table at the Armijo spread was where everyone ate—the owner, his family, all the *vaqueros,* visitors, and stray lawmen, like me. It was actually two tables, strapped together in a T-shape. The family sat on the cross section and everyone else sat facing one another on the long end. Perfecto led me to a seat next to his. There was no formality at this table. Men came in, sat down, and ate. When they finished, they got up and left the room. Dinner took about an hour at the family end, but everyone else seemed to just take a few minutes before finishing their meal. For the family, this was a social event. The *vaqueros* ate with their hats on, and everyone talked all at once; seemed like ten conversations. Two women sat with cowhands; one wore a black felt crowned hat, the other a bright red scarf. They did not sit next to one another. Both were short, about the same age. I wondered if one of them was the woman Perfecto had been talking about.

About halfway through our dinner, Perfecto leaned over. "Ora is the one with the black hat."

"Figured that," I said.

She had paid no notice to any of us at the cross-end of the table. Her skin was the color of mule hide left out in the sun too long. But, since she was sitting down, I could not tell much else about her. When she got up, Perfecto waved at her.

"Ora, *por favor*, can you join us here? I want you to meet my friend the U.S. Marshal."

As she walked over to us, I was struck by how square she was. Short, but with little change from her shoulders to her legs. She wore a long-sleeve shirt tucked into denim jeans over dusty work boots. She walked with purpose, but her short legs required several steps to reach the end of the table.

I got up as she approached and stuck my hand out when he told her my name. She took my hand with the firmest grip I'd ever felt from a woman. Not like a vice, but like she would not let go until I did. She did not smile with her mouth, but with her eyes. They flashed brightly and unflinching at me. At first I thought they were black, but up close they took on the copper brown you see on big animals, like bull elk. She carried herself the same way.

"Nice meeting you," I said.

"And me, also," she said.

"Ora, will you sit with us? Marshal Angus asked me to recommend someone on our ranch for a short job, perhaps three or four weeks. I thought of you."

She took a place at the end of the table, picked up one of the many cookies from a wicker basket, and asked, "Why me?"

"Because you have certain traits and capabilities that this job calls for. And because you have not been off the ranch for more than a year. Your father and I agree on one thing, perhaps *only* one thing about you. You need to see more of the world than this."

"You don't need to be talking about me to my father. Of course I love both of you, but this ranch *is* my world."

"Ora, Ora, this is exactly why you should listen to the Marshal. Angus, please tell her what you need. She will decide and then I will try to find someone else for you, if necessary. But she is my first choice, *que no?*"

So, not knowing how this would all come out, I told her about J. Leonard's grant from the Treasury Department, and how I figured he would try to write a report. It took longer than I like to talk.

"I don't understand something," she said, "this stagecoach with three people inside. They are riding and talking about the Navajo Long Walk? One man is an Army sergeant; he was there—guarding the Navajos. One woman, a Navajo, was being guarded. The other man, he is a professor, right? And he will write down what the other two say inside the coach? Who is going to read this report?"

It was a question I'd never thought to ask and had no answer for.

"Don't know," I said.

"This Apache boy, the one who they shot at, is he going to ride on the coach, or on a horse, when he is well?"

"No, ma'am, I'm sorry to say the boy, an Apache named Chinorero, died this morning. If you join us, you will either be on top reining the team, or maybe inside if the weather gets harsh."

"No. I don't want to be in the coach. If I can't ride my horse, I don't want to go, although I like driving a four-up team behind a wagon. I would always pony my horse behind the stage. But still, I need to know who's going to read this report."

"All I can say is Mr. Leonard works for a museum called the Smithsonian in Washington City. That's where I imagine the report will be."

She looked at me carefully, then at her father, and Perfecto. She took a bite of another cookie.

"I don't want to go with you. If the report was for us, all the people who've lived here for more than a hundred years, and if it was going to tell the truth, then maybe I would go with you. I have work to do here."

With that, she stood up and left the room.

CHAPTER 10

"A Hole in the Boat"

THE RIDE BACK TO ALBUQUERQUE from Perfecto's ranch put me in mind of my younger days, riding at night at ten-thousand feet on Ten Shoes Up. There's a feeling like no other when a man and his horse find night has laid down on them so quick it feels like the earth just spun upside down. One minute you're riding in the gray shade of a big forest, the next you're inside a cave. The blackness of a small creek gurgled as we stopped so Marathon could suck up a belly full. The lone star just over the western horizon sat there like it was glued to the sky. Took just about four hours to reach Albuquerque.

Next morning, I went down to the lobby intending to walk down to the livery bar and check on Marathon. But J. Leonard was sitting in one of the leather chairs writing in that notebook he always carried.

"Ah, Angus, it's very good to see you. I trust you had a good ride last evening and secured a good man to aid us in our travel westward."

"The ride was commendable, all things considered. But I made no progress in finding a good man. There was a woman on the ranch who Sheriff Armijo said was a possible. I'd have to say she would have fit the bill, but the assignment was not to her liking."

He gave me one of those exasperated looks I'd come to recognize as eastern management style.

"My good man, whatever do you mean, not to her liking? You interviewed a woman who could drive the stage, cook meals, give us extra security as well, but simply did not *like* us? Whatever was it that caused her not to favor our endeavor?"

"Well, maybe it was the way I explained things. I told her you'd be writing a report for your museum, the Smithsonian in Washington. She didn't favor that. Said something about if it was not for all the people in New Mexico, she'd have no part in it."

"Did you tell her our reference point was the long march of the Navajo people? They are New Mexico people, are they not? Was there some particular aspect that she took as negative?"

"Jay, this woman was born on the sheriff's ranch. She's thirty years old and as good a ranch hand as any on that fine spread. But, see, she saw thousands of Indians trudging up Tijeras Canyon twenty years ago. She was only ten at the time. But it sure made a helluva impression on her. Fired her up, it did."

"I see. Is she of Mexican descent?"

"Her father's a German, or at least he looks like one. I met him last night—he's the ranch foreman. Her mother died; she was a cousin or something to the sheriff. I suspect her family heritage is the answer to her strong reaction to the situation—like I said, it fired her up."

"How exactly?"

"She told the soldiers they were scum."

"Oh, my! Are you sure about this? She is an actual observer of the conditions under which the Indians made the trip here, across the Rio Grande, and up the canyon to the east of us. It looks like a fierce canyon from here."

"Wouldn't call it fierce myself. But this young woman, Ora Gray's her name, I'd say she could be right fierce if you roiled her. Suppose it was my poor communication skills that affected her."

"No, my good man. You are a plain speaking man of the West. I think you have made a significant discovery of error—gross error on my part! This young woman might be instrumental in the success of our endeavor. Let me explain it this way. I have a colleague at the Smithsonian who is a naval architect. He's retired now and gives our museum half his time evaluating all things naval in our archives. He has a saying he often uses in similar situations. When he finds a flaw in naval design, or in the maneuvering of a warship, he'd say it was 'a hole in the boat.'"

"Hole in the boat?"

"Yes, it's his metaphor for a flaw in design that might result in sinking the vessel. Ora Gray has identified a hole in my plan—we should not be interpreting the events of twenty years ago solely from the perspectives of an Indian marcher and a soldier guard. We should also hear from people, the people of New Mexico, who bore witness to, but were not a part of, that dreadful march. How could I have not thought of this myself? Now tell me, my good man: Is the road to that ranch suitable for Teddy to ferry us there in our stagecoach? If so, I'd like you to engage him forthwith so I can talk to the woman myself. She has identified the hole in our boat—or more *apropos* our particular situation, the missing passenger in our stagecoach."

I found Teddy at the livery barn. We hitched the team.

CHAPTER 11

"Pluggin' the Hole"

I T WAS A SOFT MORNING—the Rio Grande had a layer of fog comforting it—the eastern sky was opening up to a constantly spreading sunrise—and Teddy's stagecoach was in front of the hotel, at the ready. J. Leonard had made his intentions clear last evening in the lobby.

"Gentlemen, do let us start at the break of day in the morning. We have a seat to fill in our coach and the person who must fill it is of a reluctant frame of mind. I hope to resolve her doubts in our favor."

"Pluggin' the hole?" I said.

"Yes, that's how my sailor colleague would put it. Good of you to remember, Angus."

Once J. Leonard was tucked inside the cab, Teddy climbed up into the driver's seat, released the brake, and hollered "step out, step out!" to his team. They did and he moved them into

an easy trot up the main street and toward Tijeras Canyon.
I jumped Marathon and loped him to a position two hundred
feet in front on the well-traveled stage road to the east. We
rose at a steady pace from the cottonwoods on the river bank,
through piñon pine and juniper into the canyon. On either
side rocks, aspen, cliffs, treetops, and a steep slope measured
our progress. Three and a half hours later we topped out and
could see Perfecto Armijo's sloping spread five miles ahead.
The sun was not yet directly overhead when we pulled into
the small gate.

"Buenas Dias, Marshal," said a young boy who'd sat at the
end of the family table last evening. Didn't get his name, but
he remembered me. Teddy reined his team in alongside the
blacksmith's shop where I'd found the sheriff yesterday afternoon. To my surprise, he was back at that same shoe again.

"Buenas Dias, Perfecto," I said, tipping my hat to the boy
and his grandfather.

"Angus, my, this is a most pleasant surprise. And you're
leading such a fine parade—a Concord stagecoach bigger than
any I've seen. Please get down and tell me how it is our good
fortune to see you again so soon."

I introduced him to Teddy and J. Leonard. Teddy said
howdy, shook hands with the boy and the sheriff, and then
moved away to tend to his team. J. Leonard began to gusher
words and amazement at what a "splendid ranchero this is."
After overly long preliminaries, he got around to business.

"Sheriff Armijo, I'm here to ask your indulgence, and
that of a woman you introduced my colleague, Angus, to
last evening. Angus offered a temporary position with our

expedition, a reconstruction really, and she declined. But his description of her sterling attributes has convinced me that she is exactly what we need to advance our cause. Could you ask, please, to give me a chance to modify last night's offer? I hope to persuade her and . . ."

I'd rarely seen Perfecto interrupt anyone, but apparently he didn't suffer long speeches by Eastern professors.

"Mr. Leonard, you're here to change a stubborn woman's mind?"

"Surely I am," Leonard said, apparently taking the hint toward brevity.

Turning to the boy, Perfecto said, "Donato, would you go to the north corral? Ora is there starting two new colts. *Por favor*, ask her to come down here. I want her to see this magnificent stagecoach."

Ten minutes later, Ora came around the end of the black-smith shed. She wore yellowed chaps over knee-high boots and spurs with big Mexican rowels. Pulling off heavy work gloves and sticking them inside her belt, she approached with that same purposeful stride I'd noticed last evening. I got the feeling again this was a woman who never ambled anywhere in her life.

J. Leonard stuck out his hand. She took it. He winced. She smiled. He didn't sidestep into the conversation.

"Miss Gray, I am here to offer you a position of honor and importance. I came to New Mexico hoping to examine an event poorly understood by people here and in our nation's capital. It will be, I assure you, the chance of a lifetime. You can help us explain and reassess an American tragedy. Would you give me a chance to persuade you, please?"

"The marshal, Angus, talked to me last night and I said no. Why did you come back?"

Looking at me, J. Leonard answered her question.

"Because you were right to decline my offer last evening. It was ill thought out. You said no because of a serious flaw in the proposal. I'm here to change that."

"Let's go to the porch," she said.

Teddy said he'd stay and talk to Perfecto, but J. Leonard asked me to go with him up to the porch. I'm glad I did.

"All right," Ora said, "maybe you can tell me first, what is the Smithsonian? I did not know of it until Señor Angus mentioned it last night."

"Thank you. This is exactly the right place to start. We have been operational since 1846, as the national museum of the United States. We are part of the federal establishment but are not governed by any of the three established branches—executive—legislative—judicial. We are managed by a permanent Board of Regents, consisting entirely of private citizens. Our motto is a simple one—the increase and diffusion of knowledge. There are large volumes of written documents, mostly U.S. Army records, about the 1864 capture and incarceration of Navajos and Apaches, but no one has ever attempted to cut below the formal documents and explain how and why this occurred. The U.S. Treasury has given us a generous grant to do just that—tell the rest of America what happened here in New Mexico twenty years ago."

"I was only ten. No one would listen to a child who only saw those Indians pass. I don't want to remember that anymore."

"Why don't you? Are you afraid of what we might learn if we talked to one another about it?"

"Not afraid. But I don't trust strangers from far away to understand us."

"You are right to be skeptical. Let me ask you to read something."

Leonard fished into the leather satchel of documents and handed her a sheaf of paper bound by string.

She took it, undid the string, and asked, "What is this?"

"It is a letter from General James H. Carleton to, as he says there on the top, 'The People of New Mexico.' It was written in Las Cruces, New Mexico, on December 16, 1864. I do not know how widely this was circulated, but it was published in two New Mexico newspapers. It is quite long, but if you will read it I think you will understand why I am here."

Ora flattened the pages out on the table. One by one she picked them up, reading in silence. Five minutes passed in silence. She read several of the pages twice.

"Do you agree with what General Carleton told your people, the people of New Mexico twenty-four years ago?" she asked J. Leonard.

"No, I don't," J. Leonard said. "This is what lawyers call a suitable pretext. It was written out of a sense of grandeur, of self-importance. It is an appeal to the Spanish settlers in New Mexico to support what the Army was doing to the Navajos. I know you just read this, but let me read aloud one short paragraph, partly for Angus's sake. And, of course, I want the honorable sheriff to hear this as well."

He took the letter from her and turned to Perfecto and me, reading aloud as though he had a large audience.

"From time immemorial these Indians had subsisted upon the flocks and herds of your fathers; had, times without number, even in one single hour, reduced whole families from comparative wealth to poverty. Their ravages had impoverished not only your country, but these barbarians had murdered your people; had slain your fathers—your brothers—your children—or had carried many of them into a horrible and hopeless captivity, until there was hardly a home in the land which was not filled with mourning and with hearts made desolate."

J. Leonard read three paragraphs, not just one.

Turning back to Ora, he asked, "Ora, does this sound like the New Mexico your parents knew? The one you knew at ten years of age? Do you think very many of the people on this ranch would agree with the small part I just read?"

"No."

"I have read this letter many times. I showed this letter to my superiors at the Smithsonian and compared it with other source materials from New Mexico. So far, except for a few Army officers and some political figures in Santa Fe, I can find no one else who supports the position taken by General Carleton. But I do not wish to prejudge any of this. So what I proposed to my superiors was a fact-finding trip to New Mexico on the twentieth year after the long march. I proposed to engage a soldier and a captive in an ongoing discussion, at the actual sites where all of this occurred. By engage, I mean an exchange of views about what really happened. About why it happened. And about whether the general's letter is true. My mistake, one I can only now see, was in assuming the Army and the Navajo people were sufficient sources to answer the questions in my mind. Now I know, thanks to what you told Angus last night, that we need the perspective of a true New

Mexican. Only with all three perspectives, will our engagement lead to the kind of serious, truthful report I hope to prepare. I have many more papers and pictures to show you. But I'd like to do that when we at the places where this tragedy unfolded. Will you please join us?"

"I will. But not today. I have a young colt to finish making saddle ready. If Perfecto agrees, I could come to Albuquerque tomorrow evening. I'll be riding my own horse."

CHAPTER 12

"Sgt. Bell"

SINCE WE HAD A DAY to wait for Ora to get her tack together, I hoped to get to know Mather Bell a little better. He wasn't much of a talker. Me neither. I found him at the Range Café reading the *Santa Fe Gazette*.

"Morning, Sergeant, mind if I join you?"

"Sure," he said, but didn't put his paper down.

I ordered another cup of coffee and was happy to find it hot and strong. I added two sugar lumps from the little box in the center of the table and waited him out. A minute passed. He just kept on reading. So, I finished my coffee and pushed my chair back.

"Sorry, Marshal, I just wanted to finish that story. You got something you want to talk to me about?"

"Just a question or two, if you don't mind."

"Ask away," he said.

"What's your take on this trip so far?"

"Well, just so's you know, I think it's a waste of time. But I'm between jobs right now, and I'm getting ten dollars a day to answer J. Leonard's questions. I suppose that includes your questions, too."

"Ten dollars? Didn't know you and the Navajo woman were getting paid for this. That's a fair sum for jawboning. What kind of job are you in-between these days?"

"Most anything that keeps me outside. I spent twenty years in the Army, near all of it with a cavalry company."

"How about a beer?" I asked. "Or is too early in the day for you?"

"When I was first in the Army, in California, we had beer for breakfast when the brass wasn't around."

We walked across the street to Swinn's Gambling Parlor & Saloon. It did a good gambling business at night and opened again at eight in the morning, selling tequila, lime juice, and pickles for the hangover cure. I pointed to one of twenty-five empty tables and Sgt. Bell walked over and sat down, putting his feet up on an opposing wooden chair with padded arms. I stopped at the bar, ordered two glasses of beer, and took them back to the table.

"Beer in the morning never caught on for me, but I was never in the Army, either. You like the Army?" I asked while the man drained the top half of the heavy mug.

"It was good," he said wiping his chin with his forearm.

"You know Teddy, our stage driver, was in the Army just a few years back. He was a first lieutenant; don't think they paid him ten dollars a day."

"I joined the California Volunteers, Lt. Col. Carleton's Eighth Company in eighteen and sixty-one to fight for the Union. He was looking for men at Fort Humboldt. I got the same pay as regular army. I think it was thirteen dollars a month. How about that? I'm getting more per day for this, whatever 'n hell it really is."

"Sounds like you don't think much of the reconstructed Long Walk."

"I don't know how they found me. But I know this. I made this trip once, not for the money, but just because them Indians needed to quit killing white families. Soon as we got to New Mexico, they made Carleton a general and put him in charge of the whole state, not just one company of volunteers. My folks were Christian farm folk and the Indians out to California were bad, too. Not as murderous as the Navajo, but still . . ."

He finished his beer, picked up his mug, and said, "Another one on me, Marshal?"

"No, one's my limit."

He changed the subject when he got back to the table with a to-the-brim glass of beer. We talked about Marathon and about Chinorero. He was a horseman but had never ridden a gaited horse or one from Tennessee. He thought Chinorero was a half-breed but said he took that bullet in the gut like a man. Said he was on the right side of the Civil War, with the Union, but seemed unconcerned about Negro slavery in the South. That subject got me back to what I wanted to learn about him.

"What was your opinion of General Carleton? About all I know is what he said in a letter he wrote in 1864. Copy I saw said it was written to all the people of New Mexico. You know about that?"

"Sure, we all got a copy. It was printed up and handed out. Some newspapers also printed it. He was a fine man and just what New Mexico needed—a man with guts. Some of the regular Army officers were scared of him, but he and ole Kit Carson bloodied the field, that's for sure. He died too young; I think it was before they closed down Bosque Redondo. I kept my slot in the Army long after they mustered out thousands of men at the end of the Civil War. The right side won and all, but you had to respect the Confederate foot soldiers—they were fine marksmen."

"You didn't fight any Civil War battles, did you?"

"No, but I would have. That's what I liked most about the Army. You never had to make any damn decisions. Long as you did what an officer wanted doing, you earned your pay."

"But what if you were ordered to do something you thought was unjust, or immoral?"

"How could it be unjust? Here's the thing about the Army. If a general officer says you do the job then everyone down the line must do it. No soldier worth his salt questions an officer's order."

I left a half glass of beer on the table.

CHAPTER 13

"First Letter to Jill"

WHEN I PROMISED JILL I'd write to her once a week, I didn't take into account an important fact of my life. Something she didn't know, which I was sort of proud about, but also felt the need to keep secret. I'd never written a letter to any woman in all my twenty-eight years. Never. I'd written letters to horse traders, trapping and hunting clients, bosses of one kind or another, but they'd all be men and none expected personal details or information. I could write reports and telegrams, but a handwritten letter was more challenging than riding a skitter horse down a steep bank. So, I'd been dreading the task. Since we were heading out right after breakfast tomorrow, I knew I had to get this first one in the hands of the U.S. Postal Department.

Dear Jill,

There's hardly anything to write about, but I promised so here it is. Don't judge me by the poor hand, or the near lamentable discourse. So's you know, I just looked up lamentable in a dictionary downstairs behind the register. It fits my writing style near perfect. So far this is about as interesting as not going anywhere. The man in charge, Mister J. Leonard, is nice and all but he talks and talks. Talks so much every man in the room wants to hang up his fiddle. But when cutting time comes, he's worth listening to. He knows more than he's letting on but I believe that's because he wants everyone to hear the particulars at once. We can't do that until we get to Fort Defiance and meet up with the Navajo woman—whose name is Luci Atsidi. The other passenger, named Mather Bell, is with us already. I learned today he has his feet stuck deep in the mud—his mind is set as to what happened twenty years ago. He was one of the soldiers that herded several thousand Navajos near the whole way across New Mexico. There's an Apache boy with us—Chinorero—some rowdy shot him two days ago. A man named Teddy Bridger is handling the wagon and a lawman. Seems to have a lot on his mind. He's a good stage driver. You ought to see it—all red and yellow paint and near as comfortable as a feather bed on springs. Mr. Leonard hired another woman just yesterday—she's related to Sheriff Perfecto

Armijo—you'll remember him from the Mendoza Mendoza posse. Her name is Ora Gray. I know talking about Mendoza raises uncomfortable memories so I'll say no more.

How are you and how is the gunsmithing business? I tell people your business but behind my back they think I'm chinning them. Tomorrow we head for Fort Defiance. There's a proper stage road near all the way—probably take about four days. The regular coach can do it in three but they have horse stations where they change to a fresh team. Teddy is using big draft horses for the Concord. They step right out but take a lot of feed and water to keep them going. So we stop every three hours. I'm eating good and my sleeping is even better. Three nights so far with only my tarp to separate me from the stars overhead. I miss you—I know you don't believe that because of my affliction—riding high ridges and crossing big rivers. But I love you, miss you, and wish you could be here with me.

Ever yours,
Angus

CHAPTER 14

"From Los Lunas to Gallup"

I T HAD BEEN FIVE DAYS since somebody fired on us, or more exactly, fired on Chinorero. The Albuquerque town marshal, man named Torrez, would not investigate because it was outside the town limits. How'd he know, I asked. But he paid no mind to my little joke. Sheriff Perfecto Armijo's office took a report because it was inside Bernalillo County, so the sheriff had jurisdiction. I went to their office yesterday and asked one of the deputies what had turned up.

"'Bout the Apache boy?" he asked.

"Chinorero's his name," I answered.

"Well, we asked around but nobody saw it."

"Anybody hear about it?" I asked.

"Can't say. Fact is, the boy's a Mescalero, could be a half-breed, probably from that reservation down near Ruidoso. That ain't in Bernalillo County, so there's no one to ask up here."

"What about the bars up here? I have the feeling there's a lot of bars here, being as there's more than three thousand people living here. Biggest town in New Mexico, right?"

"Maybe, but when somebody shoots at an Apache around here, nobody wants to talk about it."

"What if somebody around here kills an Apache? That raise any questions?"

"You bet. That'd be something worth talking about. As is, there's nothing."

"Nothing? Didn't you hear the boy died, day before yesterday?"

"Now that I think on it, I did hear he did. Over to the Chinaman's place, Mr. Sarr, right?

I walked out. No need to bark at a knot on a log, right?

Everything was lined out and strapped down by eight a.m. the next morning. Ora Gray and I were mounted. She rode a spotted mare with a yellow tail. She took a position behind the Concord. I led out and Teddy followed, driving the four-up team back to the hotel. J. Leonard and Sgt. Bell were waiting on the boardwalk. Bell asked Teddy if he could ride shotgun for a while. That left Mr. Leonard alone in the coach. He chose a backward-looking seat. Never saw anyone prefer looking back at where you'd been before. He said he had to draw calculations and looking up ahead was distracting. Teddy asked his team to step out, and our adventure started all over again. But this time we didn't have a kid riding drag. We had Ora. No one would dare take a shot at her.

The country between Los Lunas and Albuquerque was a gentle down slope to the south with the Rio Grande always in sight to the west of us. We'd reach the Isleta Pueblo first, then at Los Lunas, we'd follow the train bridge over the Rio Grande west to Pulido, Cuero, Acoma, and finally Fort Wingate. Teddy's plan was to go all the way in one day, with a stop for water and rest for the horses every three hours. It was near seventy or eighty miles. Too far, I thought. I was right. We got as far as Laguna when J. Leonard decided we'd best pitch camp. He was so jarred up by the bumpy road he could not eat the stew that Teddy fixed. Sgt. Bell didn't seem bothered. Teddy was tuckered from bouncing around on the wooden seat almost seven feet off the ground. But he cooked a good trail stew.

After dinner, Teddy pitched tents for himself and Sgt. Bell. He pitched one for Ora. Don't know if she used it. J. Leonard slept in the coach. I laid my tarp out about a hundred yards away. Found a smooth sand ridge overlooking the coach, the tents, and the draft horses. I'd picketed Snow with the draft horses. He didn't bray all night. I guess the big horses were all right with him. Next morning, we had a quick breakfast of fried bread and fresh peaches, along with Army coffee. I think Sgt. Bell sprinkled a little military sweetener in his.

We reached the Rio Puerco at high noon the second day out. They call it a river because it has water in it maybe five, six times a year. Rest of the time it's a five-hundred-mile-long dry ditch. The only thing interesting about it is the quicksand that snags settlers' wagons several times each year. Sounds funny but it can be a real menace. The desert between Los Lunas and Gallup is hot in the summer and freezing cold in the winter. But we weathered on through it and made it to Fort Wingate an hour before sundown.

During breakfast and lunch, J. Leonard had given all of us an ongoing lecture about the oddities of places. Not places exactly, but the names of places.

"Take Fort Wingate," he'd said several times, as though we could. "Fort Wingate has been an army fort in two different locations and under three different names since its first naming in 1846, thirty-two years ago. Did you know that, Ora? Fort Wingate came into being two years before you were born. Isn't that splendid?"

Splendid? As was her custom, she didn't answer. In just three days, we'd all come to know Ora Gray's peculiarities, at least some of 'em. In fairness, she'd probably learned some of ours, too. The first place to be named Fort Wingate was up on the Pecos River near a little mud village called Las Vegas. I've been to Las Vegas and would not have called it a mud village, but J. Leonard did. It occurred to me that Washington, DC, probably did not have Adobe houses.

"On August fifteen of that year of acquisition, a famous Army general named Stephen Watts Kearney stood on top of one of those adobe buildings and gave himself a grand title. He was, he proclaimed to the Spanish men and women of Las Vegas, their Protector. He claimed that position because for years those early settlers, all of whom were of Spanish origin, needed protection against another conqueror. They had reason to fear, he said, the Navajos and Apaches from the west, the Utes from the north, and the Kiowa and Comanche from the east. They called all of them Indians and feared them even though the raids were sporadic and had no thought of taking over the entire country, as the Spanish did to the Puebloan Indians back in 1598."

I was fearful that the man would go on too long, and we'd miss the best part of the ride. But he said he'd hold off on telling us about the second Fort Wingate, the one we were headed toward today. He'd already announced that we would not be stopping at the one on the eastern slope of the Zuni Mountains. Seems he wanted to stop there for a full day, but not until we'd gone to Fort Defiance, picked up Luci Atsidi, and had what he called a "full complement." Still, all in all, Mr. Leonard's lecture during breakfast and lunch were much longer than I'm reciting here.

Some of his language stuck to me, never having heard a by-god professor talk before. He called the Navajos, "The Nomads of the Redrocks." We'd already started to see long stretches of country north of the stage road giving us a look at huge, red-colored sandstone bluffs. Some of 'em were hundreds of feet high. They just seemed to rise up out of the sage and scrub oak. They gleamed bright orange in the slanted sun of early morning and became apple red when the sun disappeared at day's end. At lunch he told us about a raid well known to professors like him at a place called Seboyeta, which was on the slopes of Mount Taylor. We never saw it, but took his word it was close by. According to Army records, Seboyeta had an Army garrison. It was the first Fort Wingate. His men, that is, General Kearney's men, were there "as a show of force against marauding Indians."

The show worked, I guess, because Mr. Leonard told us about a late 1846 treaty, a failed one he said, struck at another village we didn't see—in the foothills to the south of us— the Zuni Mountains. The Zunis called it *Shash 'B Tow*. The Mexicans called it Bear Springs. He had seen a copy of the

Bear Springs treaty, but didn't bring it to New Mexico with him. He read his notes of the treaty aloud to us after dinner.

"We stipulate that all warlike activities against the residents of New Mexico will cease. We swear allegiance with the Americans and that of all residents of the acquired territory will be administered by the United States Government." The agreement was made with the "chiefs of the People." The chiefs promised Col. Alexander Doniphan, who was representing Gen. Kearney, that they would "fully restore all stolen property and livestock and the release of all Mexican captives."

"Did it work?" I asked J. Leonard.

"No, sadly it did not. The Indians' animosity toward the Mexicans was too deep-seated."

"No wonder," I said. "Don't make much difference whether your skin is red or brown. If you take another man's land, he's likely to take deep offense."

"That's why the Army came here," Sgt. Bell inserted. It was unusual for him to insert himself in one of these listening sessions we were having with Mr. Leonard. Turns out, Sgt. Bell knew a little history himself.

"Mr. Leonard," the usually quiet sergeant said, "I suppose you know that lots of those treaties were signed before the big wars started when Gen. Carleton took over as military commander, don't you?"

"Why, yes I do, Sergeant. I know that Fort Marcy, where we first met, became a major staging area for the army outfitting expeditions west into Navajo land. Many treaties were signed and all were broken, as you said. And the garrison at Seboyeta just a few miles from where we are camped, was sent to construct another new fort at the east front of the Defiance

Mountains. That became Fort Defiance. Do you know the Navajo name for that place, Sergeant?"

"Can't say as I do," Sgt. Bell replied.

"It's a Navajo shrine called . . . let me check my notes on this. Yes, there it is, *Tse Hot' Sohih*. I cannot pronounce it properly. Mrs. Atsidi will help us with that soon. It means 'meadows between the rocks.'"

There was a quiet spell. Teddy went to attend to his horses and Ora gave him a hand. I asked Mr. Leonard a question I'd been thinking about for a few days.

"So, there were lots of treaties broken by Indians. Why?"

"Because the government never honored their end. They did not protect the Navajo from the Utes, Kiowa, Comanche, or from whites, who occasionally stole horses and sheep. Or from stealing young Navajo children. The slave trade among Indian tribes was quite ferocious at the time. Finally, in April 1860, the peace was broken everywhere. Two major Navajo chiefs, leading as many as one thousand warriors, attacked Fort Defiance. They nearly overran the garrison but retreated at nightfall. That began a full-scale Indian campaign. The campaign ended with killing hundreds, some say thousands of Navajos, and the removal of another nine thousand from their homeland to Bosque Redondo. That, Marshal, is why we are here today. Broken treaties."

Just about the time the sun dropped in the western horizon, we approached the biggest set of red rock boulders I'd ever seen. It was ablaze with the sun one minute and turned grey the next. We followed the stage road, which ran alongside the railroad track that followed the dry Rio Puerco. Those three things made it near impossible for a man to get lost on the way to Gallup. It was full-on dark when we pulled up to the stage stop in the middle of a town that J. Leonard said had 2,946 souls in it. Seems like those souls were from everywhere, according to a census J. Leonard had—Mexico—Scotland—Yugoslavia—Poland—Germany. Gallup had two things going for it—coal underground and two railroad tracks on top. It also had two hotels and dozens of rooming houses. We stayed at The Gibson, which was in Gallup, not in Gibson, a little coal mining town a few miles north. He didn't explain how that came about. But it was clean and had two rooms available. Ora got one. Mr. Leonard, Sgt. Bell, and Teddy bunked in the other. I rolled out my tarp in the stall with Marathon. Snow slept outside standing up in a corral with seven other mules. Some of 'em brayed back at Snow. That first visit to Gallup was uneventful. We had an early breakfast and headed north to Fort Defiance an hour after sunup.

CHAPTER 15

"Fort Defiance"

THE STAGE ROAD WE'D been traveling all the way from Los Lunas was known as the Beale Wagon Road. Settlers, travelers, and traders had been using it to make their way west from the Rio Grande to Fort Mohave in Arizona. It went straight through Gallup. But once you got to Gallup, you had to turn due north if your destination was Fort Defiance, twenty-six miles away. It was just on the other side of the invisible line separating the Arizona Territory from the New Mexico Territory. Teddy had done some mapping. He told us over breakfast there were Indian trade routes running north and south out of Gallup. They'd been used long before the Spanish conquistadores passed this way almost two hundred years before we made the turn. One of the most used trade routes was called the Zuni-Cibola trail. I asked him who called it that. He didn't know but assured us it'd been used by Kit

Carson and his mounted cavalry against the Navajo. We'd be following in his tracks. Not a comforting thought for me.

We made good progress until the sun was directly overhead. Mr. Leonard banged on the top of the stage and asked Teddy to make a stop. We'd just crossed a little stream. Up ahead we could see a mesa of some size. Leonard said he wanted to get his bearing. I'd been riding about a hundred feet in front of the coach, keeping an eye on both sides. Felt no particular danger, but we were off the traveled road here and well inside the new Navajo reservation.

J. Leonard got out and fetched a square leather case maybe six inches by a foot-square. It had shiny brass buckles on the ends of leather straps. I hadn't noticed it before.

"This is a kit put together by the mapping people at the Smithsonian for me," he said.

When he opened it and showed us the contents, Teddy gave a whistle.

"By God, J. Leonard, that's got some dollars behind it."

Leonard took the instruments out and laid them on a little square piece of canvas. Teddy picked 'em up one by one, explaining for the benefit of me and Ora, these fine-looking pieces of brass.

"All of these instruments are used by explorers and military men. Without these, you'd never find your way. The trick is to define the longitude and latitude at each point on your path. These fine instruments have been used for over a hundred years. This one is a sextant. Next, there you see an octant. This is an artificial horizon device. Besides, it is a fine surveying compass. Maybe the most important one is that gold chronometer. That's an expensive box of equipment. You can buy all the rest of the stuff for under a hundred dollars. But those scientific chronometers can run two-hundred-fifty dollars or more. Mr. Leonard, I know now for sure that the Smithsonian has real money behind it."

It took a few minutes to focus everything and start taking measurements. As he and Teddy went along, J. Leonard explained how it all worked.

"First, we have to find our latitude on the earth's surface. You all know about those, right? Lines of latitude are imaginary circles that start at the equator. That's zero degrees latitude. Imagine that there's a line from the equator at the surface to the center of the earth. Then imagine a line from the center of the earth to the point on the surface where you are standing, like right here north of Gallup on the way to Fort Defiance. The angle from zero degrees to your position is your latitude. We find that by using a sextant and a clock to measure the position of the sun at noon."

Teddy took over.

"It's noon right now. That's why I stopped here. By measuring now, we can line up the horizon by looking through the telescope on our sextant. See this little half-silvered mirror? You can see it through the horizon glass." He moved the index mirror on top with his thumb on a little drum. "I can see the sun superimposed on the horizon."

He read the angle of the sun on the scale to J. Leonard, who made a note. Using that angle, Teddy said, "We can figure this out by using a special reference book."

Teddy read the title to us, "*The Nautical Almanac*—it gives us the degrees of latitude north of the equator." Then Teddy and J. Leonard took turns using the octant.

One of them said it was a sextant with a larger scale, "One-eighth of a circle instead of one-sixteenth. The octant was used during the summer months when the sun was much higher in the sky," he explained.

Ora and I were listening. But speaking only for myself, not much of it was sinking in. They coulda been talking Greek. Teddy took up a little thing he said was an "artificial horizon."

"It has liquid mercury covered by this little sheet of glass. Since liquid will lie perfectly flat, we can use the surface to find the true horizon."

"What about the false horizon?" I asked. "Those false horizons been bedeviling me up along the Colorado border for years."

No one noticed my contribution. There was more talk about finding the right longitude. They used words like degrees off the prime meridian. Whatever that is. It made my head hurt so I checked on Marathon and Snow. They seemed to know just where they were: behind the coach headed for Arizona.

After some arguing between them, the two men took up the compass and used it, along with dead reckoning, to measure distances and direction. Finally, with some ceremony, Mr. Leonard made an announcement.

"Fellow travelers, we are at this moment physically on a point on earth defined scientifically as thirty-five degrees north and one-hundred-and-nine degrees west, more or less."

"Is the border between the New Mexico Territory and the Arizona Territory close by?" I asked.

"We are within a mile or two," he said.

"Well, then, I'd say we ought to get to it. Crossing territorial borders is high on my list of things to do."

When we got within shooting distance of Fort Defiance, I was a little disappointed. Set on a large level plain of sandy soil nearly desolate of any growth and with no obvious water source, it seemed an odd place to build a fort. There was an imposing mountain to the north, with the mouth of its canyon yawning toward the fort. We'd topped a little rise maybe a mile from the entrance. There were no bulwarks or gates. We could see several dozen adobe buildings with flat roofs and chimneys built around a large, rectangular open ground. There were cook houses and latrines on four sides, and barns, corrals, and old white Army tents lined up on the far side. There was a flag pole but no flag at one end of the open ground in the middle of the old fort. Two wagons, one open and one covered, and two mounted men were moving toward us.

Teddy reined in his team behind me, and I turned and walked Marathon back to them. He said he wanted to stop up here and take in the history spread out before us. J. Leonard knew a good deal about this fort and about its commander before the big war waged to kill or capture all the Navajo warriors and take them to the Bosque Redondo. And he had told us about one of its most famous commanders, Col. Manuel Chaves.

The fort was larger than the other forts we'd seen, but there was little activity. Turned out most of the buildings were empty. The Army gave up on Fort Defiance after the Navajo Treaty of 1868 was signed. Since then, it's been an Indian agency. I knew that from my first talk with J. Leonard at Fort Marcy. But here, in the late afternoon heat, it did not have a historic feel. Wars were fought here, men died. People were treated well or terribly depending on which general was giving the orders. This was where two great warriors clashed.

Manuelito, one of the great chiefs of the Navajo tribe, and Kit Carson, the great Indian killer. Manuelito's world began to shrink here. Kit Carson's began to thunder. Many Navajos had been fed here, during drought years. This was a place to trade, sometimes fairly. And it was a place to die when one side or the other pushed too hard.

Before Col. Kit Carson's time here, Col. Manuel Chaves was the fort commandant. He was a forty-three-year-old career soldier in the U.S. Army militia. He often told stories of his family's glory on battlefields from Portugal to Mexico. He believed his family descended from the battles that drove the Moors from Spain, and before Kit Carson came here he would be the one driving the Navajos from New Mexico. He was born along the bosque near Albuquerque and had ridden the dusty road from there to here, just as we had the last five days. Everyone knew Manuel Chaves. A man who had spent most of his life on New Mexico's borderlands, living close to the Navajo, but always apart from them in important ways. He was a sheep rancher, an occasional slave-trader, and a militia man so brave in battle with the Navajo that he earned the nickname The Little Lion. Col. Chaves claimed in Army documents that he had two hundred relatives, all who had grown up fighting Navajo raiders. Two of his brothers had been killed by Navajos and he had no love or pity for them. Navajos did not call him a lion—to them he was a "Nakai," a name the Navajo associated with New Mexican sheep herders and slave traders.

The two men rode up to us when we reached the parade ground. Without dismounting, the taller of the two said his name was

Ben Yazzie; the other didn't say. They'd been expecting us, Yazzie said.

"Yá´át´ééh," the one named Ben Yazzie said in a clipped, soft voice. "We welcome you to our land, Navajo land. You are from Smithsonian Washington, yes?"

Teddy was up top when the riders rode up, so he answered before Leonard could step outside the Concord.

"Yes. I'll let J. Leonard explain."

J. Leonard, looking not quite ready to engage in a formal way because his coat and hat were in the coach, said, "We are most pleased to be here. Most pleased. I am J. Leonard from the Smithsonian Institution. We are the United States national museum and . . ."

Ben Yazzie raised a hand politely.

"We know. The Indian agent in Santa Fe sent us a telegram. A month ago we got a letter from the Indian Affairs in Washington telling us you were coming. You are looking for Luci Atsidi?"

"Oh, yes. Most certainly so. She has kindly agreed to assist us, and . . ."

Ben Yazzie was apparently a man accustomed to being in charge. "I'm the assistant Indian agent. Mr. Donald Campbell is the Indian Agent here. He will be back tomorrow. Luci Atsidi is here, waiting for you. She's been waiting for maybe five days now. Follow me. We'll take you to the office."

Sgt. Bell had bailed out of the coach as it came to a stop near the flag pole.

"Be back shortly," he'd said, as he headed toward one of the buildings down to the left of the parade ground.

"That man," Ben Yazzie said, "has been here before."

"Right," J. Leonard responded. "Sgt. Bell was here as part of the Army guard for the second group of your people that were moved to Fort Sumner. I checked the Army records in Washington when we were planning this trip. Sgt. Bell, who was a private at the time, was part of Lt. Charles Hubbell's Company B, 1st NM Cavalry."

The office turned out to be the former commander's office—where Kit Carson stayed during the Indian Wars from 1861 to 1863. Once the Army moved out, the Indian agent ordered all the insides of the buildings painted white. We went into the large office, now yellowed after twenty years of use, to find five people waiting for us at a big table. One was the woman, Luci Atsidi. Two were relatives of hers, two were tribal leaders, and the last one was a trader who owned several trading posts on the reservation. His name was Kennedy.

To my surprise, Luci Atsidi got up when we came through the door and walked straight to us. Ignoring me and Teddy, she nodded to Mr. Leonard, but did not offer her hand.

"I am Luci Atsidi. How do you do, Mr. J. Leonard. You are very pale. I think you need a bigger hat. I'll ask Ben Yazzie to get you one."

"Mrs. Atsidi, it is so very good to meet you at last. I've enjoyed our letters back and forth. Your English is excellent, I must say."

"So is my Navajo," she said, a smile spreading out from her round face.

She wore a long heavy skirt which came almost to the floor. Later, I would see she wore high leather moccasins with straps wound from her ankle to her knee. Her shirt was dark purple, very soft cloth, almost velvet looking. She had a large necklace made of silver and a blue stone I didn't recognize. I later learned it was turquoise; the necklace had been made by her grandfather. There was a cloth string around what looked like a bunch of her dark black hair at the back of her neck. Her skin looked burnt. Her close-set eyes twinkled when she talked. Over the course of the next two weeks, I'd come to know how well she could express herself just with her eyes. They always reflected her mood and her mind.

J. Leonard pointed at me. "This is our deputy United States marshal. He goes by only one name, Angus."

She nodded at me and smiled with her mouth closed. I touched my hat and nodded back. J. Leonard pointed at Teddy, introducing him as our coach driver and trail cook. He got the same smile. Then, with a wave of his hand for her to come around Teddy and me, he introduced Ora Gray.

"This very nice woman is from a ranch near Albuquerque. She will join us in the coach for the remainder of the trip to Fort Sumner. I'm pleased to introduce Ora Gray."

Luci Atsidi, tilting her head forward toward Ora, stepped closer. She did not offer her hand, nor did Ora offer hers. The two women faced one another in total silence for a few seconds. Then, as though a ceremony were about to begin, each took another step forward, eyeing one another with obvious suspicion.

"Welcome to the Navajo Nation," Luci said.

"*Buenas tardes*," Ora answered. "I am sorry for you. I am sad that the Army treated you like they did. Maybe we can be friends, *que no*?"

Luci Atsidi's face dissolved from hesitant to accepting.

"*Hóshdéii*," she said in a quiet voice so low it was hard to hear. "That means welcome. Friends are very important to all our people, and yours, too. Come back with me to my room, before we talk about this mission of the Smithsonian. I will give you a cold cloth for your face and hands and some cool water from our well. Then, we can talk with these men."

Now, I have to say, had Jill met another woman her own age, and her own people, there would have been polite hand-shakes. But these two woman were as different as they could be—more formal, more guarded. We'd all come to understand in the coming days how close their world really was. A world where hardship was part of everyday life and women expected to stay at home. In time, they would be friends, I thought, but not just yet.

When the women came back to the big table, the rest of us had settled down to the particulars. As was the case every time we talked when J. Leonard was present, he treated it as a meeting and led the talk. He talked about our "mission," now that Luci Atsidi was with us. He asked Teddy to lay out the logistics. We were just starting to talk about the question on everybody's mind—what does the Smithsonian want?—when Sgt. Bell came through the door.

J. Leonard introduced Sgt. Bell to the group. Then turning to another sheaf of papers from his leather box, he asked Ben Yazzie about one of the papers in his hand.

"Among many things, I've been wondering about this wonderful fort for almost a year now. Our research in Washington says that a Navajo leader, Cabara Blanco, surrendered here at Fort Defiance on January 24, 1864, with 344 members of his clan. That group grew to 500. Then from here it was 'escorted' to

Fort Wingate. From there the group was marched to Los Pinos in New Mexico. The record is quite detailed. It says here that the chief quartermaster of the 'Navajo Expedition' was ordered to furnish the expedition with five six-mule teams and one four-mule team as transportation. This group left Fort Defiance on January 26, 1864. Does that comport with your records here?"

"We have no records here," Ben Yazzie said.

"None? That's curious. I assumed when the Army decommissioned the facility as an Army post and transferred control to the Department of the Interior for redesignation as the principal Navajo Indian Agency that the records would have become Agency records."

"When the Army left, they took all the papers. We have some commissary records and supply lists, but no Army documents."

"All right, I understand that. But, I'm curious. If you have no records, how did you know Sgt. Bell had been here before?"

"That building he headed for as soon as he jumped out of the stagecoach. It was for low-rank soldiers. It has a latrine on the back wall."

As if on cue, Sgt. Bell removed his hat, but not his pistol holster or cartridge belt. Sensing that he'd interrupted the talk at the table, he took a seat saying, "Sorry to hold anything up. I had business to take care of. My name's Mather Bell. Retired U.S. Army. Looks like you all been keeping good care of this old horse soldier's fort. We had us some good ole times here, back then."

The room went quiet.

Ben Yazzie got up, walked around the table, and stuck out his hand to Bell.

"Sgt. Bell, my name is Ben Yazzie. I'm Navajo. You are welcome here. But our memories of this place may conflict. The times I remember here were not *good ole times* like you say you had. Our people were captives. Captives of the U.S. Army. But we, your people and mine, signed a treaty. It is still in force. My hope, and I think you will join me in this, is that men like you and I can sit at a table without hate and war. In the Navajo language, we say peace, *hodéezyéél.*"

To his credit, Sgt. Bell did the right thing. Sticking his big ruddy hand out, he said, "Peace."

The next hour went by like molasses syrup dripping out of a cracked bowl. Mr. Leonard tried to explain the Smithsonian goals—interpreting historical events for the benefit of everyone who comes to Washington to see the museum and read the archives. Ben Yazzie said Navajo history is interpreted by storytellers.

"They don't live in museums and don't have written records. There are no archives, just drawings and markings on caves and rock walls all around here. But our people have strong memories of those times. We call them 'fearing times.'"

Leonard said the goal was information, not to cast blame. Yazzie wondered why not. Leonard said there was historical honesty in other tragedies, like the Civil War. Yazzie thought honesty was rare when the U.S. Army was involved. Sgt. Bell said something about the Army trying to save the Navajo people by giving them new, better land, and better ways to farm. Yazzie said no one asked the Navajo people if they wanted a better farm 350 miles away. Leonard wondered how the Navajos who did not go to the Bosque Redondo fared between 1862 and 1868. Yazzie said you could ask them. They are still here, he said. The two women listened but offered little comment.

After an hour, Ben Yazzie said his people had prepared food for us. We would sleep in good Navajo beds and our horses would be fed and watered by boys from the reservation school, which was two miles away. I said I'd enjoy eating Navajo food, but my horse was mighty particular, so I'd feed him special with grain I'd brought on Snow, my mule. The Navajo men thought that was wise.

During dinner, J. Leonard asked Ben Yazzie how he became the Indian agent here.

"I'm not the agent, I'm his assistant. I was born two miles from here in 1851. The same year the Army built this fort. I was five years old when the first trouble here began."

"Trouble?" Mr. Leonard asked.

"It was at a horse race. Every summer the soldiers at the fort raced their best horses against Navajo ponies. One of the soldiers was ahead in a race when one of our young riders tried to pass him. The soldiers tripped the Indian horse with a rope. We had some angry Navajos here who saw it and accused the soldier of cheating us. So a fight started out right over there, where those white tents are now. Our warriors had bows and arrows and one of them shot an arrow into the heart of the soldier for cheating. The soldiers ran back to the fort and got their guns. We had no guns then. Later I heard that thirty Navajo men were killed. No women were shot. But the warriors had to ride off. That's when all the trouble started—just because of cheating in a horse race."

"So, what happened after that?"

"I don't know. I just remember my father telling me about the horse race."

Mr. Leonard knew a lot of history about all the forts. And he had hoped to get a discussion going at dinner here for his report.

"Well, things were not good after that horse race riot. It is well documented in the Army records. In 1860, there was a big battle right here. Manuelito and Barboncito, two of the most important Indian leaders, attacked this fort with one thousand men behind them."

Ben Yazzie interrupted. "The Army lied about that, like they always did. There were many Indian warriors but not that many."

"Could be. I read the report sent to Washington by an Army captain, name of O. L. Shepherd. He drove off the attack. His report says one soldier was killed, three were wounded, and they shot twenty Indians."

"Guns are better for killing than bows and arrows," Yazzie said.

"You bet," Sgt. Bell said.

The two men glared at one another over the sweet corn the Indians had baked and served to us for dinner.

"So, what happened after that?" Ora asked.

J. Leonard pushed his plate away from him and gave her a longer answer than she'd asked for.

"The U.S. Civil War broke out. That's what happened. The Army abandoned this fort in 1861 and moved the garrison to a camp we passed by yesterday. At the time it was called Fort Fauntleroy. But General Fauntleroy resigned his commission in the U.S. Army and joined the Confederates. So, right away they changed the name of that fort; they renamed it Fort Wingate—five miles east of Gallup where we had dinner last night. It was there, at Fort Wingate, that General Carleton ordered a militia colonel named Kit Carson to make full scale war on all Navajo men. Part of Carleton's strategy was to force all the Navajo people from their lands, starting with Canyon de Chelly and working their way up here to this fort. He said it was because the Navajo would not give up their 'murderous ways.' Those are his words, not mine. His plan included moving the Indians they captured over to the Bosque Redondo, to that special fort, Fort Sumner. But Kit Carson did not agree and tendered his resignation in protest. Carleton refused to accept it and gave Kit Carson a direct order to make full-scale war or face a court martial himself. Carson backed down. He led the war here, killed hundreds of Navajo warriors, destroyed corn and grain fields, burned down houses, and shot all the livestock he could find. Then Carson and his men marched part of their captives to this fort, which was the first concentration camp. Bosque Redondo was the second, but it was intended to be permanent, whereas the one here was just a transitory place while they finished the much larger internment at Bosque Redondo. They already had Indian prisoners—about four hundred Mescalero Apaches."

J. Leonard often tried to get all of us talking. He wanted to take notes for his report. But everyone except Sgt. Bell went quiet. Sgt. Bell said, "Mr. Leonard, I ain't well educated like you, but are you saying the end of the Civil War is a big deal in the Navajo Wars we'd been fighting for ten years or more in New Mexico? That's a new one on me."

"I'm saying the end of the Civil War meant that General Carleton had nothing left to do in New Mexico. I'm saying he took advantage of the fact that he had armed troops and good jobs to offer local militia. And I'm saying that he greatly overstated the depredations of a small percentage of the Navajo warriors. He was of the mind that the American government had a God-given right to take Indian land away for white settlers. The best and perhaps only way to do that was to move thousands of Navajo innocents, women, children, and old men off their homeland to benefit white settlers. Remember his ultimatum. He told the Navajo headmen they had two choices—surrender or extermination."

I got up and went to the barn. Marathon and Snow were glad to see me.

CHAPTER 16

"Down a Steep Hill"

SUNUP ANYWHERE IS THE BEST part of the day, but at
Fort Defiance, the start was different. I had one hand on
Marathon's rump, and was giving him a good brushing with a
palm-horse brush. Without warning, the eastern sun showed
herself just barely peeking over the notch between two mountains about ten miles away. Hardly pink, and moving up in
split-seconds, it did two things at once. It rose up and then
sank down into a gray cloud lying flat along the horizon. As I
stood there, brush in hand, the sky changed the cloud's mind.
A mare's tail rode high being chased by a misshapen coyote,
all out of breath. I tried to think about what I was seeing, but
thoughts don't last when you're watching miracles.

I hobbled Marathon and checked on Snow, standing
stock still at the far end of the corral. He paid me no mind.
So, dusting off my chaps, I walked back up to the office. At

one of the tables, a young Navajo girl was setting out eating utensils and tin plates for the five of us. I knew that because Luci was already sitting down and Ora Gray was walking back from the kitchen with two cups of coffee. As I walked toward them, I heard the door open behind me. Teddy walked in with that long stride of his. We all said our good mornings. In three languages.

Breakfast was what I suppose was Navajo style. Fried bread, shucked corn fried in a dark syrup, or maybe it was just grease, and coffee. A clay pitcher of water was on the middle of the table but no extra glasses. Teddy emptied his coffee and poured water into his tin cup. Then, he proposed a change of plan for the trip back.

"I think we ought to go north from here; call it a side trip, it would add two days to our trip back to Fort Wingate, but it could be important to Mr. Leonard. He doesn't know about this idea yet, and it's his call."

"Why?" I asked.

"Why is it his call or why should we go north?" he answered.

"Why go north? The Army started their march of captured Navajos over to Fort Sumner from here; that's what Mr. Leonard told us in Santa Fe. What's north of here?"

"Well, it's actually Ben Yazzie's idea. He says we might not understand what happened twenty years ago without seeing Canyon de Chelly."

"That is true," Luci said.

Just then, J. Leonard walked in from one of the bunk rooms on the north wall of the big room. He went to the kitchen, got a steaming cup of coffee, and came to the table.

"A fine good morning to each of you," he said crisply, with his usual half-smile.

"Morning," Teddy said, "I was just telling Angus and Luci about an idea Ben Yazzie had last night after you all left. He thinks we ought to take two days off our schedule and visit Canyon de Chelly."

"Splendid. I'd been thinking about that, but was unsure of its research value. Did Mr. Yazzie offer some specifics about what we'd see there? And, of course, there are logistical considerations that would come into play, and . . ."

Teddy had developed a knack for watching Mr. Leonard talk. When he took a deep breath, it usually meant he had much more to say. Teddy took that as a sign of a good place to interrupt.

"'Scuse me, Mr. Leonard, but before you ask me about logistics and all, why don't we wait until Mr. Yazzie gets here? I expect he has good reasons why we should go north from here."

Luci tapped her forefinger on her empty tin plate. "I can tell you why he says that and why I think he's right. If anyone wants my opinion, that is."

"We do, we most assuredly do," J. Leonard said.

"Canyon de Chelly is the starting place. That's why. When Kit Carson attacked the canyon, he hoped to wipe out all of us. But the canyon is Navajo, not white. It has hiding places no white man could find. Some of my clan went there and escaped the Red Shirt and his sabre. You want to see those places? It's much closer to here than the opening of the canyon at Chinle. One place is called White House. Many Navajo people lived there. The ones who were not killed or captured, they escaped from there and went to Spider Rock. I could take you there. So could Ben Yazzie."

We ate our breakfast talking about changing the plan. Just as we finished, Sgt. Bell came in, with Ben Yazzie close behind. J. Leonard asked Ben Yazzie if he had a map of the area he thought we should see before returning to the road of the Navajo Long Walk. There was a little argument between Luci and Ben Yazzie. Luci said the Long Walk started in Canyon de Chelly. He disagreed, saying it started at Fort Wingate.

Luci was adamant. "Ben Yazzie, you are the assistant Indian agent here; I think that makes you sound like a white man sometimes. You are correct that the Army used Fort Wingate to gather supplies and wagons. But many of our people walked from Canyon De Chelly first, as prisoners. We were kept under guard here. Then we walked from here to Fort Wingate. Others started walking even further away. I remember the Army called this place, this Fort Defiance, a 'staging area.' I still don't know what that means. Some old women stayed here. Others stayed at Fort Wingate for a long time before they were able to make the march. But you forget me and my people. Some of my clan were captured at the White House, in Canyon de Chelly. No men, though. They killed the men there. But some women were captured there. I know. I was one of them; I was only ten. That is where *my* long walk began."

There was a road northwest from Fort Defiance to Canyon de Chelly, but it was more trail than road. Some wagons went back and forth. When we started out at noon that day, we could see the wheel tracks in the dust, and in the dried mud from the last rain, about a week ago. Luci asked Teddy if she could sit up top. I still don't know why, but it seemed like a good idea for me to go up top, too. I ponied Marathon and Snow behind; Marathon tied to the end of the stage with a twenty-foot lead rope and Snow hooked onto my saddle horn with a ten footer. Like always, they behaved themselves. Thinking back on it now, I guess I was curious about two things: Luci Atsidi, and just how teamsters got draft horses to do their bidding when chained to a huge coach.

Teddy sat with the reins threaded through the fingers of both hands. Luci sat to his left on the padded seat. I sat up top, behind the little iron railing, on an extra saddle blanket for padding. I needed it after hitting the first of thousands of ruts and holes in the dirt trail that barely passed for a trail these days. Right off, Teddy explained how a draft team is reined and hitched up on a big Concord rig like this one.

"Well, ma'am, it's mostly about the hitching. Managing the reins, we call 'em ribbons sometimes, is the easy part. But if your hitch is wrong, misery always follows."

"Misery," Luci said.

"Misery and worse," Teddy answered. "You see, this Concord coach has a stiff pole attached down under this seat we're on. It's called a tongue. That's what those first two big horses in front of us are connected to—the tongue. The horse on the left of us we call the near-wheeler. The other one, there on my side, is the off-wheeler. Near and off. That's important. You always hook 'em up the same. Don't be putting the near wheeler on the off side; might get you misery. The front team are the lead horses. They are not hooked directly to the tongue. They are latched onto a doubletree connected to the tongue. So all four draw the coach. The coach rolls on behind them just fine if they are hitched up properly, and if there's nothing wrong with the wood, brass, metal, and leather in between."

"And," Luci said, anticipating the answer, "what happens if they are not hitched right or if the parts are broken—is that when misery shows up?"

"Ma'am, you learn faster than a VMI graduate."

"VMI? What is that, not an illness I hope?"

Teddy explained his college days, wandered off a little into his time in the Army, but quickly returned to his teaching 'bout reining a four-up team.

"The driver, called a whip back East, or a teamster out West, controls the horses through the lines. That's what we call the four leather straps in my hands."

"The reins?"

"They are like reins on a saddle horse where one rein is hooked to each side of the horse's bit. However, when you're using four horses, the whip has four leather straps, we call 'em lines, but when you're driving a six-up team, you have six lines threaded through your fingers on both hands. It's a handful, for sure, a six-up team."

We were three or four miles out when the first piece of bad road showed up. Along the left side of the trail, a small dry arroyo had partially caved in. It was in a place where the right side of the trail was blocked by two boy-sized boulders. Teddy said the fix was either to move the two boulders over to the side about four feet or to shore up the cave-in so we could get the wagon through. Sgt. Bell offered to do the shovel work on the left side. I said I'd find a leverage tool of some kind and try to joggle the rocks away some. Sgt. Bell was handy with a shovel. Took less than a half-hour and we were back on the road. I considered climbing back aboard Marathon, but I was enjoying hearing about the fine art of driving a four-up team. So I stuck one boot on the front axle, the other in the opening for the first window in the cab, and hauled myself up over the little iron railing to the top of the Concord. I remember being surprised about how high off the ground I was, even in a cross-legged sitting position up top. It was a good ten foot drop down to a rocky trail. No place for little kids, I thought.

Teddy commenced his talk.

"You all want to know the difference between using draft horses and riding horses on a rig like this?"

Luci and I assented.

"Well, it's about distance traveled and what rate of speed you expect. Strong horses, broke to the saddle, love to gallop. And if you've got four of them trained to a wagon pull, then you can make twice the speed of these draft horses, which are not much good as riding horses. Draft horses trot faster than riding horses, except for that Tennessee Walking Horse you're riding, Angus. Riding horses, if you run 'em at a full gallop, need to be changed out on the wagon after less than two hours. Draft horses don't tire as long as you stop every three hours or so, water them, and slip a grain bag over their noses. Thing is, a running horse can't run flat out more than two, three miles before he drops. A draft horse can trot all day long and give you ten, maybe fifteen miles an hour if you stop often enough and fester about food and water at every stop."

Thinking about the stagecoaches I'd seen broke down on a road or getting worked on in a blacksmith's shop, I asked about coach equipment.

"Teddy, what's the most important piece of equipment on one of these stages, the tongue, pole straps, or the lines?"

"Do you mean in terms of misery headed your way or *just* important?"

"Since you put it that way, give me your misery answer first."

"Misery does not necessarily follow from a bad tongue or bad leather in straps or lines. Misery descends down on you like a lightning bolt when this handle here by my right elbow doesn't do its job. This is the brake. You don't need it to make a regular stop; the horses slowing down and the tongue backing up will give you a nice easy stop. But if you need to stop right fast, then this brake is the hand of God, right here with you."

"Right. Like if a gang of outlaws or a grizzly bear is blocking the road and you're running at top speed."

"Yes, but that might not be misery full blown. I'll tell you what is. If you're hauling back on a runaway team, or if you're heading down a cliff—that's misery full blown. Runaway horses can't feel the bit hauling back on a leather strap. Their brains are on fire in a runaway. And if you've gone over a cliff but still have a steep down slope beneath you, the tongue is actually pushing the horses rather than them pulling you. In either case, this brake handle has to do its job. Otherwise, it's Jeremiah bar the door, Kingdom Hall here I come."

We made fifteen miles that day. The next day, we made another ten and reached the rim of Canyon de Chelly, to the south of White Rock. Two days in the coach, with an uncomfortable sleep out in the open, gave everyone an aching back or a sore neck. Both were afflicting Mr. Leonard. Our second-day camp was marked by a warm fire on the rim, a quick supper at the drop table on the back of the coach, and a better sleep. The women slept in the coach. Teddy set up a ten-by-ten-foot tent for himself, Mr. Leonard, and Sgt. Bell. I laid out my tarp and bedroll fifty feet up the edge of the canyon rim. It was comforting to Marathon. As usual, Snow paid us no attention.

Breakfast was quick and enjoyable as Luci gave all of us a sense of this half-mile wide canyon spreading out to the north of us. It was hard to take in the scale of red rock walls rising up high into an endless sky. But any fool could see this was a mighty fine place to be. We loaded up everything and moved out, along the rim of the canyon. Luci directed Teddy to follow the rough road on a northwest tangent. At last night's camp site, the rim overlooked some three thousand feet of steep canyon walls descending into dense patches of stubby trees. They are most likely juniper, I thought, but it was hard to tell from the drop-off edge of the canyon. A dark white ribbon far below was most likely a small stream although it looked like a river from this high up.

I'd had my fill bouncing on top of a ten-foot-tall wagon. I was long-trotting Marathon and leading Snow fifty feet away from the rim. I'd guess we were a good hundred feet behind the winding path Teddy was taking. In less than two hours, the steep wall of the canyon on the far side gave way to a slope maybe only three or four hundred feet off the canyon floor. I rode up alongside the coach to hear the plan.

"How do we get down to the river? I asked.

"There, just ahead of us," Luci said. "There it is, see that small break in the shelf at the edge of the canyon? It leads down to a little mesa area. From there, you will see a road our ancestors used to get in and out without going to the head of the canyon, which is six miles further on. We used it to drive sheep and cattle so they could graze up here. My grandfather had an old mud-wagon, a single-pull harness. He had a mule that would drag that wagon anywhere. I think the canyon is only about two hundred feet below us at this point."

Teddy said, "Yeah, I see it. But before I take this stage down, I want to walk it. The grade has to be less than fifteen degrees or this high wagon, loaded down as we are, might roll over like a felled ponderosa pine. Angus, you mind riding down there with me? You're twice the horseman I am."

Ten minutes later, Teddy had Chinorero's little Morgan pony saddled. I stepped off and gave Marathon's cinch a pull upward. The road, if it could be called that, was visible because it'd been used for a few hundred years. But it was no more 'n six, maybe seven feet wide. Teddy said the axles on the Concord were exactly five feet nine inches. There was not much growing alongside except for sagebrush and some scrub acorn. There was enough space, side to side. But if this narrow road led to any tight turns down below, they'd be a challenge. We got to the little mesa Luci told us about. I turned around and could see the top of the Concord, even though we'd descended near fifty feet below the rim. The stream was now just that, a stream, with willows and small cottonwoods sticking up in areas. But the mesa was not showing any other scarred edge. We rode about seventy-five feet back up the slope of the canyon wall and found the place she'd described. It was a gentle drop-off trail. We could see a big switchback about half-way down. It looked passable from here.

"I'd put that first switchback about a hundred feet below us. What do you think?" Teddy asked me.

"Sounds reasonable. I can't tell from here whether your rig can make the turn there, though. Let's just tiptoe these horses down there and check. That'll give us a chance to see if there's any sway in the soil. Marathon's big iron shoes aren't sinking in up here, but I suppose you need to worry about those tall-girl-size wheels on your coach."

"All right," he said. "That's a plan. Let's take a look horseback."

We rode down the first switchback from east to west. It was maybe a half-mile long. At the turn point, the one we could see from up above, the turn looked less possible. We stood the horses and gauged it visually. Teddy dismounted.

"I think we'll be fine, but let me pace it off."

I watched him walk down, then stop, then take a measured pace from about fifty feet back to the one-hundred-degree left turn back. Very little dust came up from his boots. He walked back to the Morgan where he'd ground tied him, mounted up, and trotted back up to me.

"Angus, there is just enough room down there to make the turn. From there I can see the trail to the bottom. If we go slow, damn slow, we'll be fine."

We trotted back up over the rim and Teddy said his coach could navigate the turn fine, but we'd take it real slow, anyhow. We'd been told Ora had done her share of driving big wagons on the Armijo ranch, so Teddy asked her to join him on the right-hand side of the driver's seat. I nodded my agreement to that. Teddy told Mr. Leonard, Luci, and Sgt. Bell to ride in the backward-facing seats.

"All three of you, facing backward, all right? Sgt. Bell, would you sit in the middle seat and link your arms with Mr. Leonard and Mrs. Atsidi?"

He didn't offer any explanation and they didn't ask questions. He walked around the coach slowly, checking the axles and all rigging, and making small adjustments in the big horse collars on his team. Then he mounted up and invited Ora to join him. She jumped up onto the seat from the off side of the coach and took the right-hand seat next to the big hand brake. I untied the Morgan and Snow, and mounted Marathon.

"The mule and the Morgan will follow me down. I'll stay behind you, just in case you need anything. Let's get to the bottom."

I watched Teddy pull on his elbow-length, leather driving gloves, square himself on the seat, and brace his legs against the buckboard. Ora, as usual, said nothing but braced herself against the back of the seat. I could not see inside the coach but speculated there was some tension there. Teddy said "Step on, step on," and flicked the lines several times. The team pulled forward and he haw'ed them into that first right turn. I let them go down below my line of sight then nudged Marathon forward. As I expected, Snow and the little Morgan hung tight to the rear of my horse.

Since there was no wind, the big rig didn't throw up much dust. Teddy maneuvered the rig just right, staying true to the middle of the trail. As he moved to my right, I could see him with the reins threaded through his hands hauling back on his team as they headed downslope. The big draft horses were having no problem with the descent, which at this point was something in the range of a 5 to 7 percent decline. He told me he was guessing, but these big horses could maintain a slow walk down a 10 percent grade. But, he said, he'd be hauling back on the lines the whole time and adding brake to the wheels as needed.

"The whole way?" I'd asked.

"Yeah," he said, "the whole way."

He reckoned each switchback at a quarter-mile, so maybe a half-mile ride from the mesa ledge to the canyon floor. As I watched him head down, it dawned on me why he wanted Ora in the right-hand seat. She kept pumping the brake handle and cooing something I couldn't make out.

The trip down to the 180-degree switchback took about ten minutes. I tensed up some watching them negotiate the turn. Teddy had slid as far to his left on the bench seat as possible and was almost hanging off the left side of the coach. The reins were wrapped tight in his big hands, and he kept a firm hold up against his chest as the team gee'ed to the left, one slow step after another. They probably weren't going more than two or three miles an hour. Once they made it all the way through the turn and the horses and coach were now back in line, I let out my breath. I'd taken my rope off the tie at the saddle horn and had it at the ready. I'd never roped a coach before. Good thing today would not be the first, I thought.

As I watched them ahead, Teddy slid a little back to the middle of the seat. Ora was pumping the brake handle. Just then, she screamed when the brake handle flew off and swung up at her. She held on so tight it jerked her off the right side of the coach. The brake chain of the housing at the wheel itself sprung backward onto the big gray-black draft horse in front of her. It tried to rear back, but the tongue held tight. Ora flew off the seat to her side of the coach. I never saw her land.

The team bucked up once, then let fly as fast as they could go down the hill. Last I saw of 'em Teddy was braced down against the buckboard. I heard a woman's voice screaming and put the spurs to Marathon. We skidded around the switchback where I could see what happened. The coach was upright on level ground, but the driver's seat was empty. The front two horses were stock still, shuddering and stamping their feet. The horse right in front of the coach was down on its knees, all hung up in the tongue, horse collar, several leather straps, and the brake mechanism.

There was no sight of Ora. I could see one person inside the coach, moving. It took Marathon a few minutes at a fast lope to get there. Once I skidded Marathon to a stop and jumped off, I started to sort things out. Ora had been thrown from the coach forty feet back. She was barely conscious, had blood coming out of the right ear, and her right arm was badly tangled in the leather lacing from the brake handle.

Luci was out of the coach tending to Teddy's left ankle. Later she told me it was sprained, not broken. He fell off the coach, not as part of the stampede, but only when the horses finally came to a stop a hundred feet from the road on the soft sand at the bottom of the canyon. He was trying to get to his downed horse.

Sgt. Bell had an open fracture of his gun arm; a bone was sticking up through the skin. He told me he'd bounced around inside the cab like a gunny sack of potatoes inside a mud wagon. His normal ruddy complexion was the color of the sand he was sitting on, cross-legged, with no hat.

J. Leonard was still in the coach. He had his document case clutched to his chest. I asked him if he was injured. He looked at me but didn't seem to comprehend what I was saying.

We made a canvas stretcher for Ora and set her down twenty feet from the coach. She was breathing with a wheeze, didn't have much color, and was as unconscious as I've ever seen a body without being dead.

We camped there that night. I built a fire, but no one wanted to eat. We got the downed draft horse up. He was fine. Luci bandaged everyone that needed it. I got the gear all sorted out. No one had much to say. Mr. Leonard never got out of the coach. When it turned dark, Luci found blankets for everyone. I found a full bottle of brandy in Sgt. Bell's kit. Thinking Bell wouldn't miss it, in his condition, the three of us, me, Luci and Teddy finished it off and went to sleep on the sand.

CHAPTER 17

"Canyon de Chelly"

I WOKE UP IN THE TWILIGHT of predawn in the middle of a half-dozen Indians standing there staring at me. Blame it on the brandy. How could a bunch of Indians come up on me while I was sleeping without me knowing they were there? Marathon was still tied to a juniper bush thirty feet away, but the mule was down at the stream drinking. I could see Luci standing up whispering to an old man. Teddy was laying on his stomach on a tarp. As I watched he rolled over and up onto his elbows. He looked bug-eyed at the short, dark men walking around us. Then I heard Ora moaning; she was propped up against the rear wagon wheel. Her hair and face were a mess, but she was conscious. A day later she told me she saw the Indians come to her in the middle of the night.

I got to my knees, found my hat, and pulled my boots on. It was hard to get the boots on because my spurs were still strapped on tight. I tried to feel my face but realized my gloves were snugged up on my wrists. Shaking off the fog of drink, I tried to make sense of what I was seeing. Seven, maybe eight Indians, two women, two young boys, and an old man walking around touching us lightly, kneeling down close, and offering us sips of cool water. When they saw me staring, they all looked away. But the two boys were flicking their heads back and forth giving me a sideways look. I looked over at the coach. J. Leonard was still inside. An old gray-headed man with a red cloth around his neck was sitting across from him. Both coach doors were wide open. The old man was quiet; Leonard was talking low and slow. The old man's wrinkled hand was flat on J. Leonard's chest. He seemed to be blowing short puffs of breath at J. Leonard. I'd never seen anyone do something like that before. Sgt. Bell was sitting on a flat rock on the sandy floor of the canyon. Someone had splinted his arm and used cotton twine to make a sling. He just stared at the slow flow in the little stream. There was a tin of water next to him and one of the women was stacking little sticks of wood to his side.

I stood up, only then realizing the sun was not up yet. It was gray light but the predawn down here in the bottom of the canyon was gun metal gray. The summer had parched the ground. But I could see green-gray tufts on the ground, more weed than grass, spread out from the little stream toward me. The water had pooled back under a big sandstone bluff. Looking at it from this angle forced me to look up. It was something to see. The dark red rock face as wide as I could see. It seemed to be rising straight out of the earth, but I knew it was just me, leaning backward. Some tall reeds stuck out of a small pond alongside distorted tree trunks. Couldn't make out whether they were cottonwood or eucalyptus. But they were spindly and widely spaced down along the stream. I could see for maybe a half mile downstream, but not more than a hundred feet upstream. We were at a bend in the canyon where rock, water, sand and trees—all twisted this way and that in the dim predawn light.

"How are you feeling, Angus?" Luci asked, walking toward me. I hadn't realized she was there until she was five feet away.

"Like an old bull just pulled out of a sand bog," I said, trying to force a smile on my face. "Where did these people come from? How did they know we were here? And . . ."

She put the knuckled part of her hand on the side of my face. "I think you should drink something. We have water, but a cup of goat milk would be better for you. These are my people. I used to live about two miles up the canyon from here. They came to help us."

"Well, we sure need that, but how did they know we were here? How did they come on us without anyone hearing them?"

"This is their home. They know when something is different."

"What's different?"

She gave me her closed-mouth smile. "No one here has ever seen a giant red and yellow Hogan on big yellow wheels. No one here speaks American English. But these are kind people. The man inside the cab with Mr. Leonard is eighty years old, maybe more. But he can still ride a mule, and his hands can heal many things. He's in there now, touching Mr. Leonard. Soon now, Mr. Leonard will talk like the wind blowing words to the sky."

"What do you think happened to him? He couldn't think or talk last night."

"He has lived a life without ever being afraid of anything. His is an unthreatened life, one without cruelty. The runaway horses and being thrown around inside the coach made him see death. He is dealing with that. *Béésh Biwoo'ii*, the old man, is touching him to shoo death away. The Indian agent, Ben Yazzie, knows this man, too. He has two names. You can call him Charley. He will touch you after he makes Mr. Leonard well."

"What about Ora and Sgt. Bell?"

"My people know broken bones. Canyon people fall from great heights every once in a while. Sgt. Bell's arm will heal slowly. The old man held that bone coming out of his arm, and pushed it back under his white skin. The woman standing over there, she's his daughter. She made the splint for the Army man. One of the boys made the sling. Sgt. Bell said he needs some whiskey. But I think you drank it all last night."

"There's a new bottle in Snow's pack. I'll get it for him. I see Ora sitting there. She had blood coming out of her ear. Does she need a doctor?"

"She has a doctor—an Indian medicine man. Charley says her head is screaming inside, but it will be quiet in one or two days. He rubbed her ear with cactus oil. She has cuts on her arm from something on the wagon that hit her . . ."

"It was the brake handle. Looked like it broke clear off the wheel, and a wire, or chain hit her."

"Yes. *Béésh Biwoo'ii* put a paste of piñons and reeds from the river on wounds. Her head will hurt for many days. She should be still, not walking around. She will fall down easily because inside of her ear is broken. Maybe worse than the brake handle."

Luci's people moved all of us, except Teddy and me, to a small village two miles up the canyon. They gave Teddy a long stick to help him move slowly on his sprained left foot. Teddy got the big horses harnessed to the wagon, with help from the two boys. He used his hands and pointed at different pieces of the tack. They'd been hitching the family's mud wagon for years. Teddy let them ride in the cab when we rode up the canyon two hours later. When we got to the bend in the canyon where they lived, I figured out why Kit Carson's soldiers never found this place.

The bend in the canyon and the twist in the river were covered on the north side by tall cottonwoods, reeds from the river, and a stand of thick underbrush up against a cliff. From a hundred feet away, it looked like the growth was smack up against the red-rock wall. I'd say it was near a half-mile high. Anybody riding by here would look straight up and marvel at the colors and sheerness of the bald rock. It would take your eye away from looking behind the brush at the bottom of the wall. You couldn't see it from ten feet away, but there was a clearing behind the trees—snuck back under a rock ceiling covered by black smoke and scrapings on the walls and roof—it was invisible until you were inside it. I could see small fenced-in enclosures for sheep, several goats, and a dozen horses. Dogs were yapping at one another everywhere. A little further back into the dark area under the overhanging rock ceiling, I could just make out five or six small stone houses. Could be hundreds of years old. I'm guessing men and their families could hide in here for weeks and nobody would know. Smoke from small cooking fires went straight up into dozens of holes and cracks in the roof ceiling. Don't know where it went from there, but it wasn't out into the canyon.

I never knew how many people lived back there. Luci and the women who came to our rescue moved us into the stone houses. She said the owners would come back when we left.

"They want to help you, but don't want to be here with you."

"When do you think we can leave?" I asked.

"When Ora says," she answered. "The Mexican lady is very strong. But her mind is too quick for her right now. When her thoughts slow down, she will want to go back home. That's when we can all pass down the canyon to a village called Chinle."

It was midday before I felt normal. To replace his stick, someone had fashioned a sort of crutch for Teddy so he could get around the little camp. We hadn't said much to one another. They gave us water in clay pots and goat stew in small clay bowls. They had long twists of passable bread and nuts. After eating some, Teddy asked me to take a walk over to the coach. Something to show me, he said. When we got there, he fished the broken brake handle and part of the chain from the rear boot. It was a mess. The five-foot-long wooden handle was still intact, but the oval-shaped bottom was splintered. The chain was in two pieces.

"Here's how this works," Teddy said. "That oval shape at the bottom is attached to another lever which clamps down a metal brake on the right rear wheel."

"Well," I said, "I can see the power of that big rig and remember how Ora was pumping the brake for you when the team bolted. Hell of an accident. Lucky you're all alive. It could have tipped over."

"Angus, this was not an accident. The wood at the base splintered. See that bore hole through it?"

"Yes, what's that?"

"That's what makes the thing work as a brake. There's a ten-inch-long axle bolt that affixes this handle to the underside lever running to the wheel."

Teddy reached behind his vest and pulled a black three-quarter-inch bolt with a square top piece and a screwed face on the other end. It was broken in half.

"Angus, see here, look carefully at the bolt. I found it under the carriage this morning before they moved us up here."

"Looks broke to me," I said.

"Nope. Look more closely. See the smooth saw marks running a little more than half-way through? Somebody sawed this bolt, but not all the way through. Somebody knew that soon enough there'd be a real need for the brake and when that happened, the uncut metal would give way. We'd have no brake. That's what happened when Ora went to pumping the handle as we slid down the steep pitch into this canyon. The bolt gave way and the whole handle flew up in her face."

"Sabotage? Is that what you're saying, Teddy? Someone sabotaged the stage on purpose?"

"Those saw marks didn't get there by accident, that's what I'm saying."

"But who? Who would do such a thing? And why? Come to think on it, how could anyone tell when the bolt would give way?"

"Well, it wasn't cut when I picked up the Concord at Fort Union. I know that because I took this brake handle off to grease the wheel. It was fine then. I didn't check it after that, but whoever did it had to be in New Mexico. The stage sat unguarded for a few days in Albuquerque. It sat one night in Los Lunas, one near Laguna, one in Gallup, and one night in Fort Defiance. This coulda been done at any one of those places. We didn't use the brake all that much between Fort Union and the Tijeras near Albuquerque. The only hard pumping on it was when we went to skidding down the slope here, right here in this canyon yesterday."

"All right, suppose that tells us three places a hundred miles apart where it got cut. But who? Who might do that?"

"Could be the same boys that killed Chinorero. Or not. I dunno. Someone does not want us taking this trip. From now on, I'm keeping my gun rig strapped on."

"I never unstrapped mine," I said.

We decided not to upset Mr. Leonard with this news. And there was no need to bother Sgt. Bell. My guess was the Army was behind all of this. But I couldn't see Sgt. Bell as part of those outriders in Albuquerque, or involved in cutting the bolt on the Concord. He was nearly killed inside the coach. Can't see him cutting the brake bolt. He's Army to the bone, but not a man looking to commit suicide.

CHAPTER 18

"Chinle"

I T TOOK THREE NIGHTS BEFORE the noise in Ora Gray's head subsided and she could think straight. Sgt. Bell's broken arm was doing OK if he didn't move it around and he had whiskey to drink. Teddy's sprained ankle pained him some, but it didn't slow him down all that much. Luci tended to everyone and told her people how much we all appreciated them taking us in—just like family. Leonard spent all three days in the cab of the Concord, taking little to eat or drink. All of us tried to talk to him about the trip and what he wanted us to do, but not until last evening did he announce we'd continue the trip, as soon as the medicine man said Ora was well enough to travel. Old man Charley touched Ora's ears and blew a little smoke around her face. He said something in that sing-song language Navajos used when they were in the company of white people.

Luci translated, "Old man Charley says Ora can hear only from her right ear. He says to speak softly to her until she gets back home. Her head will hurt until the new moon comes up. We should go to Chinle."

We left Luci's people and their hidden cleft in the canyon after coffee and ground corn strips the next morning. It took about three hours to reach Chinle. Luci had told us before mounting the Concord that the name Chinle, pronounced Ch'ínílí, means water outlet. Her people knew it as the mouth of Canyon de Chelly. When we got to the opening of the canyon, Sgt. Bell said the stream there was the south fork of the Chinle Wash. We came to a small log-and-mud building. Scattered around it, but some distance away, I could see a half-dozen hogans and lean-to shelters for goats. There were fields of chili, corn, squash, peach, and apples trees, and melons irrigated by hand-dug canals from the wash.

When we stopped at the mud hut and everyone got out of the Concord, I asked Luci what Chinle was like when she lived in the canyon twenty years ago.

"It has been part of Canyon de Chelly for centuries. I learned at church school that this canyon was well known to the Spaniards and Mexicans since around 1790. The Spaniards and Mexicans sent expeditions of war to this place. Sometimes they came in peace, only to trade. But other times they came here looking for slaves to sell in Mexico, or in Santa Fe."

Sgt. Bell chimed in, "Yeah, I guess so, but it was American military forces who brought peace here. My old captain told us that his boss came here in 1849. His name was Lieutenant Colonel John Washington. Hell, he said, James Calhoun, who I guess was the territorial governor, made the trip here with him. That's when this place was civilized—before that it was just Indians."

Luci bristled, but kept her voice steady. "Maybe so, Sergeant, but you should know that twenty years ago, the Navajo people in this area had two chiefs, one was Chief Mariano Martinez, the other was Chief Zarcillas Largo. They were our people's headmen in this area. They could not speak for all Navajos, just the ones who lived around here. They signed a treaty with the U.S. Government. It's called the Navajo Treaty of 1849. Do you know why they signed it?"

"Can't say I do. Long before my time."

"It's because the U.S. promised to protect the Navajo from marauding Utes from the north, and Mexican slave bandits from the south. Both attacked our villages and stole women and children to trade as slaves. They stole our horses to ride and our sheep and livestock to eat. They rode this same trail we're on right now. Did you know about that, Sergeant?"

"No, I didn't. But I know about the winter campaign in 1864. Col. Christopher Carson, Captain Francis McCabe, and Captain Albert Pfeiffer accepted the surrender of the de Chelly Navajos. If I recollect right a band of fifty or more Navajos, under a chief named Humpback, surrendered somewhere around here."

Luci, fired up now, shot Sgt. Bell a fierce look. "The Chief's name was Hastiin Cholginih. My family knew him well. We also had a Navajo woman, Chief Khiniba'ih. She was involved in that surrender, as you called it."

"That's why we are here together," J. Leonard said. "The U.S. Army held council, right here in Chinle with Navajo chiefs. It all started here when the Army gathered between seven thousand to nine thousand Navajos to walk 350 miles to Bosque Redondo, New Mexico."

Pushing her food to the center of the table, Luci raised her voice. "You say it like it was merely a historical fact! I was here, that day! Were you here, Sgt. Bell? Were you in your bunk at Fort Wingate? No matter. We walked on foot. You rode your horse. We were guarded by you, not protected by you. Am I right?"

"Yeah, you're right. Times have changed since then. I guess we'll be talking about it in that big red-and-yellow mud wagon for the next month or so. But I don't know what that has to do with what's here in Chinle today."

"It has everything to do with it. Did you also know that it was a Mexican, a man called Nakhayazih, who established the first trading post at Chinle in 1882? It was just a tent. I was here with my cousin when he came. Do you know what that name, *Nakhayazih*, means?"

"Nope," Sgt. Bell said.

"It means 'Little Mexican,' Sergeant. Even after being in the Bosque Redondo prison for four years, we had to suffer a Mexican opening the first trading post here. Was that in the treaty of 1849?"

Leonard and Teddy spent the night in the big ten-by-ten tent. Mather Bell slept in the small tent and Luci and Ora bunked in the Concord. As usual, I spread my tarp one hundred yards out in a small clump of juniper and brush oak. Next morning, we awoke to the smell of strong coffee and bacon frying inside the trader's house. I'd hobbled Marathon during the night on account of the howl of a gray wolf I heard two hours after sundown. When I walked him down to the stream coming out of the mouth of Canyon de Chelly I got a better look at where we'd been. This part of the West inhabits some of the most inexhaustible sky in the world. It's high desert at its best. Reckon it's been this way forever. It's in one of the least populated areas in the whole Arizona territory. I brushed Snow down because he'd collected a mess on his hide by laying down half the night in a scaly mess of mesquite brush and hard-packed clay. Then I walked back to the trader's house for what I hoped was a breakfast of not-Army coffee, bacon, and beans. Turned out it was bacon, coffee, and burnt Navajo flat bread. No beans.

While the locals called him Nakhayazih, we learned his full name was Simon Bonito. His wife visited sometimes, but mostly lived with her parents at Jemez Springs. Her name was Valencia Giusewa—she was part Spanish, part Mexican, and part Jemez. If a man was part white and part something else, especially Indian, everyone called him a breed and thought the less of him for it. But Simon Bonito's wife had three different kinds of blood in her body. No one, not even simple-minded whites, would think of her as a breed. Came to me that red and brown mixes just fine. It's only when you mix in white that folks get stirred up.

We all sat at a long table, which usually held trade goods, but today had been cleared to hold all six of us at breakfast. J. Leonard and Luci Atsidi carried on a conversation about how the Navajo headmen and the American government came together to make the Treaty of 1849.

Nakhayazih didn't have a house, or trading post, as he called it here in 1849, but he'd been driving his little mud wagon over here from Jemez Springs six or seven times a year with trade goods. He traded for wool, mutton, and hides. Maybe a little whiskey, too, but he didn't say anything about that. We all learned more about those days than we wanted to know.

Seems there was another treaty, signed in 1848, called the Newby Treaty, which the Navajos didn't comply with. So Col. Washington demanded that the Navajos had to pay for property he said was stolen soon after the signing. Somehow, Nakhayazih remembered the exact numbers—1,070 sheep, 34 mules, 19 horses, and 78 head of cattle. The headman, a man named Mariano, agreed to all but the cattle, which he said were stolen by Apaches, not Navajos. The difficulty arose when one of the Navajos—not a headman, but a man about thirty—said he'd heard that any new treaty would demand the return of captives taken by both sides. These were slaves taken by Navajos, Utes, the Jemez people, the Mexicans, or the U.S. Army. He said some had been captured here and taken to Mexico. Others had been captured and traded in Santa Fe at the big slave market there. This man, whose name no one could recall, said he'd been captured himself when he was about sixteen and "had no wish to be restored to his people—in Jemez Springs." Luci recalled something about it and said the man had been captured by a roving band of Navajos while herding sheep near Tecolote. She said the man had joined a band at the far end of Canyon de Chelly and now had two Navajo wives and three children even though he still belonged to a Navajo named Waro, who had bought him to save him from being killed. The problem of captured slaves on all three sides, Navajo, Mexican, and white, was sensitive. So apparently they decided not to include the issue in the 1849

Treaty. I suspected we'd find out more about that when we reached the Bosque Redondo.

The number of Navajos was disputed. Col. Washington said there were seven to ten thousand Navajos stretching from the Rio Puerco in the east to the Black Mesa area on the west side of Canyon de Chelly. But the territorial governor, John Calhoun, said there were no more than five thousand. The two men agreed that whatever the right number was, there were less than two thousand warriors, but they were well mounted and well armed with bows and many arrows. They also agreed that the only long-term solution was to confine the Navajos to a reservation with clearly drawn boundaries under military surveillance. Col. Washington argued it was necessary because the Navajos had a pure love of plunder. That was only partially true—especially when compared to the Pueblo Indians who lived up and down the Rio Grande valley in New Mexico.

J. Leonard added his professor's knowledge, based on research in Washington. He told the breakfast group that from the first days of Spanish colonization, the record of Navajo aggression against Pueblo villages and Spanish settlements in New Mexico was incontrovertible. They had, what he called, "acquisitive traits, most notably but not invariably among the poor, the hungry, and the young."

Luci countered by explaining what the white world could never understand. Her people, she said, were never joined in groups like the Spanish or the Pueblo people. Navajos from the beginning of time resisted the notion of tribal governance. They lived in clans and well-defined parts of their country in self-determination—making it difficult for any group of Navajos to achieve unanimity or even a majority of tribal unity in action. This meant that some Navajos, whether in war or peace, never accepted the authority of the U.S. government, or its Army. Our people, she argued, "do not require a Navajo to accept unwanted leadership. And we don't feel any pressure to accept a majority decision or viewpoint. This explains why a few of our people raided to the east and why most of us, who live in the west, do not make war on anybody or steal anyone's horses, or their women and children. This notion always confused and enraged Army people, who took orders willingly."

Sgt. Bell could not understand this. He said without somebody giving orders, all hell breaks loose. She countered that all hell broke loose when the Army rounded up thousands of her people, just because some general ordered them to. This topic, J. Leonard said, is exactly what we need to talk about from Canyon de Chelly all the way to the Bosque Redondo. We now have about 375 miles to go, he pointed out, thinking that would be a good thing.

CHAPTER 19

"Jill Writes Back to Angus"

FIVE MINUTES AFTER WE crossed the railroad tracks and took the short road into Fort Wingate, a soldier walked up to us as we were unloading the Concord and asked if our party included a Deputy United States Marshal named Esperraza. I raised my hand. He handed me an envelope face down. I flipped it over and near burst out with a cheer! It was a letter from Jill.

My Darlin' Darlin' Angus,
    Your letter came this morning. I imagine you're riding Marathon out in front of that red and yellow stage you told me about in the letter. I can almost see you ramrod straight in the saddle, boots turned out just right for long-trotting, and with a smile on your face. You're at your best

horseback, except of course for when we're alone upstairs.

It will be weeks, maybe more, before you get this letter. I might even get one from you before this one reaches you. I'll post it to the Albuquerque hotel hoping that some kind soul will put it in your hands soon. I miss you more than any of your rides up into the high country because I know you're with other people that you feel obligated to take care of. That's a burden. When you're off on your own, I imagine you thinking of me and our home but when you're working a law job, you're thinking about the job. And, darling, how is the job—have you figured out why you're there yet? Is there someone who needs your protection or your correction?

I went to a shooting clinic in Santa Fe four days ago and took the occasion to visit the offices of the Santa Fe Gazette. They are very nice there and let me look at a box of their newspapers from twenty years ago. There were two stories about the Navajo wars and that camp the Army used to hold captured hostiles. It's the one you are going to—Fort Sumner, right? But neither story said anything about why this happened or why it ended with a treaty. They just said it was for peace in both Arizona and New Mexico. When I was just a young girl in Kansas, the teacher was a woman who studied at a university somewhere. I forget where, but she told us about American treaties. I'm sure she said they were agreements with foreign countries. But those Indians were all from New Mexico, weren't they? I know you can explain that to me when you come home.

Perhaps before you even get this, you will be writing me another letter. That possibility excites me very much. It is as though we are writing and thinking about one another but we don't know the particulars yet. I hope you are getting to see some new rivers. I don't know if they even have high mountains where you're going, but the only river I could see on the big map in Santa Fe was one called the Rio Puerco. It's quite a ways west from the Rio Grande. I also saw the Rio Pecos and that's close to Fort Sumner. I remember you crossed the Rio Pecos when you went to Fort Union, the year before I met you, right? Now, I'm thinking of when we met and how you swept me off my feet at the La Fonda Hotel in Santa Fe. Do you remember that, my darling?

I'm out of paper now so I will quit making you feel homesick. I love you so much my heart feels like a Peach Melba. Hurry home to me!

Waiting for you upstairs,
Jill

CHAPTER 20

"Fort Wingate"

W HEN TEDDY DROVE THE CONCORD underneath the big wrought iron overhead gate to Fort Wingate, J. Leonard got out first and declared in his high-pitched tone, "Today, we are at the original staging point, and at our own staging point. I'm told we will dine this evening with the fort commander. I expect it to be a learning experience for all of us."

Sgt. Bell said, "Not for me it won't. This was a miserable experience when I was here twenty years ago, in uniform. Now that I'm wearing civilian clothes, nothing will be much different. More Army coffee, boiled potatoes, and beef stew. That's my guess about dinner."

Turns out, he was wrong. It was Army coffee, boiled potatoes, and fresh-killed New Mexico baked turkey breast.

After dinner, J. Leonard asked all of us to adjourn to a spare office in the Fort Wingate HQ building for the first "formal conference" of the trip. He passed out printed maps to all of us depicting the route we'd take and a list of documents and discussion topics he hoped to cover with us over the next two weeks. To my surprise, he handed me a packet, too.

"Jay," I asked, "why are you giving me this packet? I'm not part of the research group, I'm just hired help."

"No, Angus, you're with us now—one for all and all for one, right? We are musketeers, are we not? I know you're here officially as a deputy U.S. marshal, but I think your voice should be heard on what we're doing and more importantly, why we're doing it."

"Well, I've lived in New Mexico all my life, but I have to say, I didn't know a thing about the Navajo wars, or that forced march from Fort Defiance to Fort Sumner twenty years ago. I was only nine years old."

"True. But you're a federal law officer now, and I'd appreciate your opinion on the serious matters I hope we can talk about. Do this for me, please. Come to the meeting this evening. Read the documents I put in the packet. If you don't want to continue the discussion, that's OK. But I think we need the voice of many people. Ora Gray proved that to me, and you're the one that brought her to us."

So we met that evening. The HQ building was a large rambling thing that was mostly empty now. There were two large rooms, big enough to hold maybe forty people. The one they let J. Leonard use had a long rectangular table with a large box in the middle. The table was surrounded with stiff wooden chairs. No one seemed to know what the box was for. J. Leonard thanked everyone for coming. He sat at one end of the table and Teddy, Sgt. Bell, and I sat along one side facing Luci and Ora. Wouldn't you know, he started off with a speech.

"Thank you all for coming. I first want to say how thankful I am that we're all on the mend after our nearly fatal slide down the mountain side in Canyon de Chelly. That was a dreadful accident, but thanks to Mr. Bridger's skill handling the team, we all survived to tell the tale. And what a tale it is, right? If everyone is comfortable, let me start with . . ."

Sgt. Bell interrupted. "Was it an accident? Nobody's told me that. I've been in hundreds of wagons in the Army and out of it. I've been aboard when we slid down steeper hills than that one, with teamsters clamping down on brake handles for dear life. But I've never heard of a brake handle shattering before. Can you tell me why the brake failed, Mr. Bridger? It's your Concord, right?"

Teddy looked first at J. Leonard, and then at me. Leonard started to say something, but Teddy held up his hand.

"No, Sergeant, it was not an accident. Someone sawed the bolt that serves as an axle on the brake handle. Not all the way through, just half way. But sooner or later, the handle was sure to break. It was just a matter of how much pressure you put on it. That's why you got a broken arm and why Miss Gray got her ear drum punctured."

J. Leonard looked faint. "What? Are you saying somebody tried to kill us? That's preposterous. Why didn't you report this to me immediately? This is an astounding breach of process. I'm in charge and . . ."

I pushed my chair back and stood up. "Hold on, everybody. What Teddy says is true—the brake handle bolt was cut half way through. He told me about it first thing in the morning

four days ago. I told him not to bother Mr. Leonard, because
I knew you were scared half to death and did not need to face
the question of somebody trying to harm the coach riders.
I intended to tell you about it first chance that came up. That
was not until today. He told me first because my job on this
trip is to keep everyone safe. Problem was, I'd been looking
for gunmen out along the trail, not somebody with a hacksaw
hanging around in the barn."

"Marshal," Sgt. Bell said focusing his bloodshot eyes on
me, "give it to me straight up. Do you think whoever cut the
bolt wanted to kill us or just scare us?"

"My thinking is he was trying to send a message. A busted
bolt doesn't mean anybody will get killed, probably just the
opposite. It could have busted going down a grade anywhere.
Most times, Teddy tells me, the brake helps the horses stop,
but the horses alone can do the job by holding the tongue
back on the harness hookup. I've been thinking on it some
and I think it's like what happened to Chinorero. Somebody
sending a message, by killing an innocent boy."

"What message?" Ora asked, with an ashen look on her face.

"Stop the trip," I offered.

"That's ridiculous," J. Leonard said. "Who in the world
would not want us to take this trip? It's nationally important
research. It's a story America wants to read. It's . . ."

Ora interrupted, "No, it's probably not. It's a disgrace.
People just want to forget about disgraceful conduct—especially if the government is part of it."

J. Leonard shifted back into his chair. "I just don't know
what to think. Marshal Angus, you will, of course, write a full
report. We must get to the bottom of this."

"I'll report it to my boss," I said, "and he'll send it on to the Justice Department in Washington. But I'll tell you straight up; nothing will come of it. All the same, everyone needs to be aware of this fact. Somebody does not want us to do what we're doing. The most likely place for someone to have cut the bolt was Albuquerque. I'll tell Sheriff Armijo about the bolt cutting soon as we get back there. And I'll give a copy to the U.S. marshal in Albuquerque, too."

We spent another ten minutes about the need for everybody to keep watch. We speculated about why anybody would want to do us harm. The consensus was that it was not us; it was what we were doing—looking into things that might best be left alone. That seemed to be good enough for everyone, especially Sgt. Bell.

"Everybody here knows I'm just an old horse soldier. I have no idea how I got picked to be here, but I thought it must have been because I was a good soldier back then and did my job like any trooper would. But I'm thinking the marshal is right. Someone is mighty afraid of what might come out of this. I ain't proud of what the Army did to what I came to know as peaceful Navajos. I stand by what the U.S. Army did to warrior Navajos that was robbing and killing white folk. But this bolt cutting and shooting at one of us has taken ahold of me. I say we push on and finish the mission—damn to hell whoever's trying to scare us off. I didn't shy away back then and I ain't gonna start now."

J. Leonard hoped all of us would think about how the Bosque Redondo internment camp came about. We all knew the Army built the camp twenty-four years ago, but none of us knew much about how it got started. We'd heard before that a good part of the reason could be traced to just one man—General James H. Carleton. He no longer had a Civil War to occupy his troops. So, the thinking was he and some members of the Santa Fe Ring focused on what they called the "Indian problem." Actually, he called it a menace, and insisted the only solution that would protect the white and Spanish population was to reduce that menace by gathering all the Navajos and placing them in a supervised military reservation. To accomplish that, he wrote his "Indian Policy," which included the authorization of a new Army post on the eastern slopes of the Zuni Mountains to serve as the "staging area" for his "Navajo Roundup." He called the new post Fort Wingate, to honor an Army captain, Benjamin A. Wingate. Wingate had served at Fort Lyon in central New Mexico and died of wounds suffered during the historic Battle of Valverde. Now that we were inside the gate, and settled in one of the old buildings at Fort Wingate, J. Leonard spelled it out.

"It was fought," he said, "in 1862, near a ford of Valverde creek in what was then thought to be 'Confederate New Mexico.' The Battle of Valverde was a major Confederate success in the New Mexico Campaign of the American Civil War. The belligerents were several companies of Arizona militia, and U.S. Army regulars, and Union volunteers from northern New Mexico and Colorado against Confederate cavalry from Texas. Confederate Brigadier General Henry Hopkins Sibley envisioned that he would invade New Mexico with his army, defeat Union forces, capture the capital city of Santa Fe, and then march westward to conquer California and add it to the territory of the Confederacy. It didn't work out that way. The

Confederates collapsed, leaving the Union Army with nothing to do in New Mexico. The Army had saved New Mexico from Confederate Texans. Now for want for somebody to fight, the Army decided to save New Mexico from the Navajos.

"The first Fort Wingate was at Ojo del Gallo, Spanish for Chicken Springs, near San Rafael, New Mexico Territory. They started construction in September of 1862. By the spring of 1863, it was beginning to take shape. Four companies of the Fourth New Mexico Mounted Rifles under the command of Lt. Col. Jose Francisco constituted the first garrison. Their job was to get ready for Col. Kit Carson's anticipated defeat of the Navajos in Arizona and marching them from there to be 'staged' at Fort Wingate. From there, they would be force-marched for permanent placement at Bosque Redondo, Carleton's great prison encampment of the Navajos and some Mescalero Apaches in central New Mexico. The final blow in the campaign was Kit Carson's attack on the only real stronghold the Navajos ever had—Canyon de Chelly. He rounded up more than two thousand Navajos there, and they became the first contingent of the Navajo's Long Walk. By 1865, the number of Navajos marched at gunpoint was more than nine thousand. The staging area was at Fort Wingate I, which was near Grants, New Mexico. The Fort Defiance 'Military Road' ran 350 miles to Fort Sumner in New Mexico. The 1868 Navajo Treaty officially declared Fort Wingate II, the one we are in now, was 'set aside for the use and occupation of the Navajo tribe of Indians.' By then, there were only 135 troops garrisoned there, as compared with the 3,089 garrisoned here in 1864 when Kit Carson marched that first group from Fort Defiance."

J. Leonard turned to the discussion he'd wanted to have an hour ago.

"All right," he said, "I rather doubt any of you had a chance to read the letters in your packets. So let me see if I can summarize them a little, just to start the discussion . . ."

He turned to a folder on the table before him and sorted some of the papers just as a young enlisted man, in a freshly pressed uniform, opened the door and came across the room to us. He was carrying a large tray of white ceramic coffee mugs with *U.S. Army* stamped on them. Each was nearly full to the brim with black steaming coffee. He also had two metal trays covered with a white linen cloth. He set the trays down and turned to J. Leonard.

"Captain said you all might want coffee and a little dessert. Sgt. Kitchell, our camp cook, makes these all the time. They are sliced apples, with cinnamon and maple syrup. I'll just leave them here on the table. Let me know if you need anything else."

Luci immediately got up and started passing around the coffee. No one seemed interested in the apple slices. J. Leonard blew on the rim of his cup, took a small taste of the coffee, and began.

"I brought more than a hundred letters bearing on our discussion for this trip. I'll share those with each of you during our journey, if you like. They come from the national archives in Washington, DC, and form the backdrop for our discussions. We—that is, the research and editorial staff at the Smithsonian—are hopeful that some of these letters will stimulate discussion about the events and the places we are visiting—or should I say revisiting?—on this trip.

"The first letter is from Brigadier General James H. Carleton. It's dated September 6, 1863, and was posted from Santa Fe, New Mexico, to the Adjutant General of the United States. His name is on the bottom of the letter there in front of you—Lorenzo Thomas. He was, at the time, one of the highest ranking officers in the Army.

"The second letter—dated July 14, 1864—is from Col. C. Carson, better known today as Kit Carson. He is writing to General Carleton in Santa Fe, from what he called the Indian Reservation in Fort Sumner, New Mexico. You can see he ended the letter with his official title down there at Bosque Redondo—Supervisor of Indians.

"The third letter is dated December 16, 1864, and is directed 'To The People of New Mexico' from General Carleton. It was apparently dictated in Las Cruces, New Mexico. I discussed part of this letter with Ora Gray when we first met just two weeks ago.

"The fourth letter is from General Carleton, written two years later, on October 17, 1866, to one of America's most famous generals, Lt. General William Tecumseh Sherman.

"The next-to-last letter in your packet, marked number five, is as you can see, dated June 7, 1868. It is from General Sherman, reporting to his boss, General Ulysses S. Grant, who shortly after getting this letter became president of the United States. It is the most important you will see because it encapsulates the entire experience of the Navajo's removal from their homelands and their incarceration for four years at Bosque Redondo. The last letter, number six, reflects the removal of General Carleton from command and the disbanding of his regiment. As I said, I know you haven't had a chance to read this material. Would you like me to read them aloud and then we . . ."

Ora Gray interrupted. "No, Mr. Leonard, I don't care to have you read them to me. If they are as important as you imply, I will read them for myself, privately, and with care. Perhaps if you just told us what each letter is about and why it's important, we can go from there."

No one said anything else, but Luci nodded her head in agreement. And Sgt. Bell shuffled in his seat as though his pants were too tight. Teddy was already reading the letters.

"All right, that is fine with me," J. Leonard said, clearing his throat and taking up the first letter.

"In his September 1863 letter to his boss in Washington, General Carleton reports the removal of fifty-one Navajo Indians—men, women and children—from their ancestral homes in Arizona to the Bosque Redondo, on the Pecos River, in New Mexico. He states the purpose of this removal is that, in his words, the captured Navajos can be fed and taken care of until they have 'opened farms and become able to support themselves, as the Pueblo Indians of New Mexico are doing.' He also says that Fort Sumner should be a chaplain post, so that the chaplain there could educate the Indian children. He tells General Thomas the Indians are contented and happy. He makes clear his plan to transform the Navajo from nomads to agricultural people, like the Pueblos. He calls that a *sine qua non*."

Sgt. Bell asked, "What did you say, a sine qua what?"

I said, "*sine qua non*—Latin for something that is absolutely needed."

"OK, thanks," Sgt. Bell said.

Luci asked, "Absolutely needed by who? Sounds like he wanted Navajos to become Pueblos."

Ora said, looking at Luci, not Leonard, "It's always what the white man wants. He wants the Mexicans to become whatever the white man says, the Pueblos to stay on their side of the river, and the Navajos to become civilized by a chaplain at an Army fort. That's the Army way."

"Those are good thoughts, Luci and Ora, just what we need for our report—a mix of views and perspective."

Then he returned to Carleton's letter. "It is obvious from this letter that General Carleton did not trust the Navajos or respect their traditions. He says in the middle of the letter that the Navajo people are perfidious, and after two centuries of experience, we can put no faith in their promises, and they have no government to make treaties. They are patriarchal—one set of families may make promises, but the other will not heed them."

Luci looked first at Leonard and then slowly panned the room. When she brought me into view, I swear she had smoke in her eyes. Turning and squaring herself to J. Leonard, she said, "Right, that's what I told you in the trader's house at Chinle. We have no need for a government that speaks for all the people."

"Wait, Luci, there's more than just not needing government. Carleton says in this letter that your people only understand the direct application of force as law. If its application is removed, your people will become lawless again. He says the Army tried over and over. He says your people can no more be trusted than you can trust the wolves that run through your mountains. He says all this can be changed only if we, the U.S.

government, take away your hiding places, teach your children
how to read and write, teach them the arts of peace and the
truths of Christianity. He wants your people to become happy
and contented. He recommends to Washington that feeding
your people will be cheaper than fighting you."

Luci got up from the table. "I do not wish to hear any
more tonight of General Carleton's rant, or his beliefs in the
white God. I need to talk to my ancestors. Tomorrow we can
talk again."

She walked out, followed by Ora. Sgt. Bell said he'd stay
and listen but only if Leonard could get that orderly to bring
them a bottle of Army whiskey. Leonard didn't like that idea,
so Sgt. Bell left the room. I said it was time to water Marathon
and check on Snow. After I did my horse chores, I went to my
room. I took the packet with me and read all six letters. Slowly.

The first letter in the packet raised my blood a little. I'd been
riding the mountain ridges and rivers for many years and had
contact with all manner of people—Mexicans, Indians, foreign-
ers, mountain men, soldiers, traders, hunters, cowboys, and
a few outlaws. There'd always been stories of Indian attacks,
but they were few and far between. General Carleton's letter
to General Thomas sounded more like he wanted to build a
big army than he wanted to solve a real problem. He wanted
the government to set aside a reservation "forty miles square"
in the middle of New Mexico, far away from Navajo country.
He argued Navajo country wasn't fit for a reservation, and
even if it were, he said, those Indians would just "steal away
into their mountain 'fastnesses' again, and then, as of old,
would come a new war, and so on, *ad infinitum*." I don't know

what "fastnesses" means but I was mighty impressed with Canyon de Chelly. Expect the Navajos who lived there were, too. Seems a shame the Army drug them off mountains and canyons they had lived in for centuries. His position on New Mexico people versus Indians was not to my liking, either. He thought white people here were "suffering people." He said the Army was chasing and rounding up "aggressive, perfidious, butchering Navajoes." Hell, he couldn't even spell their name right. His plan became clear in the last sentence. "If I can have one more full regiment of cavalry, and the authority to raise one independent company in each county in the New Mexico territory, they can soon be carried to a final result." He wanted more soldiers, more killing, and more capturing. What else is an Army good for?

The letter he wrote "To The People of New Mexico" on December 16, 1864, was something I think most New Mexicans had never considered. We'd just fought and won the Civil War. Carleton wanted to start another one. He said it was his "fortune, under Providence, to have been instrumental in the removal of the formidable Navajo tribe of Indians." Expect he thought God was telling him what to do. He said, "From time immemorial these Indians had subsided upon the herds and flocks of your fathers." I guess he believed the sheep, goats, and cattle herded by white people had always been food for Navajos. He called the Navajos "barbarians, murderers, and ravagers." And he said they had "carried many of your children into a horrible and hopeless captivity, until there was hardly a home in the land which was not filled with mourning and with hearts made desolate." Now I may not have traveled everywhere in the territory, but I have not heard of hardly any families who lost a child to Navajo raiders. But I have heard about the slave markets in Santa Fe; they were full of Indian children being sold off as household servants.

The thing I don't know much about, but was in General Carleton's letter to all of New Mexico, is the history part. He talked about our ancestors under the Spanish Government making campaigns against the Navajo people and making treaties with them. He made it sound like the Navajos always broke those treaties. But other people think it was the other way around. He named five other Army generals who'd made campaigns against the Navajos. Called them "our best men." But they all ended with broken treaties—in his words— "Navajo Faith, like Punic faith, became at length a scoff and a jeer." I suppose that's Army poetry. But that don't make it right.

This letter was the longest letter I've ever seen—more than five printed pages—letters so small it was hard to read. He said he'd personally met with eighteen Navajo chiefs who begged him for a peace treaty. He said he would, but "if they committed any more murders and robberies, as surely as that the sun shone, so surely would the troops come and, this time, make a war upon them which they would long remember." And he did. He sent Kit Carson to make that war. And he built Bosque Redondo to make sure the Navajos never saw their homeland again—that was how Carleton's last war ended. He went on and on in his letter. He speculated about what ought to happen if the Navajos were to "rise up" again down in the Bosque Redondo. He said that would "give good reason to cut the Gordian knot which has been so difficult to untie, with one terrible blow, and to wipe out the whole

Navajo nation from the face of the earth." I'm not sure what a Gordian knot is, but I'm damn sure the people of New Mexico could not stomach wiping the Navajo nation from the face of the earth. It was supposed to be a prison, not a killing field for thousands of men, women, and children who belonged to a mostly peaceful tribe.

Two years later, in October of 1866, Gen. Carleton wrote a three-page letter to Lieutenant General W. T. Sherman. Seems like there were some Army generals, including General Sherman, who were questioning what was going on in New Mexico. Carleton wrote back defending his ideas. He told General Sherman that New Mexico was "infested by predatory bands of Indians." He wanted more Army posts so they could "pursue the marauders and robbers from the jump." He must have believed the problem was still bad, two years after he began marching large numbers of Navajos to the Bosque Redondo.

He said, "As a rule, the Indians of New Mexico and Arizona are scattered in little bands over an immense extent of country." He envisioned many little Army posts so that they "could encroach on the country possessed by Indians." He said he knew new settlers were coming to New Mexico and Arizona. The little Army posts, if there were sufficient numbers of them, could make sure the Indians were "little by little brushed back before this advancing tide of civilization, until at length they will either become lost in its depths, as has been the case in California, or they will become settled upon reservations in the midst, as upon islands." I just can't fathom what he means. His plan would help the most people, he said. "It soonest covers the Indian country by white men."

On the last page of his letter to General Sherman, Carleton said, "I thought I would place myself on the record, and leave it to time to vindicate or condemn my views and my judgment." On that point, he added, "The true economy is to put troops enough in this country to drive the Indians to the wall at once, to exterminate them if they won't give up; and have done with it. This country is claimed by white men—and they will have it. The spread of our people and the spirit of enterprise make the points of contact between the white and the red man so numerous now, that you can have no peace until the Indians are wiped out, or gathered up and fed." I read this page three times to make sure I was getting his point. We'd just finished the Civil War. The Southerners had their slaves. Carleton had his. The US Army freed the black slaves. But now it was doing the opposite to red slaves.

A knock on my door an hour later was a welcome thing. As I moved the chair away from the little writing desk in my room, I heard Teddy's voice.

"Angus, you still up? I see your light on under the door."

"Yep, I'm up," I said as I opened the creaky door, "come on in."

He came in with the packet of letters in his hand. "You read these yet?"

"Just about, I just finished the one Carleton wrote looking for more money for troops and a bigger reservation for the ones he'd already rounded up. Take a seat, if you want. Is your room like this one, equipped with a little writing desk and a curtain to hide the night bowl?"

"Yeah, about the same," Teddy said. "These rooms were for officers at a time when this fort had a much larger garrison than it does now. There's less than a hundred men now, probably no more than three or four officers. They used to have ten or more officers back when they were fighting Indians everywhere. I would like to hear what you think of these letters."

I shook my head at Teddy. "They tell a sorry story, far as I'm concerned. I know some Indians did not come to peaceful ways easily. It's always seemed to me that they were here first and we didn't give 'em much respect for that. But you're from Virginia. Maybe it's different back there."

"No, not much different, except that the Indians back there were subdued forty, maybe fifty years ago. Our problem in Virginia was not hostile Indians. It was Southern gentlemen who were hostile to black people, but had the law on their side. It took a war to upend the old way of the South toward black slaves."

"Same here. It took a war to get the Navajo land away from them. That reservation down there in Bosque Redondo was a slave camp for several thousand people—red skinned instead of black skinned. That's about the only difference I see. Teddy, I'd like a straight answer. Do you see the same thing here, or am I seeing slavery when I should be seeing white fear of the red man?"

"Angus, I think you got it straight. Those letters from General Carleton were not surprising to me because I'm a Virginian. I've seen that same argument against black people. It's about God giving white people dominion over black people in Virginia—here it's God giving Carleton dominion over red people. It's just prejudice and money. That's what drove the

South to secede from the Union. It's what drove the Army and probably rich landowners to boot the Navajos out of their homeland."

"I was just about to read a letter from General Sherman to General Grant when you knocked on my door. I hate to read that stuff. Mind just telling me what it said so I don't have to read it?"

"It is a rebuke of Carleton. Gen. Sherman told Ulysses S. Grant, the year before we elected him president of the whole United States of America, that Carleton and his friends were 'half crazy.' He also said the Bosque Redondo, where we'll be in a week or so, was a mere spot of green grass in a wild desert. He believed when he went there that the Navajos had sunk way down into absolute poverty and despair. He did not see them as hostile or dangerous. He and the other officers who'd been there seemed to think the problem started with Mexicans invading the Navajos and stealing their children. They turned them into peonage. And here's a point I was very surprised at. General Sherman learned that out here in New Mexico, if a citizen loses a horse, or some cattle, instead of calling on his neighbor to help and go find whoever took those animals, they would call on the closest military fort to deal with it. Hell of a situation."

"I agree with that, Teddy. Hell of a situation. Not any good news in that packet Leonard gave us, was there?"

"Well, the last letter, the one dated February 25th, 1867, was good news, I'd say."

"Didn't get that far. What was good about it?"

"It said General Sherman was relieving Carleton of his command out here in New Mexico. He also said the Fifty-Fifth, which had been in New Mexico for fifteen years, should be decommissioned along with its commander. It doesn't say whether anyone bothered to tell the Navajos. You were just a boy out here then, what do you think?"

"Doubtful."

CHAPTER 21

"Back in Albuquerque"

W E GOT BACK TO ALBUQUERQUE one week after our
expedition began and we were definitely the worse for
wear. The livery stable owner was sitting on the bench at
the livery stable next to a woman wearing a large floppy hat.
I didn't pay any particular attention to her. The owner jumped
up and trotted out to us. The woman sat with her legs crossed,
her hands in her lap, and her face in the shadow of the late
afternoon sun. I was twenty feet out in front of the Concord
and wasn't looking for anyone to welcome us. I didn't pay any
never mind to the woman until I got about thirty feet in front
of her. She stood up and smiled. I put the spurs to Marathon.

"Jill," I hollered, "what in tarnation are you . . ."

I pulled Marathon up in a pile of dust five feet from her
and jumped off to sweep her up in my arms. After she gave
me a proper kiss, she explained.

"Angus, darling, I thought I'd just catch the stage down here. I was in Santa Fe two days ago intending to send you another letter when I got a telegram from Perfecto Armijo. He'd sent it to Chama first, and they forwarded it to me at the La Fonda. It's in our room at the La Posada. Want to go see it?"

I introduced Jill to everybody and promised to meet them for a late supper at the hotel. Then Jill escorted me back to the hotel where we got reacquainted. Afterward, she said Perfecto was worried about Miss Ora Gray, but that he'd told her I was not hurt in the wreck we had in Canyon de Chelly. And she asked me to do her a big favor.

"Sure, sweetheart, anything you ask."

"That's wonderful," she said, pointing to a good-sized leather suitcase on the other side of the room. "I'm all packed and ready to see Bosque Redondo. I'm so glad you said I could make the rest of the trip with you."

"I never said any such thing. Why in tarnation would you . . ."

"You did, too. You just said, 'Anything you ask, sweetheart.' You were reading my mind, which is already made up. I'm going with you. Besides, you need me. Perfecto thinks Ora Gray should not make the rest of the trip. He's worried about the injury to her head in that awful rollover of the big stage-coach. Was it just an accident coming down a steep hill—what exactly happened?"

It took a half hour to explain what happened at Canyon de Chelly. I gave her my suspicions based on the half-cut bolt that Teddy discovered. I told her I had no idea who might have done it, but that everything seemed fine coming from Chinle to Fort Wingate, and on to Albuquerque. As for her coming along for the rest of the expedition, well I ducked. Told her that decision could only be made by J. Leonard. She said she'd take care of that—she'd ask him herself.

We went downstairs to dinner about eight o'clock. Seems like everyone else had things to do, too, 'cause only Teddy and Sgt. Bell came into the lobby at the same time. The four of us walked across the big lobby, past the red velvet couch and the big stuffed chairs into the dining room. The waiter with that wispy mustache strolled over our way and said Mr. Leonard had a table for us. He motioned to the back of the room. I could see J. Leonard, Perfecto, Ora Gray, and Luci sitting at the table set for ten people. Wondered who else was coming. They had a bottle of wine, a bottle of whiskey, and a pitcher of beer. Looked like they'd been having a fine time waiting for the rest of us to arrive.

J. Leonard stood up, beaming at Jill, just like every other damn fool was doing. She always drew the looks when she dolled up for dinner in a hotel dining room. "Ah, Mrs. Esperraza, delightful to make your acquaintance. Sheriff Armijo's been telling me of your proficiency with firearms, but he did not warn me as to your beauty. So glad you could join us for dinner."

Jill extended her hand to him, "Mr. Leonard, so nice to make your acquaintance as well. I have a favor to ask of you."

Leonard beamed. "Anything, Madam, you have only to ask."

I knew he'd regret that open-ended permission. Jill, held onto his hand. "Wonderful. I've always wanted to visit Little Black Water and that wonderful blue lake they have there. It's on the way to Fort Sumner. I am so glad you want me to be part of your grand experiment. Angus has told me so little about it, but I'm sure you are the right man to clarify everything."

For once, Leonard seemed speechless. But he did what I'd done just an hour earlier. He ducked.

"Madam, I did not quite mean to . . ."

Not risking losing her advantage, she said, "Jill, my name is Jill. I will be no trouble, I assure you. And while you have two men skilled with guns, the circumstances may call for another gun. I have brought several."

Smiling, Ora Gray stood up and offered both hands to Jill. "Jill, I'm Ora. It will be a pleasure to have you on the road, but you should also know that I've been shooting since I was six years old. I'm still not a good shot. I will be honored if you will teach me some of the skills you've become famous for in New Mexico. Perfecto already told me about your shooting clinics in Santa Fe. It's wise, unusually so, for Mr. Leonard to ask you to join us."

And with that buy in, the deal was cut.

There were more surprises to come at dinner. After wine was poured for everyone except Sgt. Bell, who ordered whiskey and beer, both at the same time, we had a new guest show up for dinner: Mr. Sarr, the little Chinese doctor who had taken care of Chinorero just before he died. There were welcomes all around. Mr. Sarr took the seat at the far end of the table. Turns out that Mr. Sarr was more than just a Chinese healer and dispenser of Oriental medicines. We learned during dinner he and Perfecto were old friends. Apparently, Mr. Sarr had no first name. Everyone who knew him addressed him as Mister.

Perfecto, speaking from the far end of the table, asked how Mr. Sarr's patients were doing.

"Good health, bad heath is our world, is it not? But healing, that's more important than health. Most of my patients heal quickly and listen patiently. Not like you at all, old friend. You heal impatiently, and listen quickly. How is your chess, have you mastered the Queen's gambit yet?"

"No, old friend. I have not. But Ora has. She beats me more often than anyone, except you. I propose a match between my ranch and your ranch. My player will be Ora and you can choose any of your many business partners. We will make a suitable bet. What do you say to that?"

Over the course of dinner, it became clear that Mr. Sarr owned most of the property in Albuquerque's Chinatown and that he was as well known for his gambling skills as he was for his medicinal skills. He and Perfecto had been placing bets on many things for years.

Perfecto chimed in. "Angus, I was waiting until after dinner to tell you something. My deputies arrested two men a couple of days after you and Mr. Leonard left in the Concord. They were in the Cinches Bar down on Fourth Street, drunk, and bragging about doing something 'real bad' to that fancy red-and-gold stagecoach. The bartender, who's married to one of my cousins, told her that night. One of my deputies, a new man from Colorado, found them there the next night. He bought them two rounds of drinks and they repeated their boast to him. Then, he showed them his badge, arrested them, and we have them still locked in our jail. I told the judge we should wait until you come back to town, and then we can have a trial. I think they could be the same men who killed Chinorero. They are *mui malo hombres*."

"That's some news, Perfecto. Can I talk to them?"

"*Si*, Angus, come to the jail after breakfast tomorrow morning."

"How about tonight after dinner? Catch them unawares. And I'd like to bring Teddy Bridger along. That be all right with you?"

"*Si*, tonight's OK with me, but I don't let anyone except lawmen in the back part of the jail. Why do you want Mr. Bridger there with you?"

I turned to Teddy. "You want to tell him?"

"Seems a good time. Yes."

Turning toward J. Leonard, Teddy continued, "I been meaning to talk to you about this in private, but this situation changes things. Mr. Leonard, I'm the man the Treasury Department picked to handle the big stage for you because I'm an experienced teamster. But I'm also a U.S. Secret Service agent. I'm here as part of your protection team. I showed my badge to Marshal Angus and now it's time for everyone to know I'm wearing two hats on this trip."

Teddy passed his wallet badge and ID card down the table to Perfecto, who looked at it and passed it on to J. Leonard. Leonard did not seem surprised. "Mr. Bridger, I initially thought it odd that Treasury, as part of its grant, would select a Virginia gentleman to handle the coach and related duties, but when I met you, I decided you were the right choice. I cannot say I suspected your law enforcement role, but your provenance seemed beyond what you were billed as. I must say now how pleased I am that Treasury thought so highly of our mission as to assign a Secret Service agent to the team."

No one pressed Teddy further, accepting his law enforcement role as extra protection for a trip across what everyone back East thought was still the Wild West. Later that evening, I learned that Perfecto Armijo was not so easily persuaded.

The dinner conversation continued, mostly about the terrain and the coach wreck in Canyon de Chelly. When coffee and dessert came, J. Leonard made an announcement that surprised everyone at the table.

"Gentlemen and ladies, I have something of a substantive nature to tell you regarding our continued expedition in search of the truth about Bosque Redondo and all it entails for our nation. I have two telegrams from Washington asking after our welfare and mission status. I read them in my room as soon as we left the coach. They have generated a change in plan for me. Rather than continue after one day's rest for the team, I think it best that we stay here in Albuquerque for the next five days before taking the next leg of our journey. We need, I think, to reconsider both the mission and the protocol for achieving that mission. This will take some time to explain, but coffee and this delicious-looking baked apple tart should help you digest what I'm about to say."

It took almost an hour. He had been overly confident, he said, about acquiring an 'on the ground' assessment of the Navajo people's ordeal. He thought, from the perspective of how things are done in Washington, that he could assess the situation on the road by simply engaging two people who made the trek—Mrs. Atsidi and Sgt. Bell—in discussion.

"However, now the events over the last nine days have given me considerable pause. I have to admit my plan was flawed. The fact that news of this mission prompted an attack on the first day, and a nearly disastrous crashing of the coach in the first week, proves the flaw. What we must do now is widen access by engaging other people."

To do this, he said he'd spend the next five days engaging local newspaper reporters, politicians, city leaders, and ordinary citizens to ask for a broad perspective. The Smithsonian Institution needs to answer overarching questions about the removal and incarceration of thousands of Indians. His mistake, he admitted several times, was in thinking this problem could be analyzed by a small team. Now that he'd gotten a better sense of the enormity, that was his word for it, the base travesty, also his words, he must not fail the Smithsonian by minimizing the harm done and the long-term impact on how America integrates Indian populations. It was a one-hour monologue. Everyone at the table understood how serious he was. From my standpoint, it meant spending almost a week in a hotel with Jill. I was all for it. The part I didn't care for was his insistence that the original team—me, Teddy, Sgt. Bell, Luci, and Ora—meet with him every afternoon for the next five days, at four in the afternoon, for tea and what he called "adjustment of the learning protocols and outcomes to inform and influence a fair and positive report to the Smithsonian."

True to his word, J. Leonard met with all three editors of local newspapers, six of the city's leaders, four members of the state legislature, two local judges, and a federal judge who came down from Santa Fe. He also learned a great deal, he said, from more than thirty local citizens who had opinions on, and some actual knowledge of, the events that led up to the roundup of Navajos as well as their "deplorable" stay at the Bosque Redondo. All of it, he assured us, will be part of his eventual report. Most of it he shared in our daily tea and catch-up sessions in the dining room of the La Posada Hotel.

It was good that J. Leonard had things to do because that busy work allowed me the freedom to investigate Chin's shooting and the sabotaging of our coach. True to his word, Perfecto Armijo gave me and Teddy access to the two men he'd arrested for shooting Chin. At ten o'clock that night, we interrogated the men in their cell at the Bernalillo County Jail. We woke them up from a sound sleep. They were hostile to the interrogation. All we knew about them were their names. Jack Evans, the older man, appeared to be in his fifties. His sidekick, a surly kid barely out of high school, went by Kid Lucifer. Sheriff Perfecto said we could interview the two inside their cell, but we'd have to leave our guns outside, with his night deputy sitting five feet on the other side of the bars.

I'd been in lots of jails, always on the outside of the bars, but this one was more dismal than most. The building looked from the street to be a single story, but once inside the main feature was the open metal stairway down into the basement where the cells were.

Sheriff Armijo explained, "This jail is about forty years old, maybe older. It was built by the Mexican government as a prison for deserters and anyone who the bishop said was unholy. There are no windows down there, and the only heat comes from what drops down from the two fireplaces up here. This is an adobe building and retains heat well, even down there. We have five cells—one big one—twenty-by-twenty feet—and four smaller ones—eight-by-ten feet. The small cells have two metal bunks, stacked one atop the other. The big cell has no bunks. We use the big one for drunks and the others for prisoners being held for trial. Your two suspects are in the corner cell, furthest away from the metal stairway and closest to the piss and shit pots that get stacked up every day. One of the drunks, usually the first one to sober up, gets out early every morning in exchange for hauling those copper pots up and out to the back where the shit and piss mellows every morning. We have electric lights up here, but only gas lanterns down there. It's dim, but you don't want to see those hombres up close, anyway."

We gave him our guns. A toothless deputy, named Changa, picked up a ring of keys and led us down the stairway. Half way down, the stench hit us. By the time we reached the back corner, it was near overpowering. The cell was dark; Changa struck a match across his boot heel, lit the gas lantern on the wall outside the cell, and used his key to open the cell and let us in. Then he locked the door behind us.

"Who 'n hell are you?" the older man asked, looking up from the lower bunk at us.

"I'm a U.S. marshal. Name's Angus. This man is a U.S. Secret Service agent. You can call him 'Sir.' Sit up and put your feet on the floor. You, in the upper bunk, wake up."

The lower bunk inmate sat up, dropped his feet over the side, and started slapping his own face as though he couldn't quite make out what was happening. Jack Evans looked older in the dim light. His mean streak came out right away.

"Fuck you, Angus. And you, too, 'Sir.' Got nothing to say to either of you."

The upper bunk man had his back to us and barely stirred. Teddy went over, grabbed his leg, and jerked hard, nearly pulling him down onto Jack Evans. He said, "Kid Lucifer, what fool would claim that foolishness for a name? You want to see

Lucifer in the flesh? I can arrange that if you don't behave and answer the marshal's questions."

Then, turning his attention to Jack Evans, he rapped his right ear hard with a short knuckle punch. "Don't sass a U.S. marshal, Mr. Evans. It always turns out bad. He is much more patient than I am. If you don't answer his questions, he will leave and go upstairs for a nighttime brandy with the sheriff. That will leave you boys alone down here with me. I'll be the only one thinks that's fun."

Both men got it. They couldn't wait to talk to me.

"Why'd you boys shoot the Apache boy? His name is Chinorero, and he was a friend of ours. You mean to kill him, or just scare the folks in the stage? What I want to know is who you're working for."

Jack Evans rubbed his ear and started blubbering. "Hell yes, that's right. We was only told to scare him and some ass-hole from Washington. Dunno why. They just gave us forty dollars to send a message."

"What message?"

"Go back to Washington? Hell, I dunno. It was a forty-dollar deal. I kept thirty, like always, and gave the Kid ten. We kept quiet about it for two days, and then the kid here, stupid little shit, started bragging about gut-shooting a breed and chasing that Washington asshole the hell out of Albuquerque. That's all I know. The kid don't even know that much. He ain't good at thinking. But he's a fine shot and didn't mean no harm. Just a scare, that's all. Then the breed fired five shots at me. Missed all five. So I had to plug him before he could reload. Hell, he was a hollerin' and fixin' to run straight at me. Shot him in self-defense. That's all I got to say about it."

"Where did you go right after you shot him?"

"What? Where'd we go? Why you want to know that?"

Teddy took two steps toward the man in the lower bunk. "You want a rap on the other ear, you turd? Answer the man's questions, or this is gonna get hard for you."

Evans turned back to me. "We went back to the Cinches Bar to report to the man from Santa Fe, like we was told. Got the other half of our money, and spent two days drinking it away. Then the kid got us locked up with his big mouth in the bar."

"There's more to it than that, Mr. Evans. And you were paid more money, right? No sense lying now. You cut the bolt on the brake handle that night after the shooting. What did the man from Santa Fe pay you for that?"

"Never cut no bolt. I don't do manual labor. Got the kid for that, but he didn't do nothing like that, neither. What 'n hell you talking about?"

Kid Lucifer wasn't as stupid as he looked. But he was a mean little turd. "What the shit," he yelled down to Evans, "you got more money? And you cut something on the stagecoach? Never told me and never shared the money? You bastard."

With that, Kid Lucifer swung his right leg down from the top bunk and kicked Evans square in the face. Blood spurted out Evans's broken nose and he screamed.

"For God's sake, Kid, don't make this worse!"

"I'll tell 'em everything now, you cheatin' asshole. OK, Mr. Marshal, ask me whatever you want. Then get out of here so I can kill this asshole that cheated me out of money and lied to me, too. I'll tell the judge, too, soon's we get a trial. All I did was miss on purpose, I didn't kill no one. I didn't do no sabotage."

We left the jail ten minutes later. Upstairs, we filled in Sheriff Armijo. A man they knew as Mr. Sanchez, in Santa Fe, had paid the two drifters, Evans from Texas, and Kid Lucifer from Missouri, forty dollars. They had a room in a rundown brothel he owned on the south side of Santa Fe. They worked as bouncers in that bar, and two others that Sanchez said he owned, one of which was in Bernalillo. They beat people up once in a while; mostly other drifters who owed the Sanchez family money. Sheriff Armijo said he'd send a man up to Santa Fe and find out who this Sanchez was. Evans did not know why Sanchez wanted the man from Washington to go back where he came from. All Evans knew was it was worth forty dollars to send two messages—one by a 30.30 rifle—the other with a hack saw.

Teddy and I walked back to the hotel. On the way, Teddy said we'd done the Lord's work getting that "carpetbagger trash to talk."

"Carpetbagger trash?" I asked. "What's that mean, Teddy? The men in your family were Union officers twenty years ago, right? Were they deployed in Virginia after the War in the reconstruction of the South?"

"Angus, you don't know about what reconstruction really was, do you? Once Lincoln was shot and a new president put in, the U.S. Army stayed in the South for two years, maybe more. Reconstruction brought carpetbaggers, and carpetbaggers nearly destroyed Southern tradition. It wasn't just Negro slaves after that. It was carpetbaggers destroying a way of life in my home state, Virginia, and the whole damn South."

Next day, at four o'clock in the afternoon, we met for tea in the La Posada dining room. Everyone had tea except Sgt. Bell who insisted on a mug of beer. J. Leonard gave us the day's collection of opinions he'd gathered from people Leonard was sure knew what they were talking about.

"Well, fellow travelers of the Navajo Long Walk, I have some very interesting perspectives to pass on to you. These are from local citizens, mostly white, modest people, but who are keen observers of their own community. One would expect them to be mostly supportive of the Army's protective efforts vis-à-vis the Navajo problem. But they were skeptical of the Army's solution, even before the mass surrender in Arizona, because they did not feel any danger here in Albuquerque. Back in Washington, when I first began to study the subject, two years ago, I erred in seeing New Mexico as a whole. What I know now is that New Mexico consists of two sizeable communities and many small settlements spread over a large state. The raids the Army used as the rationale for rounding up and killing many Navajos did not occur here, or in Santa Fe. Or even in Las Cruces. They occurred in small outlying areas, and mostly in the 1840s and 50s. Horses were stolen, and some sheep as well, but the raids were not massive or widespread. It was talk about them that spread. It was also true that by 1863, at least two thousand Navajos, mostly children, had been enslaved as domestic help by settlers, often on large Spanish haciendas. There are records, although I haven't seen them, of the Catholic Church that suggest the number could be as high as five thousand children sold in New Mexico and the Republic of Mexico, south of the Rio Grande. The truth appears to be that there were raids by Navajos as retaliation for raids by Mexican bandits. New Mexican settlers were alleged to have conducted such raids as well, although this is doubtful. What is certain, though, is that many New Mexican haciendas had household help in the form of Navajo children sold in what was a slave market in Santa Fe. The extent of that market is a subject of great debate. But no one denies its existence."

Ora and Luci both spoke up almost simultaneously.

Ora asked whether the Santa Fe slave market was known to the Army. J. Leonard said yes.

Luci wanted to know whether the Army was involved in taking children during their raids. She said many children were killed in those raids and that some children were not accounted for after the soldiers left. J. Leonard had no information on either question.

Sgt. Bell said the real problem was the Indians' refusal to accept civilized ideas. He said it was a clash between white settlers and Indians over religion and land ownership. He remembered officers saying that the Indians refused to share any part of their vast holdings of land and that was the biggest cause of the hostility between the Army and the tribe. J. Leonard said the notion of clash of culture was a smokescreen for those who wanted to take Navajo land away from its natural owners and make it available to settlers. Sgt. Bell said he'd been west and no settler would want to settle on that land—it was all harsh desert and no place to raise a god-fearing family. J. Leonard asked why, if that was true, the Army rounded up everyone who lived on that desolate land and moved them hundreds of miles away in a prison camp. The afternoon tea discussion lasted for almost two hours before everyone rebelled and returned to their rooms. Neither Teddy nor I had much to say. It was mostly a political discussion.

Two days later, the guy at the hotel registration desk knocked on our door at 8:00 a.m. He handed me a note from Sheriff Armijo's office asking me to come see him whenever "I got up." I walked down the hall to Teddy's room. Not surprisingly, he was up, too. Lawmen never sleep late, except when they don't sleep at all. Ten minutes later, we were in the sheriff's office.

"*Buenos días*, gentlemen," Perfecto said when a deputy showed us into his office.

"Morning, Sheriff," I replied, for both of us. "Got anything on those two jailbirds downstairs?"

"I released them the day after you and your ferocious friend talked to them."

"Ferocious, me? Don't know what they were talking about," Teddy said.

"Señor Evans said something about a knuckle punch that nearly blew out his ear drum. However, I never heard of such a thing. Besides, I wanted them out on the street to see who they talked to. Yesterday, a man named Sanchez asked for Evans in two different bars in town. Both bartenders sent a kid to me about this man. I found him at the stage line yesterday afternoon, waiting for the return stage to Santa Fe. We had a short but productive talk. He is a man who likes to ride two horses at once."

"Whose horse is he riding up in Santa Fe?" I asked.

"Mostly a rancher's named Stonker and a state senator who I shall not name. He's a compadre of mine, sometimes; other times he's not. However, between the rancher and the legislator, I have discovered something you probably don't know anything about. Twenty-five years ago, the rancher bought two Navajo boys and they are still working on his ranch. They probably came from the old slave market up there, but it's been closed now for a long time. The legislator, whose name I cannot tell you, was the man who protected the auctioneer at the market. The auctioneer was only a go-between. That's what I heard about him. No one knows who really owned the market. Nevertheless, here is the most interesting thing. One of the reasons it closed down is because the auctioneer was getting American dollars from buyers of household and ranch help, and keeping the money himself. He was paying the Mexican banditos who stole the children in counterfeit money. I guess it went on for several years. The banditos knew it was phony money but could hardly complain to the authorities. And in Sonora, the counterfeit money looked real enough.

I asked, "Sheriff, wasn't that slave market illegal? I mean I guess it was legal in the South with Negroes and all, but it was against the law in the rest of the country, right?"

"The slave market was not actually illegal, but it was not accepted, either. So, my confidant thinks some very angry Mexicans came across the border and kidnapped the auctioneer. If that's what happened, he's probably in a Mexican prison, perhaps he died there. That's why no one knows where the auctioneer is. I don't know if that helps you, or not."

Teddy spoke first. "Sheriff, now I have to tell you something. You may not know, but the U.S. Secret Service is the primary enforcement agency for counterfeit money in this country. We do more than that these days, but during the Civil War, counterfeit money was a very big problem, especially in the South. We also knew that soldiers in the U.S Army, mostly in the enlisted ranks, were trading in counterfeit money out here in the West. We think it was used in trades between soldiers and banditos. Some officers thought there was a connection with the slave trade, but there was never any real evidence of it. The problem went away when the war ended, or at least it went underground. Then, only a year ago, we discovered counterfeit money being used in the weapons trading across the Mexican border. That's part of the reason the Treasury Department sent me along with the Smithsonian research group. It's a good cover for me to ask questions here as part of a research team, rather than as a Secret Service agent."

"Señor Bridger, does your agency think there was counterfeit money involved in the Navajo Long Walk?"

"Not for sure, no," Teddy answered. "But there were always rumors about somebody in the Fifty-Fifth regiment being involved in both the slave trade and the transfer of counterfeit money."

"Teddy," I said, "I never thought about that before today, but is there any way we can find out the auctioneer's name and whether he had anything to do with the Army company that was moving the Navajos from Arizona to Bosque Redondo? Is that a possible connection?"

We talked about it for a half-hour, but none of us had any answers. Perfecto said he'd ask around and try to find the auctioneer's real name and whether he was in a Mexican prison. Teddy said he'd send a telegram to Washington asking similar questions. I said I wanted to get back to the hotel in time for lunch with Jill.

J. Leonard continued to talk to people, have afternoon tea meetings with us, and finally, on the fourth day, said we should have dinner because we'd be back on the road Monday morning. And he said there'd be more changes. He decided one stagecoach was not enough, given what happened at Canyon de Chelly. Perfecto Armijo offered his six-passenger wagon that had a ranch cooking box, with a drop-down table built into the back of the wagon. He invited two more people to join us. Ora's cousin, a twenty-one-year-old man named Johnson Ortega, would be driving the Armijo ranch wagon, and a rancher in his midthirties from San Pedro. His name was Anderson Kipfer. He'd asked for permission to go with us.

The big news was that we would be taking a different route than originally planned. It was called the Canon Blanco Route and was shorter by almost fifty miles. It was not used as frequently as the mountain route because the Army thought it was a rougher trail, given that the Navajos were walking on foot, and there was not as much water. But J. Leonard had been assured by Mr. Kipfer that there was plenty of water for two wagons and three outriders. Besides, he said his ranch was halfway between the Bosque Redondo and Albuquerque. We could stop there for needed supplies or rest. The longer routes used by the Army needed lots of water. They were using dozens of mules and even more oxen to pull the heavy wagons with building materials and supplies for Fort Sumner. They seemed confident we could make the trip in six days. It was unclear how long J. Leonard planned on staying in Bosque Redondo before returning to Albuquerque. But he said he and Teddy would be taking the train back to Washington in two weeks.

CHAPTER 22

"New People"

TWO DAYS BEFORE WE packed up for the last leg of the trip, J. Leonard convened a private dinner meeting for the six of us that came from Canyon De Chelly, plus Jill and the new people, Johnson Ortega and Anderson Kipfer. That would make nine of us headed for Bosque Redondo. "We'll be bugs under a microscope," J. Leonard said. No one could guess what he meant by that. The dinner was in the lobby of the Grant Opera House, which had been constructed in 1883. The hotel would supply the food and drink. Neither Jill nor I knew there was an opera house in New Mexico. But Perfecto did.

Jill took it in stride, just as though she'd seen rooms like this all her life.

"Angus, darlin'," she said, "I went down this afternoon and took a peek at the Grant Opera House. Just wait until you see it! Mr. Leonard's dinner is going to be held in the lobby.

Of course, I've been to the opera before, back in Kansas, but this one is special."

"What makes it special?" I asked, even though it was not a subject I had any interest in. I'd never seen or heard an opera before, but I'd been in plenty of lobbies, which I thought was a little room before you went inside a saloon, pool hall, or house of ill-repute.

"Well, because this city, which is really the only city in New Mexico, was founded in 1706 and named after Don Francisco Fernández de la Cueva. He was the eighth Duke of Albuquerque; born in Barcelona into one of the most aristocratic families of Spain. *Villa de Albuquerque* was the original name for the old town, two miles from here on the Rio Grande. Then, in 1880, the railroad came here and a new Albuquerque was built around the train station. This hotel is in the new Albuquerque. It got electrical lighting in 1883, at the same time they built the Grant Opera House and the Charles Ilfeld Building."

"Who told you that?"

"It's on a big plaque, inside the lobby of the Opera House. It's very historic, that plaque."

"Historic? Does that mean the plaque is old, or that the Don is old? You're confusing me."

"And Angus, darlin', you're teasing me when you ought to be paying attention. We're having dinner in a beautiful room this evening and we need to respect New Mexico's traditions."

"Jill, darlin', to be a tradition it has to be a century old, and this new Albuquerque is only eight years old now."

When we walked in the lobby two hours later, I have to say it was respectful as all get out. The room was probably forty feet square, with a polished wood floor so shiny it looked like it was made of yellow ice. There were four dinner tables with fancy white linen cloths and a flower base in the center of each one. Right off, I counted the chairs—six at each table. That meant J. Leonard had invited two dozen people. I couldn't identify the flowers, but each table had a different color. The chandeliers sparkled light over everything. Someone said the chandeliers cost more than all the livery stables in the whole state. There was a podium set up in front. They had a poster on it depicting the Smithsonian Institution in Washington, DC, with its famous motto in big print: *The Increase and Diffusion of Knowledge.*

The lobby had its own bar and everything was free. I'd learn later that free meant the Smithsonian was paying. Our group sort of moved off to one side of the room and the invited guests took the other side. Teddy, with a glass of red wine in his hand, asked Jill how she liked being a bug under a microscope. I'd told her about J. Leonard's strange comment.

"Oh, Mr. Bridger, I don't think we're the bugs. The bugs are local people sitting over there at the other two tables—the Smithsonian is the microscope and *they* are its bugs."

Teddy looked at Jill sort of slant-wise. "Pardon, ma'am, but I'm a Virginia man, through and through. We know a lot about bugs. And we know a lot about northern Yankee justice. The War's over back home, but there's a lot to do before the South can ever raise its head again."

"Mr. Bridger," Jill said, in a tone I rarely heard from her, "the South should never raise its head again because it thought more about cotton than human life. We fought a civil war to emancipate and eradicate human slavery in the South. And we are now part of a group that sees a different kind of slavery that was practiced here in New Mexico. The enslavement of a whole tribe of Indians. For a short time, the Army here became like the Confederate Army. It thought more about land than human life. It's not about bugs, it's about human dignity."

J. Leonard had told us the day before that the dinner would be in a grand place, "entirely consistent with the mission we are on." He'd sent little handwritten notes to all our rooms telling us that drinks and hors d'oeuvres would be served at 7:00 P.M., with introductions and a brief program at 7:30, followed by dinner at 8:30 and dessert at 9:30. I asked Jill what kind of a program would take an hour and why couldn't we eat first and program later. She tut-tutted me and said something about giving Mr. Leonard a chance to preach to the choir.

Once everyone was seated with a glass of wine or a snifter of brandy, a waiter wearing a black wool vest over a white long-sleeved shirt carried around trays of little bits of food. Then J. Leonard went up to the podium and gave a little rap on the wood to get everyone's attention.

"Good evening, old friends and new. My name is J. Leonard. I am a senior researcher on staff at the Smithsonian. If I may, let me start with a special welcome to the new friends who are here this evening to learn more about the Smithsonian Institution and the very serious mission we are on here in New Mexico. Let me begin, if I may, by directing your attention to the Smithsonian's 1846 motto, which you can see here on this poster. It is at once motto, mission, and everlasting hope. We are a private institution not supported by government funds, and what we do is embedded in this motto— 'Increase and Diffusion of Knowledge.' We are educators, researchers, social reformers, and opinion makers. We increase knowledge by researching events, people, scientific problems, and natural phenomena, wherever knowledge is to be found, discovered, or lies buried. With that grand purpose, we are here in New Mexico for a special reason. We are here to discover and report on an event that took place in your wonderful territory over twenty years ago—between the years of 1864 and 1868. It is well documented in U.S. Army records, even though the perspective therein is entirely that of the U.S. Army. It is poorly documented, and if I may be so blunt, almost unknown outside those records save for a scant few newspaper articles and writings of some of the people involved in it. The Army called it a 'social experiment' after the fact. New Mexicans saw pieces of it, and there is one document, a letter written from an Army general to the 'people of New Mexico' that rationalizes the undertaking. We shall spend the evening discussing this social experiment and perhaps probe both its claim of governmental validity and its undoing after only four years. It ended with an historic treaty, the first of its kind for the American government."

J. Leonard took a sip of mineral water from a small cut glass on the table next to the podium. Then he spent about twenty minutes describing the details of hunting down, and rounding up, somewhere between eight and nine thousand people, and forcing them to walk 350 miles from Fort Defiance to Fort Sumner to a new Indian reservation, the first of its kind in America. He used maps and charts, and read from Army documents. And, he tried to explain why the Smithsonian was given a grant from the U.S. Treasury to investigate and document the trail from west to east.

"You may wonder why our Institute would take on a project such a distance away from Washington, DC, and at a considerable expense. It is simple in one sense but remarkably complex in another. First, a bit of current history. The native people in this part of America were its first inhabitants. They were here for centuries. Early in this century, adventurers arrived. They established towns, ranches, farms, and new ways of life. The people who had lived here for centuries viewed these people as trespassers on their lands. The native population knew nothing about Spanish land grants or purchases made by the United States government of lands they thought were theirs. The settlers, on the other hand, saw the nomadic Indians, and even the more settled Puebloans, as a threat to their way of life. It was in every sense a clash of cultures. Consequently, a series of Army installations was established to protect the settlers. Those forts and supply depots, from the government's view, were supposed to integrate new territory into the ever-expanding United States of America.

"However, the Civil War interrupted that process. The South wanted to secede from the Union. New Mexico became a target of the Civil War, and the Union Army was substantially increased to resist your neighbors to the east—Texas—which was a Confederate state—from taking over New Mexico. The Civil War here in New Mexico was short lived, and once won by the Union Army, left a rather sizeable standing Army here with no war to fight. That Army took on a new mission—to disarm and dismantle a tribe of Indians they thought especially hostile. That thesis is debatable, but the consequence is not. The Army took on the Navajos in a battle fought by stealth and bows and arrows on one side, and a determined, heavily armed, and mobile Army of soldiers on the other side. The eventual outcome was predictable—the U.S. Army won. However, the consequence of winning was not only not predictable; it was almost a secret solution.

"The Army built a prison compound in central New Mexico, rounded up thousands of Navajos, and forced them under armed guard to move permanently to Bosque Redondo. The Army's plan was to keep them there permanently as farmers rather than nomads, and as Christians, rather than allowing them their heathen religions. The Army did not act independently; the U.S. Congress sanctioned its conduct. Some argued and many believed that subduing native populations and settling their lands was our destiny. A 'Manifest Destiny,' some called it. With this understanding, an Army general from California, with little knowledge of or interest in the people of the New Mexico territory, established a new Army fort, called Fort Sumner. Its sole purpose was to manage the permanent incarceration of thousands of Navajos and a few hundred Mescalero Apache on a forty-mile square piece of land called the Bosque Redondo Reservation. Between 1863 and 1866, Navajos were forced to march to this reservation. Nearly all of them passed through this part of New Mexico. Some of the people here this evening bore witness to those marches. Others are here this evening because they want to know more about what happened, why it happened, and what lessons were learned that will live on in American history in a good way."

J. Leonard paused to take another sip of water. Before he could resume his speech, a man at the table next to ours stood and asked, "Mr. Leonard, I don't mean to interrupt, but are you going to take questions from us? Speaking only for myself, I think you're leaving out some important parts of the story."

"Quite right, sir. Quite right. I tend to verbosity; my traveling companions here in the room will no doubt confirm that. I'm leaving out much, to the end of including only the vital. To your point, I welcome questions. However, if I may, perhaps this would be a good time to make brief introductions, following which I will take your question, sir. Would you defer for a few minutes, sir?"

The man nodded. I turned to Jill and whispered, "What's verbosity?"

"Too much talking," she whispered back.

"Well, then," J. Leonard said, "let me introduce our new friends, the five people who have been traveling with me for the last three weeks. I'll ask each of you to stand briefly, so that names can be matched with faces, the better to know one another during the evening.

"Starting with a native New Mexican, a man who now lives in Chama, New Mexico, Deputy U.S. Marshal Angus Esperraza. This fine gentleman has been tasked with security and navigation for our trip. He has also proved to be quite resourceful and helpful in understanding both cultural and logistical matters.

"Teddy Bridger is a native of Virginia, an expert teamster, camp cook, and military historian. He is also, I learned recently, on loan to us from the United States Secret Service in Washington, DC.

"Luci Atsidi is from Arizona, specifically the Canyon de Chelly area. She is the *raison d'être*, the very reason for our expedition. As you all know, we are reconstructing the 1864 to

1868 forced march of many Navajo people across this territory to the Bosque Redondo. Mrs. Atsidi was one of those forced marchers. Her insights regarding the overall experience, down to the small nuanced details, are invaluable to the people of New Mexico, her own people, and those who will ultimately read the report we will eventually write.

"Sgt. Mather Bell is a man with a long record of military service. He is a widely traveled man who offers both a similar and a startlingly different perspective. You see, Sgt. Bell was in the Army that guarded the Navajos on the march across your state. Between Luci Atsidi and Sgt. Bell, we are learning first-hand the fine details and the larger questions of why and to what purpose these events unfurled. Their original memories and views are priceless to a researcher such as myself. And to hear them *in situ*, so to speak, is a rare and invaluable experience."

Another lean toward Jill's available ear. "Sweetheart, what's *in situ* mean?"

"Latin, I'm pretty sure. Sounding it out, I'd guess it means on site. You know, on the ground instead of up in the clouds."

J. Leonard continued, "Miss Ora Gray, a woman who has more talents and skills than almost anyone I know, lives close by, up in Tijeras Canyon, on the Armijo Ranch. I'm sure all of you know Sheriff Perfecto Armijo, who is in the audience tonight. When we needed another person to join our merry band of adventurers, he suggested we talk to her. Among many other perspectives, she was eyewitness to one, or perhaps more than one, of the marches up the rocky road to the ranch on which she was born and on which she still lives and works. She was only ten when the march passed by, but her memories of that day are vivid and valuable to our ultimate report and conclusions.

"Therefore, ladies and gentlemen, those individuals, plus myself, are the original group making the trip in our magnificent red-and-yellow Concord stagecoach. We have completed the first half of the trip—from Fort Defiance here to Albuquerque. There will be an additional coach, a covered wagon actually, joining us for the next part of the trip from here to the Bosque Redondo. Three new people will join us. They are here this evening. Would each of you please stand when I call your name, for a brief introduction?

"Johnson Ortega is a twenty-one-year-old ranch hand on the Armijo Ranch. He's seated between Ora Gray and Sheriff Perfecto Armijo. As I said, I'm sure everyone here knows the sheriff—but hopefully not professionally. No one here has been arrested by the sheriff, right? Mr. Ortega will handle the horse team pulling the additional coach.

"Seated at the far table in the magnificent straw hat is Anderson Kipfer. Mr. Kipfer owns the Long K Ranch near Little Black Water. When we first met, I asked how large his ranch was, which I *now* know was an impolite question. He would only say, 'It's a sizeable spread.' He knows the country well between here, his ranch, and the Bosque Redondo. He will make the trip for many reasons. One reason he wants to join us is personal, but he has given me permission to share it with you. His mother passed way twenty-five years ago, when he was eight years old. She was a Navajo woman but was raised from age six to nineteen in Mexico, in a Catholic ranching family south of the Rio Grande. She was fluent in Navajo, Spanish, and English. She taught all three languages to her son. Mr. Kipfer's first language is English, his Spanish is good, but his Navajo, he says, 'is barely passable, though I think this is modesty.'

"Now, ladies and gentlemen, let me introduce the third new traveler on our reconstruction of the Navajo Long Walk. Some of you may already know her. Jill, would you wave to our group, please? She has gained a wide reputation in New Mexico for her remarkable skills in building and fixing guns of all types and for teaching people how to use guns safely and effectively. The reason I saved her for last is because she is married to Marshal Angus, who was the first team member I introduced to you a few minutes ago."

Jill leaned toward me, whispering, "It was not a few minutes ago, it was forty-five minutes ago. That's not a few, that's a bushel-bag full."

J. Leonard sipped from his nearly empty water glass, and squinted toward the last table.

"Now, sir, thank you for your patience. If memory serves, you asked about certain questions I left out during my introductory remarks, is that right, sir?"

The gray-headed man in the dark suit and string tie waved his hand for recognition. "Yes, I questioned why didn't you talk about all the raids by Indians on ranches and against other tribes, going back as far as I can remember. My family ranched here in the 1840s and I can tell you we had some fearful times. Some of that came from Navajos stealing and burning. You looking into those, too?"

"Thank you, sir, for that important question. For three long centuries, there were depredations, slave raids, reprisals, and outright war, by and against Navajos. The treaty of Ojo

del Oso, the U.S. Army's campaigns of 1847 through 1849, and
the massacre at Fort Fauntleroy in 1861 all speak to the Indian
Wars, especially raids by Navajo warriors. The Smithsonian
Institution and the U.S. government have done a good deal of
documenting and researching the many quarrels, both great
and small, between Navajos and white colonizers. Raids and
reprisals, by *and* on the Indians. Those events followed a pattern
first established by the Spanish in the early seventeenth century.
The Spanish colonizers were here in what is now New Mexico
long before the East Coast ever heard of white settlers. Some of
those early Spanish settlements were subjected to Navajo raids.
They retaliated by visiting on Navajo clans the ancient slaving
practices of Mediterranean Europe. These hostilities intensified during the second half of this century when many settlers
came from the East and Midwest to New Mexico. However, it
was in this century that enslavement on both sides was coupled
with appropriation of Navajo land. Losing both their children
and their land posed a different threat to native people. This
threat came from a much larger belief by American citizens
and government. It was the notion that it was our destiny, our
right, our heritage, to seize land or anything else owned by
large groups of Indians, like the Navajos. That overarching
sense of righteousness forced some, although certainly not
all, Navajos to choose between unconditional surrender to
General Carleton's demands or face extermination. That, sir,
led directly to the battle at Fort Fauntleroy, which resulted in
fierce raids and plunder by Col. Kit Carson, the roundup of
thousands of Navajos, and their forced march to the Bosque
Redondo. Most scholars who've studied the Navajo Problem,
writ large, believe the attack on Fort Fauntleroy resulted in a

massive action by the Army then headquartered at Fort Macy to hunt, burn, capture, or kill. The many, the Army decided, should be punished for the misdeeds of a few. It is the case that some, only some, of the Navajos marched to the Bosque Redondo were warriors. Thousands of the marchers were women, children, and noncombative men and boys. When scholars say the social experiment was an overreaction, it is in part because of the disproportionate punishment of innocent women and children, who lost not only their homeland, but their sense of both place and existence. Does that sufficiently answer your question, sir?"

"It does," said the man in the dark suit. "But, I'd like to hear from someone who didn't get his opinions out of a book. You introduced a man, an Army sergeant, who was one of the troopers guarding the Indians on the march. I wonder what he's got to say about this?"

"Certainly, my good man," J. Leonard said, turning his gaze toward Sgt. Bell, sitting next to me.

"Sgt. Bell, would you care to lend your own personal experience to the discussion?"

Mather Bell shuffled uncomfortably in his chair, took a sip from the whiskey glass in front of him, pushed his chair back, and stood up.

"Yeah, I guess I got something to say 'bout all this. Twenty-four years ago, I was ordered up to that god-forsaken duty station, Fort Defiance. We all knew about the battle there that started this whole thing. I was a one-stripe soldier ordered to do a job. I did the job. Not one I liked. No pride in it, no sir, no pride at all. But we were troopers and we were given a job to do. We did it. Hell fire, man, there was no choice in the matter. We didn't think it was our destiny to march those Navajos three hundred damn miles, in the middle of winter, from one hell hole to another. Far as I could tell, they were no danger to us, or anyone else. They were defeated souls just trying to push one moccasin out in front of another. We were there to keep them from running away. But getting them there, after a long slough through ice and snow, was the worst goddamn duty I ever pulled. That's all I got to say on the matter."

Sgt. Bell plopped back in his chair and drained the brandy in his glass. J. Leonard, looked over the room, and then glanced down at his notes. In the silent moments that followed, we all wondered about the mood in the room. Then, without suggestion from J. Leonard, Luci Atsidi slowly stood up. She didn't talk at first, but just stood there, looking first at the man who'd asked the question. The silence in the room was getting uncomfortable. J. Leonard found whatever he'd been looking for in his notes and was starting to continue his lecture when he noticed that Luci was standing. Everyone in the room was looking at her, not him.

"Luci, would you like to say something? I'm sure that all of us . . ."

Luci nodded her head at J. Leonard and slowly moved her gaze first to Sgt. Bell, and then back to the man who'd asked the question.

"I don't like to talk in a place like this, where I have no family to listen. But some words have been spoken from you, Mr. Leonard, and this man at the other table asked a question. And Sgt. Bell has said some words, too. But I don't think I'm here for words. I think I'm here because I survived. Where are the words for those who fell by the side of the road and never got to that Bosque Redondo? Who asks about the words of the hundreds of my people who died after they settled us there? Mr. Leonard has shown us many words written down by soldiers of great military rank. Where are the words of my people? We had no written language then, or now. We did not write things down on paper. We draw things on the sand. And we tell our children and grandchildren stories about our lives. We marched in the snow, huddled together, but at least we had heavy wool blankets stamped with the name 'U.S. Army.' Some of the soldiers were kind. Some were not. I have talked with Sgt. Bell. I was afraid of him at first. And he was not sure of me at first. I don't think we are friends now, but we have talked. That's something. He told you he only did his duty. So did I. My duty was to give up my home for years. Give up my way of life—with the sheep and the goats—walking down the stream at the bottom of Canyon de Chelly. It was not my destiny to take the white man's land. I do not understand why it was his destiny to take mine. I have no more to say right now."

J. Leonard picked up his notes from the podium and suggested we have dinner. With that, the waiters began carrying trays of food to the tables. People talked at the tables, and an hour passed without anyone standing up. Then J. Leonard returned to the podium.

"My friends, I trust you all enjoyed the marvelous repast served by the staff at the Hotel La Posada. While dessert and coffee are being served, perhaps we can use our remaining time productively by taking questions or commentary from the other guests here this evening. We are fortunate to have with us this evening an editor from the *Santa Fe New Mexican* newspaper, which as you all know has been publishing weekly news here since 1864. We also have your estimable Sheriff Perfecto Armijo and three citizens who own local businesses. There are others here who are guests invited that I have not yet had the pleasure of meeting. So, let me just say this, anyone in the audience who wishes to speak can just raise his or her hand. Anyone who has a question to pose is encouraged to do so."

At first, no one raised a hand, then a woman dressed in a fashionable evening dress asked why the Smithsonian cared about "little" New Mexico and "a bad thing" that happened here two decades ago.

"Good of you to ask," J. Leonard said. "An excellent question. One thing we hope to build in Washington, at the Smithsonian, is a collection of both physical artifacts and an understanding of the Native American way of life, as it was both before and after the advancement of white people onto and around Indian lands. We hope to involve Indians in a dialogue that will enhance both our ongoing relationships and a broader knowledge of how we will build this great nation together. Language is a barrier. The lack of written documentation is a barrier. The sense of entitlement by both our government and by many citizens is a barrier. The lack of opportunity to share in the bounty of the land is a barrier. There are many more barriers, too many to mention this evening. But the short answer to your question, Madam—why has the Smithsonian come here?—is one I'm very happy you asked. We came here because our mission demands it. No more. No less.

"At the risk of repetition, I draw your attention again to our motto on the placard here in front of me. To *increase and diffuse knowledge*. That's what we are doing all over America. Your robust territory, comprising both Arizona and New

Mexico, is not well known in the rest of the country. We want to increase knowledge of New Mexico. And we want to *diffuse* that knowledge. These verbs are very important—increase and diffuse. It is not enough to simply *acquire* knowledge of the incarceration of thousands of Navajos, hundreds of miles from their homeland. It must also be the case that knowledge of what happened and why it happened is diffused throughout the nation. We understand the difficulties associated with the transmission of knowledge and the limitations of diffusion. How do you explain the upheaval of an entire tribe of Indians to advantage white citizens who live around tribal lands? The Smithsonian is examining how diffusion of knowledge contributed to the blending of cultures in New Mexico—Indian, Spanish, and settlers from back east. The problem is acute after decades of war, retaliation, and treaty. The social experiment some call *Manifest Destiny* resulted in the capture and removal of Navajos from their homelands. That was supposed to solve the problem. It could never have worked. The Peace Commission at the Bosque Redondo realized that after just four years of forced internment. The final leg of our trip across the state will be to examine that treaty and the Peace Commission that led it—General William T. Sherman and Samuel F. Tappan. Let me read to you Article 1 of the treaty. 'From this day forward all war between the parties to this agreement shall forever cease. The government of the United States desires peace, and its honor is hereby pledged to keep it. The Indians desire peace and they now pledge their honor to keep it.' Those words connect the concept of peace to the reality of 'forever.' That promise, on both sides, will be measured by honor—on both sides. What the Smithsonian hopes to do with this trip is dig deep into the narrative that pushed the country to a drastic remedy—forced permanent internment—and then quickly reverse course to give back the land that was never theirs to keep in the first place. It rejects the Manifest Destiny thesis, which research shows was only held by a small element in the American population, and never by the American government."

The audience posed many more questions. Not all of them were answered. Some questions were never asked, like why a U.S. marshal was involved in a political quest. Would the Smithsonian Report be provided to the people of New Mexico? And, if it was, would there be any changes in how New Mexicans and Navajos treat one another? Nobody asked me questions like that. Good thing. I had no answers to high-minded questions. I was still trying to figure out who was behind shooting Chinorero and cutting the brake axle on the Concord.

I woke up early the next morning, needing a good cup of coffee. Jill was still asleep when I went downstairs hoping the dining room was open. It wasn't—the sun was up. Why don't people in hotels know that's a sign to put the coffee on? I walked out front but there was no one about on the street. From behind me, someone said, "Marshal, good to see you're a man who appreciates the rising sun. Best time of the day for me."

I turned to the man and was happy to see it was the rancher, Anderson Kipfer.

"Morning, Mr. Kipfer. Yes, I'm a sunrise man. My horses pay attention to sunrise because they know I'll be giving them a nose bag with sweet grain. Come sunset, they only get hay. Is that the way it works on your ranch, too?"

"No, I don't grain my horses. But then, I'm not riding them all day, like you do. At least that's what someone told me last night. Heard that you're a man that likes long rides in high country."

"I noticed that you were sitting at Perfecto Armijo's table last night. Was he the one telling you about my fondness for mountain rides?"

"Yes, sir, it was. He gave me a short version of you chasing a man he called his least favorite cousin up to the top of the Valles Caldera a year or two ago. I wouldn't mind hearing more about that. You looking for coffee? I know a little Mexican café the other side of the livery stable. Wanna join me?"

We walked two blocks down and one over to a café with no sign on the door. But you could tell it was a café by the smell of roasted coffee beans and bacon on the stove top. There was a Mexican shopkeeper at one of the three tables, and two old men at the other. We took the third table. A short, stout man with a drooping mustache came out of the kitchen with a covered basket and two cups of coffee. I was surprised that he knew what we wanted, but then he took the coffee to the two old men.

"*Buenos días, Señors,* would you like some coffee, too? And some of my wife's fresh baked tortillas also, *por favor*?"

In response to my question about his ranch, Kipfer said it was good land, in a green valley, with a good stream running not far from the barns, corrals, and the main ranch house. He ran a cow-calf operation, bred his own horses, and had had no trouble with Indians.

"You know, I'm half Navajo myself."

"Yes, sir, I heard you mention that last night. What's the other half?"

"Call me Anderson. That was my father's name. He died two years ago. So I guess I don't need to say I'm Anderson Junior any more. My dad's folks came to Texas from Germany. They first settled in West Texas thirty years ago, came to Agua Negra Chiquita and settled on 160 acres of good farm land, fit for cattle, too. How's your Spanish?"

"Middling, I'd say. I worked two ranches up north when I was a kid. So, your ranch is near some black water?"

"Close. Full translation would be *Little Black Water*. Our ranch is twelve miles south. The people in town are thinking of renaming the town Santa Rosa because a man named Don Celso Baca, who was the first settler there, built a little adobe chapel and called it Santa Rosa. He's still the boss there, and will likely rename the town his way."

"Is the water really black?"

"No, we're on the Pecos River; a damn fine river—good fishing, and lots of water for farming."

"I've ridden the Pecos north of you. I think it's one of my favorite rivers, third-favorite behind the Rio Chama and the Rio Grande. I've always thought I might ride the Pecos all the way to the Gulf of Mexico someday."

"You could get close, but the Pecos empties into the Rio Grande in Texas, at a little town called Del Rio. Went there once with my dad, to buy a bull. Pretty place."

"So, Anderson, what's your interest in this ride we're on? I suppose you know Fort Sumner, since it's what, maybe fifty miles south?"

"Just shy of forty miles from my ranch. But the fort's gone now. The old buildings are owned by a rancher named Maxwell. My grandfather knew all of central New Mexico well. My dad loved growing up there. The Pecos runs straight down from Little Black Water, past my ranch to Fort Sumner. Dad used to sell grain, a little hay, and a few horses to the Indian agent down there before they closed the place when the Navajos were moved back to Arizona in 1868. There is still an Indian agency there, mostly for Mescalero and a few Kiowa from Texas. But I was never there when the Bosque Redondo was full of Navajos. I talked a little about that last night at my table. It always surprises people to hear I'm half Navajo. I can still speak a little Navajo, but I was only eight years old when they closed the Bosque Redondo down. I've been there maybe three, four times since then."

"Are the buildings still up? And the farm land; is it still plowed and fertile?"

"The buildings are there, but the fort is just a name now. It's good land for cattle, but I'm not sure about large farming. The Apache grow good crops and they raise fair horses, too. But it has a bad feel for me."

"If you don't mind me asking, why are you going there with us?"

"For my mother. She died when I was eight. She didn't know exactly how old she was. I'm going because she can't. Mr. Leonard asked me the same question when I knocked on his door at the hotel day before last. It's not an easy story."

"I've got time. I heard J. Leonard say your mother was Navajo. Taken from her home and family by Mexican bandits as a young girl. Can't say we knew much about Indian or

Mexican slavery up near the Colorado border. But I know it was a bad problem for Indians and Mexicans."

"My mother, Angelica, had a Navajo name, but it got lost down in Mexico. The bandits that took her sold her to a Mexican hacienda who needed help in a big kitchen—lots of *vaqueros* on that ranch, she remembered. My father bought horses from the patrón there. He was on a horse-buying trip when he saw her carrying food to the patrón's big porch while they were negotiating terms. Dad said he thought his mind was in a stampede, she was so beautiful. She was about sixteen or seventeen then."

"Did your dad buy her from the patrón?"

"No, the patrón could see dad was bolloxed just looking at her. Turns out, the patrón treated her like his own daughter—the two girls grew up together on the ranch. My mother learned Spanish on that ranch. The patrón asked my father to stay on the ranch for a week. He needed advice about breeding horses, the patrón said. After three days, so the family story goes, Angelica and my dad stampeded together right out of Mexico and up to the ranch. She died first, and then when my dad died he left the ranch to me. That was six years ago. I'm the third Kipfer to own the brand."

The little kitchen cook brought us more coffee but we passed—*Nada, señor*—on more tortillas. I told Anderson a little about my part of New Mexico and my folks in a little Mexican settlement north of Espanola. In time, he came back around to his reason for coming on this trip.

"I always wondered what my mother thought when the Army marched nine thousand Navajo men, women, and children down the road to the west of our ranch. I wondered whether some of her kin folk were there, at Bosque Redondo."

"How'd you find out about this Smithsonian trip?"

"Hell, Angus, everybody within fifty miles of Fort Sumner knows about it. Everybody's curious. But for me, it's more than curiosity. I want to know who was there, and whether any of them were related to my mother—and so, to me. Like I told Mr. Leonard, it's personal. He said they have records and names for many Navajos, but that won't help. My mother never talked about life as a little girl over west of us in Navajo country. Maybe she talked to my dad, I don't know for sure. But neither of them ever talked about it. And then, there's the other reason."

"Other reason?"

"You bet. There's a retired Army chaplain living in Little Black Water now. He never served out here in the West, only in Maryland. He was English by birth and didn't come to the U.S. until he was about ten. He used English words Americans don't know about. Once, when we were talking about places people were from, I told him about my mom, you know, being stolen from the Arizona Territory, living in Mexico as a servant, then meeting my dad and moving up to New Mexico. He said it was *serendipity* that my *mum* was stolen, else I wouldn't be me. I asked him what serendipity meant. He said a famous English author invented it. It means 'fortunate happenstance.'"

"Well, yeah, guess I can see how fortunate it was for you, and your mom. That's reason enough to be on this trip."

"Angus, I'm thinking the other way around. If she *hadn't* been stolen over there near Canyon de Chelly, she would have been living there when the Army came in killing the men and stealing the women. They might have taken her to Bosque Redondo, forty miles from my Dad's ranch. Sure, I would never have been born, but I can't get it of my head that she could have been in that damn prison camp. I need to know more about that damnable *unfortunate* happenstance."

We spent a full hour talking about Chinorero's shooting, the wreck at Canyon de Chelly, and my job on this trip. We talked about Ora and her reaction to that march she saw when she was only ten. I told him what little I knew about Luci. We talked about my wife Jill, and how she got to New Mexico from Kansas. Anderson was curious about everything and had an easy way about him.

CHAPTER 23

"The Last Leg"

SATURDAY MORNING, we took our bags downstairs to the
lobby right after breakfast. At eight-thirty, Teddy drove the
Concord stage to the boardwalk in front of the hotel. He had
washed down the outside with river water and given the seats
inside a good brushing. The four-up team looked fit after a
week of rest in the big corral behind the livery barn. A few
minutes later, Johnson Ortega drove up in the two-horse rig
and we got our first look at the Armijo Ranch wagon we'd
heard about a few nights ago. I'd assumed it would be a typical
covered wagon, 'cause that's what J. Leonard called it at the
Grant Opera House dinner. Should have known better. Perfecto
Armijo always did everything a little better than most folks.
Besides the driver, two passengers could sit behind him on a
padded seat. The middle part of the wagon was for gear and
a large chuck box had been hung on the end.

Perfecto had joined us for breakfast and seemed delighted by my surprise at what he'd called "our Mexican chuck wagon."

"Perfecto," I said, "that doesn't look like the covered wagons we have up north in Chama."

"*Si, Angus, mi amigo*, it is something my foreman, Marcelles Gray, Ora's father, has been building and changing for a long time. We bought a freighter express wagon ten years ago. There were many for sale here when the Army pulled out after the Civil War. This is lighter than the big ones from the mines. You can see the wagon bed hangs on three elliptic springs. I think this one came from Indiana. Marcelles liked it because it has a fixed oak box, and bottom rails cut from hickory, with paneled sides. You know those panel sides make it possible to do many different jobs with this wagon. It has Warner wheels, which are much stronger than ordinary ranch wagons. We use it as a three-passenger wagon to haul supplies from town, and as a chuck wagon for longer cattle drives, or hunting trips.

"I see you've got a two-up team out front—looks like a fine matched pair of draft horses."

"*Si*, but the linkage allows four horses, when we need them for heavy hauling."

"So, Marcelles turned it into a chuck wagon by adding that big box on the back?"

"He did. Do you know who built the first chuck wagon in the West?"

"Probably a cook named Chuck. That'd be my guess."

"No, *señor*, it was Mr. Charles Goodnight, a Texas rancher. A *vaquero* who worked his ranch over there in 1866 said Goodnight used a Conestoga wagon to build the first one.

Here's another question most Texas cowboys know, but New Mexican cowboys don't. Why is it called a 'chuck' wagon?"

"Well, my first guess—that the cook was named Chuck—was wrong. So I ain't gonna guess again."

"In Texas, from the time the first cattle were introduced there, chuck was what they called food served out on the prairie during long cattle drives. Texans are not civilized like New Mexicans. All they had for chuck was things that were easy to preserve such as salted meats, coffee, beans, and sourdough biscuits. They didn't have chili until after the Civil War and they still don't have tortillas. And they don't like pinto beans, either; they grow round black beans in Texas. Very sad, don't you think?"

"You bet. Lots of things we take for granted in New Mexico are lacking in Texas. Like mountains. Whose idea was it to tarp only the back half of the wagon bed?"

"That was Ora. She told her father to leave the passenger seat and the driver's seat open to the sky. She does not like to be closed in, *que no*?

Over dinner last night, J. Leonard decided who would ride in which coach. He assigned Luci, Jill, and Sgt. Bell to ride in the Concord. That left Ora and Anderson to ride behind Johnson in the Armijo wagon. I hitched my mule, Snow, behind the Armijo wagon, with a spare riding horse in case we needed one. Teddy would drive the big Concord, and I'd ride lead on Marathon. Teddy assured everyone the brake handle was functional again, with a new brake-bolt locked into place. We headed southeast up the long pull through Tijeras canyon toward Little Black Water or Negra Chiquita. We'd cross the Pecos River there and turn south, past Anderson Kipfer's ranch, and on to Fort Sumner and the Bosque Redondo.

It was about 150 miles away, Anderson said. Teddy said we could make thirty miles a day, so we'd be there in five days. Anderson asked me how long it would take me and Marathon if we didn't have to ride guard for the wagon train.

"Marathon's a long walking horse, so I think I could do fifty miles a day in flat country. That'd make it a three-day ride, long as there was plenty of water, grain, and grass for my horse, and elk jerky for me."

We camped out each night for the next four nights. Teddy, with a little help from Jill, cooked breakfast and dinner. After dinner, all of us would gather around the camp fire and J. Leonard did what he said he'd do back in Albuquerque. We'd talk about how the Navajo Treaty of 1868 came to be. J. Leonard had three copies of the treaty with him. He'd given one copy to Ora, which she and Jill talked about in the Armijo chuck wagon. Luci and Sgt. Bell listened to J. Leonard talk about it in the Concord.

A man named Theo H. Dodd was the Indian agent at Bosque Redondo. He wrote a letter to General Sherman and Colonel Tappan, the Peace Commissioners, on May 30, 1868, giving them a sort of census taking. Contrary to what I'd been thinking before I read this letter, there'd been a hand off by the Army to the Indian agent of a large bunch of Navajos seven months before that—on November 1, 1867. The letter, as was always required when dealing with the Army, was specific, "2157 Indians under 12 years of age, 2693 women, 2060 men, and 201 age and sex unknown."

Mr. Dodd also accounted for "the amount of produce raised on the Government farm during 1868." He counted

"201,420 pounds of corn, 2,942 pounds of beans, and 29,152 pounds of pumpkins. He said they'd produced 423,682 pounds of corn in 1865. The year 1867 was a total crop failure. He told Gen. Sherman he'd made a personal count of the animals owned by the Navajos, "horses, 550, mules 21, sheep 940, goats 1025."

Those numbers didn't surprise me, but this did. Dodd estimated that "since June 30, 1867, the Navajos have captured from the Comanche Indians about 1,000 horses making the total number of horses on the reservation about 1,500." He said there were 1,850 families living on the reservation. A majority of them are "living on the reservation peaceably and are well disposed. Some thieving ones have occasionally committed depredations by stealing stock from citizens. Often, however, the stock has been recovered and delivered to owners."

Dodd offered Gen. Sherman several opinions on the situation. First, he said, "Navajo families have attempted to cultivate patches of their own for corn, pumpkins, melons, etc. but have never succeeded in raising very good crops. The cost of maintaining them from November 1867 to May of 1868 was $280,830.07. About half of the land cultivated at the Bosque Redondo is productive; the other half I consider unproductive in consequence of containing a large amount of alkaline matter. The most serious objection to the reservation is the scarcity of timber and fuel."

Those numbers made me think the government was counting its cost rather than thinking about keeping the Indians interned.

Second, Dodd told Gen. Sherman, "For nearly two years the Navajos have been very much dissatisfied with their reservation and they state their discontent is in consequence of frequent raids being made upon them by Comanche and other Indians. Scarcity of fuel, unproductiveness of the soil, bad water, and unhealthiness are here. During the past year they have been constantly begging me to endeavor to have them removed to their old country where they say the soil is more productive, where is an abundance of timber, where mescal, mesquite beans, wild potatoes, and fruits are found in abundance and where they would be far removed from their old enemies, the Comanche, Kiowa, and other Indians. I am satisfied the Navajos will never be contented to remain on this or any other reservation except one located west of the Rio Grande and I am also of the opinion that if they are not permitted to return to their old country that many will stealthily return and in doing so commit depredations upon the people of N.M. and thus keep up a state of insecurity."

Dodd offered what J. Leonard called a cost-benefit analysis. "I therefore believe that it would be better for the Indians and the people of N.M. and a saving to the Government and in the end more likely to succeed in civilizing them to relocate them upon a reservation west of the Rio Grande."

We had a good talk about this after dinner that night. Sgt. Bell said the Army was never good at saving money. "We were good at doing what the Generals wanted—round 'em up and march 'em away."

Luci said, "Our people just wanted what we already had— land of our own. But the government letters didn't say what the storytellers in our tribe recorded in our oral tradition. The march from Canyon de Chelly in the winter of 1865 was brutal. Stragglers were shot. Women who were with child were killed if they could not keep up. But they had hope and so they kept marching. Four years later, they had no hope. Some of the people left early. It says in the white man's papers that after the treaty was signed, 7,176 people left with an Army escort. What about the two thousand who died or disappeared there? What about them? Did the government care about those who died of disease or not having enough to eat?"

J. Leonard said it was a kind of reverse Manifest Destiny. The government was giving back land it never owned to people whose Manifest Destiny was to stay on that land.

Ora was thankful. "At least they used wagons to take the Navajos home and didn't make them march on foot in the dead of winter. Again."

Anderson Kipfer, who'd been quiet up to now, had a lot to say.

"I have been waiting for a long time to learn about this Navajo roundup because of my mother. She was not captured or interned at Bosque Redondo because she lived and died on our ranch. She was not at Canyon de Chelly with her clan because she'd been captured by Mexican banditos before the Army raided the canyon. But she could speak Navajo, Spanish, and English. I keep thinking about that. None of the troops at Fort Sumner could speak Navajo, or Spanish. So at the council before making that treaty, they relied on a few people who could understand what the Navajos said. One of those was a man named Jesus Arviso. He was born in Sonora, Mexico, not far from where my mother was taken in the raid when she was just a little girl. It says in the council documents that he was a little child in 1850 when Apaches from Arizona stole him across the border in Mexico."

Ora interrupted, "I don't understand. If the Apaches stole him from the Mexicans, how did he end up translating for the U.S. government at Fort Sumner?"

"It says in the treaty documents he was badly treated by the Apache but finally exchanged for a black pony to a Navajo named *B'ee Lizhini,* which translates to 'Black Shirt' in English. A Navajo family living with the headman, Tlaii, which means 'Lefty,' raised him. He was with a band of Navajos who held a peace conference in 1860 near Oak Springs, south of Fort Defiance. The commander at Fort Defiance gave Arviso a chance to stay with the troops as a guide. In 1863, he served as a Navajo interpreter at Fort Wingate. He spoke no English before becoming an Army guide. In 1865, he married a Navajo woman at Fort Sumner named *Yohazbaa*, of the *Nanash 'ezhii* clan. He was the main interpreter at the council in 1868, translating from Navajo to Spanish. He went back to Navajo land in 1868 and settled with his wife east of Tohatchi. Anyway, my interest in him comes from how my mother came to live only a few miles apart from him at the time the treaty was negotiated. One was a Mexican captured by Apaches. The other was a Navajo captured by Mexicans. It's interesting to me that both spoke their native tongue plus two other languages and both lived through captivity to a better life when they married."

Luci, Ora, and Anderson talked every night after dinner. Sometimes they invited J. Leonard and me into their conversations. One night, Luci relayed Manuelito's story.

"He kept running away from Carleton's army and Kit Carson for more than a year after Carson burned our crops in Canyon de Chelly. Carleton did not want Carson to capture him. 'Kill him,' he ordered. Finally, when his horses and blankets were stolen, he left his hiding place near the headwaters of the Little Colorado. He went to Fort Wingate in September of 1866, with twenty-three members of his band, mostly relatives. He'd been wounded a few weeks before that and had lost almost entirely the use of his left arm."

Anderson was also interested in Manuelito because he'd seen a picture of him taken in 1886, eighteen years after he made the treaty, and marked it with his X. There is a record, the rancher noted, about what Manuelito said twenty years after his surrender at Fort Wingate. Anderson read it aloud to everyone.

"We fought for our country because we did not want to lose it, but we made a mistake. We lost nearly everything, but we had some beads left, and with them we thought we were rich. I have always advised the young men to avoid war. The American nation is too powerful for us to fight. When we had a fight for a few days we felt fresh, but in a short time, we were worn out, and the soldiers starved us out. Then the Americans gave us something to eat, and we came in from the mountains and went to Texas . . ."

I interrupted, "Texas? Never heard of the Army taking them to Texas."

Ora laughed, "That would have been even worse for the Indians. I think he probably did not know the Bosque Redondo was still this side of the Texas border in 1866."

Anderson continued reading Manuelito's story. "We were there for a few years; many of our people died from the climate. Then we became good friends with the white people. The Comanche wanted us to fight, but we would not join them. So the white men came in twelve days to talk with them, as our people were dying off. We promised to obey their laws if we were permitted to go back to our own country. We promised to keep the treaty you read to us today. We told General Sherman we would try to remember what he said; "my children, I will send you back to your homes." The Americans gave us a little stock to start with and we thanked them for that. Then we left. We told the drivers to whip up the mules; we were in such a hurry. When we saw the top of the mountain from Albuquerque, we wondered if it was our mountain. We felt like talking to the ground, we loved it so. And some of the old men and women cried with joy when they reached their homes."

During the ride from Albuquerque, we had talked about many aspects of Navajo life, and death. When Anderson asked about Navajo spirits and her family's views of death, Luci said, "Navajos believe that the souls of people who die go to a marsh, where they remain unsettled for four days. Then they discover a ladder leading them to a world below the one we now inhabit. Some souls never reach this place. They are lost forever."

Anderson said his mother believed in the Christian God, but did not speak to him about Indian spirits or about religious beliefs. Ora said her ancestors were Spanish, who had deeply held religious beliefs. Sgt. Bell said he believed in a fast horse and a quick and easy death.

This bantering back and forth came to rest when Luci shushed everyone, saying, "We worship different gods than white people do, even Mexicans who may be white, compared to us. We have two great spirits, Father and Mother. They live where the sun rises and sets. That's where the ladder goes. That's where they can see both Father and Mother combing their hair. Sometimes departed souls who reach the bottom of the ladder spend days in silence looking at Father and Mother."

J. Leonard asked Luci and Ora about the widespread slavery of women and children. He asked about Mexicans taking Navajo children, Navajos taking white children, and about Navajo children finding their way to Indian Pueblos up and down the Rio Grande River. While I can't say they agreed on everything, the rest of us were surprised to find how common slavery between Mexicans and Indians was during the fifty-year period before the Treaty of 1868 was signed.

Luci repeated a story known to her family. Ora said she'd heard the same story, but couldn't remember who told it. It was about a white soldier who owned a Negro slave. Neither Luci nor Ora could remember when it took place, but the soldier's name was Brooks. He was a major and was in charge of the 311 Infantry stationed at Fort Defiance. Luci said a Navajo man had lost his wife—she deserted him. Navajo women have always been at liberty to leave their husbands. But, if they do, the husband can wipe out the disgrace by killing someone. The husband lived near the fort and felt the Negro slave should be killed for some real or invented slight. Once the Negro was killed, the Army demanded that the headman surrender the husband, who had only been trying to erase his disgrace. The Army said if you don't produce the murderer, it will be war. But the Indians killed some other man and took his body to the fort. The Army did not believe the other man killed the Negro. Meanwhile, some Navajos near Albuquerque were killed and robbed by Mexicans. The Navajos at Fort Defiance demanded that the soldiers make the Mexicans surrender themselves. This was after the time that the Santa Fe slave market was selling Indians that came from Chihuahua for less than fifty dollars. War ensued. That, they said, is what caused Gen. Carleton to order Col. Kit Carson to go to Indian country and kill Indians if they didn't agree to go to Bosque Redondo.

J. Leonard was quick to draw a distinction between the widely practiced "peonage" in New Mexico, and outright "slavery" in the Southern States. Most of us had never heard of it. He explained peonage debt slavery or debt servitude. It was a system where an employer compels a worker to pay off a debt with work. Peonage, he said, "was a construct of the Santa Fe slave markets. Legally, peonage was outlawed by Congress in 1867. However, after Reconstruction, many Southern black men were swept into peonage though different methods. It was not unlike selling women and children in Mexico, or Santa Fe to ranches, haciendas, or families who needed household servants."

We could all tell that J. Leonard's academic explanation pained Anderson Kipfer a good deal.

CHAPTER 24

"The Pecos River to the Long K Ranch"

I T TOOK US THREE FULL DAYS to get to Little Black Water where we crossed the Pecos River and headed south toward Anderson's Long K Ranch. We were a full day behind because J. Leonard decided we would have a full lunch stop every day so we could eat cold biscuits, salted ham cuts, and olives. That man sure loved his olives. The only thing he liked more than food was talking. Every day at lunch, instead of asking folks about the country we were riding through, or the events we were supposed to be recording for the Smithsonian Institution, J. Leonard gave us a geographical and historical talk about the topography and geology of wherever we were. The horses liked it because we could hobble them near good grass. Snow liked it because I'd take the heavy bags off his pack saddle.

And Sgt. Bell liked it because he could wander off, saying he was going to make a nature call. I knew it was also so he could take a couple long pulls on that never-ending supply of brandy half-bottles he carried in his satchel.

One place J. Leonard had been talking about was a natural water hole deeper than anything else in the middle of New Mexico. Folks called it the blue hole on account of the color and the fact that no one had ever measured the depth. The Army surveyors had tried throwing measured ropes with iron hooks out but they didn't have a rope long enough. It was more than a hundred feet deep, we all eventually agreed, and maybe ninety feet across. Anderson said he'd hear about an Apache boy only thirteen years old. Story was he tied a rope around his waist, held onto a big boulder against his stomach and jumped in feet first. He never came up again. But the coiled rope stretched out to over ninety feet before it stopped snaking into the water. Apparently, everyone knew that story.

Getting there was tricky. We'd crossed a col, but Marathon had never heard the word col before. I told him it was the lowest point of a ridge between two peaks. It's how we get from one side of that mountain range over there to the one in front of us, I said. Then we just followed a worn wagon track, which kept winding back and forth on itself until we hit the Pecos.

It was maybe forty feet wide, but shallow and easily crossed. Spring runoff was over with, so the water wasn't muddy no more. To the south, we could see a long stretch of brown mountains and far-off forests of juniper and maybe some piñon pines.

We journeyed on, past the winding Pecos and up and down slopes and little acacias off the river. It got hotter the further south we went. We crossed a log-framed shack buried in a sand drift; only one roof joist was visible. By late afternoon, we entered a gorge cut by the Pecos with the sun falling down into it and the shadow of the bank hitting the middle of the river. Darkness came two hours later, like a sheet pulled over two coaches, nine horses, a tired mule, and a dozen souls trying to remember why 'n hell we'd agreed to this trip. Truth was we were getting a little tired of one another. Before the cook fire burned down, and within two minutes of finishing our supper, I took Jill, two tarps, our sleeping rolls, and a water sack down about a hundred yards to a spot where we could hear the river rustling and the wind wheezing. We decided not to talk until morning.

I rode point the next day, down the east side of the Pecos for just over thirty miles. So much had happened in the last three weeks that I needed this long ride to get my mind back in balance. I'd been focused on all the bad things that happened on this trail twenty years ago—the end of the Indian Wars—their capture and internment—the loss of life, land, and dignity. But being out in front of a small wagon train headed toward what was for me a new part of New Mexico, I was able to doze off on a fine horse and just think about where I was.

Life in the American West was hardship and toil, solitude and monotony. But it was also living life as big as a man could stand. Made me think about what the word cowboy really meant. I'd been one, and still was in some ways. Anderson Kipfer was one for sure. Ora was, too, although she was damn sure not a boy. Sitting on top of a fine horse, looking at landscapes I'd never seen before, was uplifting. Got me away, at least for a while, from thinking on all the misery the U.S. Army handed out to mostly peaceful people who got here first.

More than just taking my mind off what we were here for—to visit and talk about the Navajo Long Walk—this day's ride got me thinking about what made cowboys different from everyone else—soldiers—prisoners—storekeepers—lawmen—outlaws—politicians—all of 'em. Cowboys were square shooters, upright, and honest as all get out. Mostly. 'Course, we had cowboy renegades, men who fell back on their principles, and some who turned against the law. And cowboys were known for smoking, drinking, cursing, and no table manners whatsoever. They knew it was a hanging offense to steal a man's horse because without a horse, a cowboy's life was threatened from every direction. Still, our simple way of life meant never disrespecting a lady, no matter her color or tribe. The West was rapidly changing now, twenty years after the Civil War. The range was being closed off by barbed wire. But when a cowboy came across a downed fence, he knew what to do. Knowing right from wrong and willing to work hard would take a cowboy a long way in life.

I kept coming back to that speech at the opera house dinner. The one by Sgt. Mather by-the-goddamn-book Bell, who did wrong because some general ordered him to. Doing what he was told to do just plain mowed down doing what was right. Can't say I expected him to disobey an order—that's a court martial offense. But it didn't mean he had to justify it. Then I remembered him proclaiming aloud that he wasn't proud of doing it. Was relieved to hear that. I guess the difference was a cowboy could quit the brand if the range boss ordered him to do wrong. A soldier was stuck, I guess. So, I wasn't going to hold it against Sgt. Bell.

I decided not go back to the wagons for the lunch stop. I had some salt tack, elk venison jerky, and a half-full water bag. Marathon was relaxed, not sweated up at all, but all horses need a little stand-to after hours of steady riding. We were probably a hundred miles north of the Mexican border and pretty near dead center of New Mexico. This was hardscrabble ranching county, but it had a nice little river floating by on my right side. The sky here was bigger than up north, along the Colorado border. Mostly scrub oaks along here with a few cottonwoods on the river bank, but spread out like outposts of underground water wells. I found a little spot of shade, dismounted, and squatted while Marathon nibbled at roots and shoots of green, spread thinly around rocky ground.

I was startled out of my "reverie," that's a word Jill used once in a while when she'd catch me day dreaming, by a sharp crack behind me. Then, two more in rapid succession. First thought was Jill. Then, in an instant, I realized it was too far away. "Were those Santa Fe boys back?" I thought. Marathon heard them, too; he raised both ears straight up and turned back toward the wagons behind us. I ran to him, cinched him up, unsheathed my rifle, and swung my leg over the cantle. Putting my spurs to Marathon, we reached full gallop in twenty feet. The wagons were five hundred yards behind me, not quite visible because we were down in a little draw. When I came up over the short ridge, I could see they'd stopped. When I got to less than a hundred yards from them, I tugged back on Marathon's reins, bringing him to a walk. Teddy was still up in the driver's seat, but he had his rifle stock buried deep in his shoulder, panning from right to left. Anderson Kipfer had jumped out of the Armijo wagon, and was waving his arms at Teddy and me.

"Hold up, fellas, that's probably my foreman. He's firing a hello shot—one quick, and two more, ten seconds later. It's a signal. He spotted us from the top of that ridge over there past the bend in the Pecos. My ranch is a mile past the bend."

A minute later, Jill ran to me, as Luci dismounted the stagecoach. Twenty minutes later, two men rode up on the west side of the river, forded it, and rode into our little standstill.

"Afternoon, boss," a tall grizzled cowboy said.

"Too-Tall, it's good to see you. Nice of you to warn us you're out here. Everything all right on the ranch?"

"Well, we could use a little more rain, but otherwise the cows are calm and the creek isn't rising. Glad you're back. A little late this time, ain't it?"

Anderson introduced all of us to his foreman, who he said was called Too-Tall by everyone he liked, and a longer, less descriptive name by those that didn't. The man with him was a Long K *vaquero* who said nothing, but nodded in turn, as each of us was named.

Introductions done from his side of things, Anderson said, "My friends, you're looking at every cowboy on the Long K Ranch. We do it all, except Too-Tall does the cooking, in addition to being foreman over that tough little Mexican *vaquero*. I hired him five years ago but he prefers to go unnamed around strangers. When he feels like it, he might volunteer his name. Or he might not. It's up to him. He'll answer to Señor."

J. Leonard, now outside the coach and greatly relieved this was not another rifle attack, jumped ahead of Anderson by giving a five-minute speech to Too-Tall about what this grand expedition was doing here in what he called "the living heart of New Mexico."

When he finished, Too-Tall turned to Anderson. "Boss, why are you're doing such a fool thing as this?"

Anderson didn't respond to Too-Tall. That's the way cowboys talk to one another without doing the talking part. You only need to answer back if you disagree. When a man says, "Can you get that mother cow out of the bog?" you just go do it. No need to say you can, or you agree the cow needs to get out of the bog. He turned and asked if he could ride the rest of the way to his ranch on the spare horse tied to the coach. When I didn't answer, he walked over, untied the lead rope, and hauled out the saddle, pad, and bridle from the boot at the rear of the coach. He saddled the mare in two minutes and swung up on her. We headed south, toward the Long K.

It took another hour before we reached the northern line separating his ranch from open range. There was no fence.

"How long you think this open range will be unfenced?" I asked Anderson.

"Surprised it's still open now," he said. "A Texas rancher I know told me last summer that barbed wire was patented by a Kansas farmer in 1874. He said it would fence near everything off in ten years. Texas has a lot of wire, but there are still millions of acres to go over there. Our ranches are all small around here, and we have no need to fence our cattle in. We all honor the brands here. 'Cept for the occasional rustler—we have a short rope and no patience for those boys."

"Did you have trouble with the Navajos at the Bosque Redondo when they were there, twenty years ago?"

"No, no trouble, if you mean rustling our herd. A few times, there'd be a crossing of a small group on horseback, but they meant us no harm. Mescalero Apaches have been here for, hell I don't know, maybe a century. Once in a while, they'd get real hungry and steal a calf, but they weren't a danger. The Kiowa and the Comanche over in Texas were fierce and they raided this direction a fair amount. But we were lucky I guess. Did you know the Goodnight-Loving cattle trail runs not far from here?"

"No, can't say as I did."

"It is just a few miles over there, on the west side of the Pecos. Goodnight has been running a drive a year through here from his big spread over in San Angelo, Texas. It goes all the way up to Cheyenne, Wyoming, where his cows get on the railroad either to California or Chicago. Depends on cattle prices, I guess."

"How far south of here have you ridden the Pecos? Did you ever make it to the Rio Grande confluence?" I asked, realizing this was the first man I ever knew who might have done such a thing.

"No, sir, not that far, but I rode it twice all the way down to the Mexican border. To do that you have to cross two fine rivers, the Seven River and the Black River. The Pecos turns east at the border and goes all the way down to the Gulf of Mexico. But I never wanted to go that far. Way too much Texas to suit me. You thinking about riding that far?"

"Been thinking about it for a long time. But my duties as a lawman and a husband man seem to get in the way. Maybe when I get to Fort Sumner, I can talk Jill into keeping on going south from there. Any idea on how long it'd take us to see the Gulf of Mexico horseback along the Pecos?"

"No real idea, but my guess is you could do it in two weeks on that long-stepping horse of yours. I've not seen how your wife sits a saddle yet, but expect anyone riding with you might fall behind sooner or later. Perfecto Armijo says you're known for long lonesome rides."

"He's right about long, but I've never been lonesome with a good horse, mountain ridges, and rivers I can ford."

CHAPTER 25

"The Last Ride to Fort Sumner"

OR THE LAST THREE NIGHTS, before, during, and after
supper, J. Leonard spoon-fed us what he called the mani-
festation of America's first Indian concentration camp—the
military called it Fort Sumner. Others, he assured us, called it
Navajo hell. Luci interrupted often and Sgt. Bell spoke up a few
times. Ora smoldered, but seemed oddly quiet. She watched
Anderson Kipfer out of the corner of her eye—I guess she was
watching to see how much of this he was buying. The rest of
us just sipped from our cups, ate what was put before us, and
learned several sides of the story.

J. Leonard reminded us that besides the Navajos, the camp
included Mescalero, which he called "Plains Apaches." They were
familiar with central New Mexico, but still hated being herded
like cattle away from their home as much as the Navajos did.

Ora said it was different as night from day. She reminded everyone how the "scum" soldiers paraded the Navajos past Perfecto Armijo's ranch, like they were no better than the oxen that pulled the Army wagons loaded down with supplies for Fort Sumner. But she agreed that "bastard Kit Carson" was as hard on the Apache as he was on the Navajo. J. Leonard tried to make this sound like another chapter in the book of American advancement into the New Mexico and Arizona territories.

He went on for ten minutes describing the geography, weather patterns, current population, and such as that when Anderson broke in.

"Mr. Leonard, I live close by. But people on the ranches around here, including the family that bought the old Army buildings on Fort Sumner, don't know much about the 1868 treaty. It was only with the Navajos, right?"

"Well, Mr. Kipfer, that's a splendid question. The Mescalero Apache left the Bosque Redondo in November 1884, in the middle of the night. They eventually returned to their homelands in the Sacramento Mountains. The Army tried to recapture them but failed. Back at the Bosque Redondo, the Navajos were learning to farm the way the Spanish settlers had for many years. But the soils along the Pecos were very alkaline. It was made worse because the Army overseers tried to impose European conventional farming methods that did not work in dry climates. But, that was not the real problem at the Bosque Redondo. The Army had grossly underestimated how many Navajos would be brought there. Even though Kit Carson only caught two-thirds of the Navajo people, it was twice as many as Fort Sumner had been planning for. The Army had to feed way too many people when the crops started to fail. Back in

Washington, by the summer of 1865, the government was tiring of General Carleton's idea. Vice President Lafayette S. Foster visited the camp that summer. He and the other visitors from Washington were critical of the Fort Sumner operation and condemned the treatment of the Navajos. Unfortunately, they did not have an alternative, so not much changed for the next three years."

"Why did making changes take so long?" I asked.

"Because, Marshal," he said, "the U.S. Congress was not yet engaged. Reconstruction of the South following the end of the Civil War was what Congress cared about. It had little interest in the western part of the country. However, by November of 1867, things began to change. General Ulysses S. Grant ordered that custody of the Navajos be turned over to the Indian Bureau of the Department of the Interior. That order made the Navajos no longer prisoners of war. Six months later, a group of Navajo headmen went to the Indian agent, Theodore Dodd, and asked him to take them to Santa Fe to meet with the new general there. Carleton had been dismissed. The new general was George W. Getty. Their request was simple—let them return to their homeland. That meeting changed everything. Washington established a 'Peace Commission' led by General William Tecumseh Sherman and Samuel Tappan. Mr. Tappan was well suited, even though he was a civilian at the time. He'd been a colonel in the U.S. Volunteers during the Civil War and was well known for his investigation of the 1865 massacre of Cheyenne women and children at Sand Creek, Colorado. The combination of Sherman and Tappan drove what eventually became the most significant treaty between an Indian tribe and the U.S. government—the Navajo Treaty of 1868. We'll talk about that at breakfast in the morning, before we get to Fort Sumner. Mr. Kipfer, how long do you think it will take to get there?"

Anderson said, "Five, maybe six hours. I can ride it in three, but my new friend, Angus, could get there in two on his trusty Tennessee walker."

CHAPTER 26

"The Navajo Treaty of 1868"

T HE RIDE SOUTHEAST FROM THE Long K ranch to what used to be Fort Sumner was dusty and without structures of any kind, until we got to what was left of the many Army buildings at the old fort. Now it was the Maxwell ranch that grabbed everyone's attention. Lucian Maxwell bought the buildings when the fort closed down in 1869. He hired a crew of carpenters to completely rebuild the old commanding officer's quarters and turn it into a very large, family ranch house. It was still a large, imposing wood building, but instead of the parade ground in front of the house, the family had put up a picket fence. It was the largest building for fifty miles in any direction. The second story had a large balcony in front big enough, I'd guess, to sit a dozen people. It faced the river to the west and a mountain range behind that which likely gave them a mighty fine sunset view. The large sloping roof was shuttered, with dormer windows cut in along the sides. The ground floor had a wraparound overhang covering over what looked like an eight-foot-wide boardwalk all around the house. Months before, J. Leonard had arranged permission via mail for us to make camp on the north side of the main house, near what they called the "issue house." He explained that was an adobe warehouse where they stored foodstuffs and agricultural equipment. There were sizeable trees around, some cottonwoods and a few scrubby oaks. We set up camp and had a quiet dinner around our campfire. The family in the ranch didn't come to our camp, but J. Leonard paid a courtesy visit to their house, in the company of Anderson Kipfer, who knew Pete Maxwell, the owner now that his father Lucian died two years ago.

Next morning after breakfast, J. Leonard passed around four grainy photos on stiff paper. He'd already shown us a stiff paper copy of the treaty the Indians signed with the Army twenty years ago. The photos, he said, "would pair faces with names in the treaty, and give you a look at the same ground you're sitting on right now." I suppose he thought it would help me, Teddy, Ora, and Anderson reconnoiter the ground and get a better feel for the situation. But while we passed around the pictures, I noticed Luci Atsidi did not look at them; she just passed them to Ora, sitting next to her on the little adobe wall. Ora looked at them quickly, turned them face down, and passed them to Anderson, who sat on the other side of her. Luci's face contorted like a vice was gripping the sides of her head. Her usual sad look when we talked about this place changed dramatically. She clamped down her upper jaw bone, making her face tight, and her dark skin wrinkled. Her eyes flashed, telling us exactly why she would not look at those damn pictures. I'd admired those eyes because I thought she was a handsome woman. Not like my Jill—not beautiful—but a face that showed pride and narrow eyes that could have been curved fighting swords coming at you. But, now, with the pictures past her, I could see what she was thinking—don't show me a picture—damn your hide—I was here—those men and this place are burnt into my soul and I'm crying inside now. Don't you look at me—look at your photos. I hope they make you cry inside, like I'm doing. I turned away, fearful she'd look my way and slice me up.

Since I was last to sit down on the little adobe wall, by the time the pictures got to me, I had no one to pass them to, so I took my time studying them. The first one was of Barboncito, a man in his fifties who looked like he'd ridden a fast Indian pony a million miles. I could tell, even though the picture was of a seated man, that this guy was a horseman. One I wished I could have ridden with. His skin was black from the hot Southwestern sun. He sat on a stump like he was sitting a fine young stallion. Shoulders squared, right hand pushed a little forward, he wore a a knife sheath that seemed to be strung by a wide leather band across his chest. There was a fierceness about this man, but his stare was slightly off from where whoever was taking the picture must have been standing. His left arm was outstretched in front of him with a small, bony hand wrapped loosely around the barrel of a fine long rifle. It looked to be a flint-lock musket with a fancy curved trigger guard of dark metal and a stock that glinted a little from a flash of some sort. Probably on the camera, I thought. The barrel was near as long as the sitting man was tall, and supported a long ramming stick underneath the large bore opening at the business end of the rifle. He wore a white headband, and small wisps of brown, greasy-looking hair showed below and above the band. His leather moccasins looked well-worn and were tucked under leather leggings reaching up nearly to his knees. His pants looked to be made of a dark canvas with silver buttons running down both sides from waist to knee caps. He wore a necklace, made of either beads or light-colored strings. Hard to tell in the photo. It could have just been a bad picture, but he seemed to have crossed eyes over a thin nose. Below the nose he sported a wispy mustache. His eyes were dark and had some of the same anger I could see now in Luci. The oddest thing about the picture was that it was taken in a studio of some kind, on a seat on a dark patterned carpet.

While we were in Albuquerque the second time, J. Leonard had told us about many of the Navajo headmen, but he was always corrected by Luci until he got the history right. Between the two I got a glimpse of what kind of warrior Barboncito was. They think he was born around 1820. They were sure he died in 1871, just three years after the treaty he helped negotiate was signed. He was captured in Canyon de Chelley in August 1864, Luci said, "only a few miles from the place where the Concord went crashing down into the canyon."

"It was Captain John Thomson that trapped him," Sgt. Bell added. "He had a small troop with him. I wasn't there, but I knew two men in that troop. They were damn proud of catching a major chief like him. I remember them talking about the peach orchards they destroyed and how surprised Barboncito was to find them in his camp just before daybreak. Seems like I remember they gathered up more than eighty young bucks. And they took them to Los Lunas, over to the Rio Grande, right where we camped three weeks ago."

Anderson asked if Barboncito stayed here from then until the treaty was signed. J. Leonard didn't know, but Luci did. "He was here until June 1885. One night he and five hundred men and a few women from his band got up and left. The soldiers were mad at us for not telling them for two days. One girl who was my friend went with them."

"But, am I correct that soldiers from Fort Sumner tracked them down a few days later? Have I got that right?" J. Leonard asked.

"No," Luci answered. "When Barboncito left he joined Manuelito. It was more than a year later, sometime in the fall of 1866, when Barboncito went over to Fort Wingate and surrendered. He had twenty-one warriors with him. They were starving by that time."

The group went quiet for a while. So I took another, longer look at the second picture. It was of the famous general, William Tecumseh Sherman, and it had his big fancy signature covering the bottom part of the stiff photo. This one was for sure taken inside a studio. Only his head, neck, shoulders, and a little bit of his upper chest showed. The rest of the print was gray smoke. He was wearing his Army uniform, with gold stars on his epaulets, and a black bow tie over a stiff starched shirt with the collar sticking up on both sides. Whoever the photographer was, he decided to shoot from the general's left side so it was almost a profile of a man looking away from the camera. I thought he looked sad; dunno why. He had short dark hair, back over his left ear, but clipped close to his skull. He wore a full, neatly trimmed beard. He had no neck, just beard down into his stiff collar. Thin eyebrows provided cover to eyes that seemed soft, contented. He didn't look mad like Barboncito; guess that's because he was on the winning side of the Indian Wars, just like he was the big winner in the Civil War when he burnt most of Atlanta to the ground.

The third picture was of Manuelito. I studied it a good long while because I'd heard a lot about him before I ever heard of J. Leonard or the Bosque Redondo. We'd talked about him after dinner several times on the way here. Almost everyone in New Mexico had a Manuelito story to tell. Unlike the Barboncito portrait of a fierce but slight man, Manuelito's highly staged photograph presented a Navajo who, in a prior life, might have been a Roman emperor. Large, heavy, bare-chested, and demanding undivided attention. This was a portrait of a full-blooded war chief the day after winning a decisive battle. His eyelids hid his eyes, but somehow made you feel safer. Anyone directly in his glare would wilt. The set of his jaw, the cocked backward angle of his neck, and the way he held both arms out and away from his body suggested a history of war and conflict that escapes ordinary understanding. He almost looked like he was horseback. When you're trotting or loping a horse, you naturally stick your elbows out on both sides of your body—gives you better balance. That's the way he was sitting the photographer's stool, like his mind was horseback. Far from looking inscrutable, Manuelito took a pose in this picture that told his story. "I will agree to peace only when I can no longer fight." The staging of a Navajo in full was finished when someone laid a beautiful Navajo rug across his waist and legs. The stripes and angles in the rug blended with a tall but slender leather pouch. It could have held a lance, or perhaps a long rifle. Like Barboncito, he wore a wispy mustache, but displayed a bigger string of beads around his neck.

J. Leonard told us Manuelito had evaded capture longer than any other Navajo chief—almost fifteen months after General Carleton's ultimatum to get him dead or alive. When he finally surrendered, it was not because the Army captured him. He left his hiding place near the head waters of the Little Colorado and rode to Fort Wingate, where he surrendered on September 1, 1866. He brought with him twenty-three family members, a few horses and mules, and his great dignity. By then he had lost, almost entirely, the use of his left arm. This came from a skirmish several weeks earlier with troops trying to capture him. Until the day of his surrender, his family said, he vowed to suffer death rather than go to the Bosque Redondo camp.

The fourth picture got everybody's attention because it was about as sad a chapter as any of us had ever seen. This was a copy of the photograph J. Leonard had sent to us in the first letter. It was a big open field. J. Leonard's note said it was the parade ground inside Fort Sumner at the beginning of internment. The man taking the photo stood behind a single soldier with his back to the camera. He was looking forward at maybe a hundred or more Navajos—men, women, children—all huddled under wrapped blankets. The sheer desolation was what made it fascinating. A patch of raw dirt, a low adobe wall, which might have been the side of a ditch. At first I thought the huddled piles were just blankets; then I realized these were people squatting on the dirt waiting for someone, maybe the soldier, to tell them to get up and go somewhere. Beyond the sitting Indians, a few dozen men, some with hats, some not, stood motionless as though they were old trees waiting to die for lack of water. That one soldier, his rifle laid across his arms with the barrel pointing sideways from him, seemed to be in charge. But I knew he wasn't. The ground was in charge. They were hundreds of miles away from home with nowhere else to go except this cold mud under a cloudy sky. There was no need for the soldier to aim his gun. He was the only one who hadn't been taken away from his home.

J. Leonard said these photos were from the Smithsonian and some might have been taken by the Army's photographer at Fort Sumner.

"Why did they have a photographer?" Teddy Bridger wanted to know.

"It was quite common for the Army to record its goings-on, its successes, you know. Actually, there were at least four photographers identified in the Army records, who took pictures here. These were most likely shot by a man named J.G. Gaige. He was a daguerreotypist, ambrotypist, and photographer who worked in Arizona and New Mexico from 1862 until his death at Camp Goodwin in 1869. He lived in Santa Fe at a studio built on the plaza in 1863. Pity we don't have any pictures of the little grove of cottonwoods you can see down there about a mile from us. Can anyone guess why that grove is important?"

"Probably because those cottonwoods are a sure sign there's water close by. That grove is nourished by the Pecos River," Anderson Kipfer said.

"Yes, indeed, you're right about what they signal. But they are also on a little mound. That grove gave this camp its name. Bosque Redondo means 'little mound,'" J. Leonard said proudly.

We camped outside the old fort's crumbling walls that night. After breakfast the next morning, we visited some of the rubble of the main building. And we learned a little about how the Maxwell family had turned this into a working cattle ranch. When Maxwell and his son came here in 1870, there were only a handful of soldiers here as caretakers. They left when Lucian took possession of the buildings. He spent $10,000 to add wooden roofs and floors to the buildings. What Maxwell wanted, he said, was the land on the reservation, now that all the Indians had gone back home. They built line shacks for cattle herds, but did not have legal ownership of the land. Eventually, Kipfer thought, the ranch would go bust. While he could not have foreseen it at the time, the railroads were quickly opening the West to American settlors. They would homestead the vast acres it took to feed huge cattle herds. Cattle feeding lots would be the end of big ranching in New Mexico.

"The Army has been gone from here for eighteen years," the rancher said. "The officers' quarters held two dozen officers. But it's now one large, twenty-room house for his family and some men who helped him build this ranch."

Ora asked, "When did you say the father died?"

"In 1875. Peter still lives there, but is away this week in Texas trying to buy a bull. Peter's wife homesteaded the section of land immediately to the south of us."

Sgt. Bell asked, "How big is a section of land?"

Teddy had the answer. "It's one square mile—exactly 640 acres."

"Well, even so, I expect there ain't enough water in the river to sustain a big cattle herd down here," I said.

"There's one more thing some of you probably know about this place, and especially Peter Maxwell's house. Since he gave Mr. Leonard permission to camp here, I don't think he'll mind me telling you about this. Just seven years ago, there was a big fight going on in Lincoln County. They called it the Lincoln County War. A famous outlaw, Billy the Kid, was killed here in that house you're looking at. The sheriff, a man named Pat Garrett, did him in. He tracked the Kid to this ranch, in the dark of night. Or so the story goes. Sheriff Garrett shot the Kid twice. He's buried just up the road, in the old post cemetery."

J. Leonard decided he wanted to walk down to the Pecos River, which was about a half mile west of the big yard where we'd set up our camp. Teddy said he'd saddle a horse and ride down to the river and catch up with him. Said he wanted to ride across the Pecos and check out a little adobe hut we could see over on the far side of the river. That gave Jill and me a chance to walk the opposite direction, due east up the bluff where another mound of trees was blowing in the late afternoon breeze. We walked for a half hour before turning around to look back at the ranch, the river beyond it, and the late afternoon sun dropping into a cloud bank on the western horizon. Jill had packed a small basket with crackers, a little jar of raspberry jam, and a small jug of tea. We had no ice, but it tasted good even though it was warm. I could tell Jill was bothered about something.

"Angus," she said as we sat on a stone shelf looking at the ranch, the river beyond it, and the hazy sheen over the hills, "do you feel safe out here, in the middle of such a big space of land?"

"Sure, why not? Open space is protective just because you can see in every direction and no one can sneak up on you."

"Well, that's true, but I don't feel safe here. There's tension in our group. While Professor Leonard tries to put on a courageous face, he's scared. Has been ever since we all learned that Chinorero died. He cannot accept death the way people here do. He told me he is very worried that someone wants to kill his research project, and that the men that shot Chinorero are really after him."

"He said that? To you? Straight out?"

"No, he's too Eastern for that. I've been talking to him little by little because I can sense his fear. He doesn't know how to deal with people outside a university very well. He lives in a big city with police everywhere and there are no coaches to rob. Earlier today, when they were talking about Billy the Kid, the outlaw, and how he was shot right there in the ranch building where we're camped, it hit him. I watched his face go all pale and his hands start to shake a little. I think Teddy can see that, too. Maybe that's why Teddy followed him down to the river."

"Can't say I noticed any of that. But do you think Teddy feels the same thing? That maybe there's danger here, now that we are about to the end of the trip?"

"Teddy? Honestly, Angus, Teddy is a mystery to me. He's not once mentioned the boy's name, Chinorero, since he died. And he's always asking questions about proof when he talks to the professor. He asked me questions about you, too."

"Me? What kind of questions?"

"Oh, just little things, like whether you ever went to college and whether you ever looked into the members of the group. I got the feeling that maybe he thinks you know something about him you shouldn't know."

"Well, now that you say it, there is a lot I don't know about him. He says he has two missions here—one to help me guard the professor, and another to look for government misconduct in counterfeiting, slave trading. Who knows what else?"

"Maybe that's because of his father, the Confederate colonel."

"Confederate? He told me his father and an uncle were Union men."

"Maybe so, but Sgt. Bell thinks different. He told me Col. Bridger was a slave owner from Virginia."

"How'd he know that?"

"Don't know. Maybe he's making it up. But I know Sgt. Bell doesn't like Teddy, and I think the feeling's mutual."

I didn't know what to say to her. Jill always had a better feel for what people are thinkin' inside.

Boom! Boom! The sound of two far-away shots coming from the west stopped our talk. We ran fast as we could back to the ranch yard. Ora and Luci were up on top of the Concord. Ora had a pair of binoculars and was panning from side to side down toward the river.

"What's going on?" I yelled when we got close enough for them to hear us.

Ora answered. "We don't know. J. Leonard walked down to the river an hour ago. Teddy saddled up and followed him.

We heard two shots. Sgt. Bell borrowed a rifle from the ranch foreman and went down there. And nobody's coming back here from the river."

"Is the sergeant on foot?" I asked as I ran from the stage to the barn so I could saddle Marathon.

"No," Anderson said, "I let him take my horse."

"All right, everyone stay here," I said as I swung my leg up over the cantle.

The ride to the river only took a few minutes. When I pushed through the thick stand of willows and cottonwoods, the first thing I saw was J. Leonard down on the bank, with his legs and half his upper body laying still in the river. No one else in sight. I jerked Marathon up to a sliding halt a few feet from the man. His hat was snagged on a little jangle of brush and river rock and his face was down on the rough sand of the bank. Bending over to pull him up out of the river, I got a real shock.

"Don't you touch me again," J. Leonard said in a growl. He had a long scrape across his forehead, with dried blood and mud smeared down his face and neck. The shock came from his right fist which was curled around a small derringer. He raised it toward me and I grabbed it out of his clenched fist. He acted like he didn't know me.

"Hold on, Mr. Leonard, let me pull you up out of the river."

As I wrenched him up and onto the little shelf next to the river, he began to moan, which quickly broke down into a full-throated cry. Can't remember when I'd heard a man cry before. His ankle-high city boots and socks were neatly set on a rock about five feet from the water's edge.

"Angus, is that you? Oh God, where is he? Where is Mr. Bridger? And Sgt. Bell? I think he saved my life. He was just here. And, oh God, my head hurts."

"Just try to calm yourself, Mr. Leonard, and tell me what happened here."

I propped him up against a young cottonwood and gave him some water. I wrapped my kerchief around the scrape on his head. Slowly, in a halting voice, he answered my question.

"Mr. Bridger tried to kill me. He was crazy and screamed at me like I was the devil. And he choked me and drug into the river. But I bested him, Marshal, I did. I was so scared, but he didn't know about my derringer. It was a loan from my colleague at the Smithsonian, you know, I told you about him—the naval architect—and . . ."

"Take another sip of water, Mr. Leonard. I think you're alright. You got a nasty scrape on your forehead, and I can see bruising on your neck, but you're OK. Where's Sgt. Bell?"

"He was here. But Mr. Bridger heard him coming and rode off after I shot at him. I told the Sergeant what happened and he just started cursing Teddy. Called him a lying Confederate bastard and he tore after him like . . ."

"Slow down, man. Start with what happened when you and Teddy first got here."

"I walked down alone, but Teddy actually got here before me. He tied his horse to that dead tree right over there. When I got here, he had taken his boots off and was cooling his feet in the water. I thought that was a delightful idea, so I took mine off, too, and sat down right here. Oh, thank goodness, they're still here. Would you help me put them on Angus, and . . ."

"That can wait a minute, Mr. Leonard. I need you to concentrate and tell me what happened here."

"Well, I can hardly believe it, but Teddy is not who we thought he was, Angus. He arranged for those men to kill Chinorero, although he said it was a mistake. Remember you said they missed on purpose? Well, you were right. Teddy told me so. He said it was just to scare me, but Chin was stupid and jumped up and fired and that's why the man shot him in the stomach. 'Cannot allow a breed to shoot at a white man,' Teddy said. Those were his actual words, Angus. He snarled when he told me that. He is a different man, Angus, I told you that already, right?"

"Yes, you did, Mr. Leonard. But why did Teddy talk about that at all? I don't understand how you ever got to talking to him about it?"

"Because, Angus, it is about Teddy's father. Col. Theodore Stanford Bridger. He's the reason Teddy volunteered to come on this trip. He was a Union Army man in Virginia who sided with the Confederates in the Civil War."

"Hold up there, Mr. Leonard. Teddy told me his father and uncle both fought for the Union."

"Yes, he told me that, too. Back in Albuquerque. But here on the riverbank today, he told me the truth. His father turned Confederate while his uncle stayed with the Union. That broke up the family."

"What in tarnation does that have to do with Teddy trying to kill you here?"

"Well, you know I've been sharing many records with everyone all along the trip. I told everyone last night that I had more documents and would be sharing them as we talked about the 1868 Navajo Treaty now that we are finally here on the Bosque Redondo reservation. That scared Teddy."

"Scared him? Why? I can't see any connection between your records and Teddy's father."

"Neither did I, Angus, but Teddy is paranoid about it."

"Paranoid? Crazy? What do you mean?"

"Teddy knows his father was one of the Confederate officers who ran a large counterfeit money operation for the Confederacy. They used that fake money to pay for many things in the South. And they used it out West to support the slave trade with Indian babies and wives. That's what he told me. He was afraid I already had records about that. He asked me, when we were sitting here with our bare feet in the river, if I had lists of Union officers who joined the other side—the Confederacy. I told him I had brought some lists with me from our archives, but they didn't seem to bear on the Treaty, so I hadn't shared them with anyone."

"And then what happened?"

"That's when he drew his pistol and hit me. Then he tried to choke me. He was screaming that I wanted to destroy his family name, and that this whole trip to New Mexico could harm many Virginia families. And he was just unhinged, I tell you, Angus, unhinged."

"Did you shoot him?"

"I did. Oh my god, I've only fired a gun two times in my life. I brought the derringer—it only has two bullets, one in each barrel—out here in my valise. But once those men killed Chinorero, I've been carrying it in my inside vest pocket. So when he was choking me, I was able to grab it. I thought I put it against his chest, but it was only his arm. I fired right into his upper arm. And the blood spattered all over him, and me."

"Lord, Mr. Leonard, I've never heard a story like that before. What did Teddy do then?"

"Well, sir, I can say now he was mighty surprised at me. He thought I was a defenseless, fifty-year old professor. So I think the shock of the bullet was not as big a shock as seeing me with a gun in my hand. He screamed more obscenities at me, but he let go my throat. He threw me down into the river, but I still had my gun. He turned and ran for his horse. He had a rifle scabbard there. I aimed at him, but missed and hit his horse on the rear. The horse screamed something awful, but he managed to mount him and ride off."

"Which way?"

"That way, down the river," he said, pointing due south.

"All right, tell me about Sgt. Bell."

"I must have passed out from the pain of being hit in the head and being choked. But I heard Sgt. Bell come crashing through the brush, just there, where you did a moment ago. He felt my head and took my pulse. I told him what happened. "

"All right, Mr. Leonard, tell me what you told him."

"I said Teddy had just tried to kill me and he was a traitor and he'd lied to all of us about the war and his father being in the Confederate Army and everything. I told him Teddy was the man who hired those two men in Albuquerque who killed Chinorero. Then, he spun around on that little Morgan horse he was riding, screaming that he'd get the 'lying Confederate bastard.' Then he ran his horse right into the river. I don't know which way he went. I think I passed out."

I told J. Leonard to just sit there a few minutes while I went back to get the buckboard to ferry him back to the Maxwell ranch house. Once we got him inside and settled down in one of the bedrooms, I told Jill that I had to go after Teddy Bridger.

Marathon had been watered by one of the hands. I pulled my big stock saddle off Marathon and borrowed an old McClellan army saddle from the foreman. It was twenty-five pounds lighter, had no saddle horn, and only one brass ring on each side to tie down small burlap bags. I put three water bags in one bag, along with a loaf of Apache bread, two raw potatoes, a brick of cheese, and the case holding my binoculars. I hung that one on the on-side of the saddle. I stuffed a nose bag and five pounds of sweet grain in the other bag, and tied it to the off-side. Then I hooked an Army-issue shoulder strap to my Winchester and slung it cross-way on my back. I stuffed the pockets in my chaps and vest with extra bullets, a pair of handcuffs, two boxes of matches, my compass, and a large folding knife with a six-inch serrated blade. Kissing Jill hard, I jumped Marathon and spurred him into that long trot of his toward the Rio Pecos.

CHAPTER 27

"Chasing the Rio Pecos"

Took Marathon a scant ten minutes to reach the river bank. I sat on him for a couple minutes while he sucked up a bellyful of cold water, stamping his hooves in the mud. Scanning the opposite bank, I thought I could see where Sgt. Bell had climbed the opposite bank. I figured the old horse soldier could reckon Teddy's track by riding slow, and paying attention to the dirt and freshly broken brush. They had a little over two hours head start, with Teddy riding hard, and Sgt. Bell riding careful, looking for sign. Thought I could just long-trot Marathon and keep Sgt. Bell's track in easy view ahead of me. I'd catch 'em both. And I was hoping I'd get there before the angry horse soldier caught up with his sworn enemy, a Confederate soldier.

The sun went down two hours later, and I lost sight of the horse tracks following the bank of the Rio Pecos south, toward Old Mexico. From time to time, I could see that there were two horses, one following the other, crisscrossing every quarter mile or so. Both were heading south and both on the west bank of the Pecos. I tracked the pair of them until I lost the light and couldn't risk going on without a track to follow.

So I stopped alongside a stand of juniper a hundred yards west of the river bank. Unsaddling Marathon, I led him down to drink his fill, and then back up to the trees. I hunkered down into my sleeping posture, back up against the saddle pad, which was up against the tree trunk. It'd been a good long while since I felt the need to sleep sitting up. It's a good way to hear what's going on, and still feel completely rested when the predawn light lowered itself down onto the earth.

As I sat there in a nearly moonless night, I thought about Teddy and his treachery. I knew the next day would be like no other in my life. Once the black night gave way to predawn light, I'd have a good hour before dawn, and two hours before full-on morning. I knew Teddy was a Virginia gentleman, and not an early riser. He'd complained about me up and making noise in the morning for the last three weeks. Sgt. Bell was a heavy drinker and likely taking pulls on his brandy flask as he tracked Teddy southward. So, he'd sleep through the predawn light and maybe a bit past sunrise before he took up the track again. I hoped the combination would get me three, maybe four hours closer to them.

As the black sky retreated and light gray penetrated the juniper and piñon forest, I could hear the river gurgle. Wildly twisted juniper branches, some dead, but captured in place by live ones, came into close view. Soon, the sky to the East would turn silvery blue, but only for a few minutes. Then the pink would slither up into a welcoming sky and I'd be five miles south, on the hunt, following the scent of fresh horse dung, and the sweat of tired horses.

One side of the river was rolling grass and scrub oak country, but up ahead I could see a burned-out piñon forest spiked with charred trees. Two coyotes yipped as they darted away from a fresh kill, over a small hill. They'd hide until I passed. Then they'd finish the first of many small meals before retreating to a den somewhere, to wait out the rising moon. With one eye on the track, and one ear to anything sounding strange, I leaned forward in the saddle tasting the bile produced by a man I thought was my friend. I knew better now. Teddy was a man who killed with abandon, and ran from my badge and my handcuffs. He'd soon face both, I hoped. But I also knew I had a barrier to cross first. Between me and him was another man of the horse who had a different goal. Sgt. Bell would kill Teddy if he caught up with him before I did. Or Teddy would kill Sgt. Bell. Either way, I had two men, likely with guns drawn, to face before the sun went down this day.

As it often happens, July in New Mexico brings an early monsoon—not a gully-washer, but short spells of sputtering sunshine, peppered with squalls in the distance, and sometimes a sudden rain that glistens everything without soaking you to the skin. This rain came on just after high noon. Looking dimly through it, I thought I could see a loose horse, on this side of the river. Another forty yards and it was clear. It was the horse Sgt. Bell had ridden trying to catch up with Teddy. He stood stock still in a thick stand of scrub oak brush beside the slow-moving river. One rein snagged on a beached log, the other dropped down into the flow on his far side. The saddle bags had badly shifted, likely from loose tie-downs. The on-side bag hung down almost to the horse's belly while the other was visible on his back. No sign of Sgt. Bell. As I walked Marathon to him, I cooed softly.

"Easy, old son. Easy boy. Shoo, shoo, easy now."

He'd spotted me fifty yards up river, and didn't see me as danger. I dismounted, ground tied Marathon, and stepped over to him, ten feet away. He eyed me indifferently, and let me walk up, take hold of his halter, and reach under his neck for the off-side rein. I untied the other one, and led him up onto the bank. Then I saw the blood on his cantle.

"Where's the sergeant, little horse?" I asked more to the wind than to the horse. It didn't take long. And it wasn't hard. I took the rope off the saddle horn and used it to lead him behind Marathon. I just followed that now-familiar short-stride track back, up the river, for about two hundred yards. Sgt. Bell was waiting for me.

"Heard you coming, a mile off, Marshal," he said in a raspy voice mixed with exhaustion and brandy. He was sitting on a flat rock, holding his gun-hand, which was wrapped in a dirty brown cloth.

"You OK, Sarge? What happened?"

Between dismounting and tying up both horses, Sgt. Bell filled me in. He'd followed Teddy from yesterday until late in the night. Then he dismounted, without unsaddling his horse, and tried fitfully to sleep till dawn. Then, he picked up the trail, followed it to this little spot, when he was knocked out of the saddle by a rifle boom. The shot hit the side of his saddle horn and ricocheted into his gun hand. He did the right thing. He jumped off, grabbing his rifle from the scabbard. Firmly planted on the ground, he jacked a round into the chamber and fired in the direction he thought the shot had come from. That caused the "fool horse" to spook and run off.

Although he couldn't see Teddy, he screamed at him, "Come get me you traitorous bastard!" He hunkered down behind a rock shelf, facing down river toward the shot that could have killed him. He heard what he thought was a horse crashing down into the river.

It happened more than an hour ago, he said. But he'd stayed put.

"Like any smart soldier stays put. Inside the walls of the fort when there's hostiles around. This is my little fort, Angus. You want to hunt down Teddy, that's fine with me. My mad at the bastard ain't got much steam left."

I rewrapped the bandage on his hand with a clean hand- kerchief, my only one. I adjusted the bags on his saddle, gave him one of my water bags, the loaf of bread, and checked his rifle. He assured me he could ride back to the Bosque Redondo.

I found the spot a hundred yards away, where Teddy had fired on Sgt. Bell. Like the bushwhacker he was, he'd staked out a little hide this side of the river. He had not bothered to police his brass, making me think he lost his VMI military bearing. The 44.40 cartridge gleamed in the sand. The horse dung by the tree where he'd tied the stolen horse, and the little fire hole he'd foolishly dug last night, were signs of an overly confident adversary. He was no more than an hour ahead of me now. I'd square him face on before sunset.

As I followed him south, on the east bank now, I tried to put myself in his boots. He'd know I had the better horse and a strong motivation to run him to ground. So I guessed he'd look for another hide; a place to make a better ambush than the one he'd tried on Sgt. Bell. I didn't think he'd go more than an hour from here. And when he found a place where he felt safe, I would be at the same disadvantage Sgt. Bell had been. But next time, he wouldn't miss and hit the saddle horn. Maybe he'd nail me center mass. He'd hunker down and wait for me to get real close, so he couldn't miss.

So, I did what I didn't think he'd figure. I crossed back over the river to the west side, rode a mile past it, then turned south and followed the river's track instead of his horse trail. I had a plan. It would take the rest of the day and all night to put in place. The only flaw was whether Teddy would act true to his nature—find a hide—shoot from cover—run away.

I got far enough away from the river to keep the big cottonwoods in sight. They gave the river's path away. But I wasn't close enough to be seen or heard from a man in an ambush hole on the other side of the river. I was hoping Teddy would find his hide well before sunset. If I was right, I'd ride on past it, from a mile to the west of him while he sat there, eyes glued on his back trail, with his rifle safely benched on a shooting stand. He'd sit the evening through and then start worrying when it got dark. By then I'd be long past him but still following the winding river as it ebbed down toward the Gulf of Mexico. At some point, he would give it up, thinking I'd either lost his track, or my nerve. Then, he'd panic, saddle up his horse and ride south at a good clip. Plan was to meet him head on, from the front. A place he'd never think of. Back stabbers always look over their backs. But by midday tomorrow, with a little luck, I'd be miles south of him, waiting for the bastard. It nearly worked out that way.

I rode the rest of the day, Marathon jiggling along with his agitated gait, likely doing seven, maybe eight miles an hour. Then, when I figured I was south of Teddy by a good ten miles, I turned down toward the river and found a bluff, a hundred feet away and about the same distance above the river bed. When I dismounted and hobbled Marathon, I could smell the water, faintly hear the gurgling, and had a clear look back up the river on the east side for at least a mile. This sandstone bluff was the most important piece of the puzzle—a natural low place where a man could walk across the river and never feel the water topping his boot. A horse could thunder across at a full run without danger. And while making a pile of noise doing it. If I was guessing right, Teddy would be coming down the west bank straight across from me between midday and early evening tomorrow. Or maybe he'd hole up longer in his hide, and it'd be dark before he got this far south. Either way, I'd be ready for him, but not in a hide. He'd hear me first, then he'd see me. And I'd have him out in the open, where I wanted him.

Once I'd picked my spot on the east bank, I spotted a large cottonwood tree; probably fifty feet high. It had strong lower branches. I could climb up about ten feet above the bank and see both sides of the river. Also I could see up river for a good three miles. I had no intention staying up there in the dark, but come sunrise, it would be a fine place to scout the opposing river bank for a good distance. I hobbled Marathon, gave him a large nose bag full of grain, and settled in. With no fire, I ate my last potato and nibbled on the last brick of cheese for two hours in total darkness. The moon didn't come up until somewhere around midnight. But it was just a sliver, so the dark blanket covered things in every direction. When the blanket broke, and the silver light that always came before the sun came up peeked over the eastern sky, I saddled Marathon, tied the burlap bags to the copper rings on the back of the McClellan, and bridled him. I looped the rawhide lead rope from the saddle horn around the big cottonwood. Snugging Marathon up against the tree, I slung the Winchester over my back, and shinnied up to the lowest big branch, about six feet off the ground. Finding a strong branch to hold me, I straddled it and focused my binoculars on the other side of the river. I could see everything clearly through a few trees for at least a mile upriver. What looked like a deer trail ran down part of the trail about seventy-five feet away. So I kept panning from there up, and then back down to the fording place just below me. Marathon settled in. Damned if he wasn't the most patient horse I'd ever been around.

I'd just brushed a bug out of my right ear when I saw Marathon's ears flick up. Panning as far as I could north, up river, I saw movement in the brush about a hundred yards away. As I adjusted the lens, he came into view. Teddy Bridger rode slumped forward in the saddle with the reins in his left hand and his borrowed rifle in the other. He was bent toward the left, away from my side of the river, and looked back over his left shoulder three times as he moved thirty feet down the trail. The horse walked with its head down, almost to the ground, nibbling shoots of grass on the side of the trail. He had not fed this horse all night, I thought. And he had not slept well himself. I thought he might fall asleep in the saddle. As I sharpened the lens focus, his face came into clear view. Haggard, pallid, with a slack jaw and a drooping neck. Not at all like the proud VMI graduate I'd met on that first day in Albuquerque. I watched him sit the horse for another minute. While he looked nervous and kept looking back, he didn't seem at all attentive. His horse could have walked under a tree with a chest-high branch and it would have knocked him off the saddle before he looked up. This was an exhausted, fearful man, I thought.

I skinned back down the tree, put my hand over Marathon's nose, and cinched up the saddle. Gathering up my lead rope, I looped it around the saddle horn. Then, slowly, I eased myself up into the saddle. Hoping Marathon wouldn't whinny to the approaching horse, I eased him out of the tree stand and down fifty feet to the river's edge. There, I reversed the rifle sling so the big Winchester's trigger guard, lever, and breach were chest high in front of me. I jacked a round into the chamber and inched Marathon forward to the bank of the river. Then I fired the first round straight up in the air, knowing it would spook Marathon. He reacted just like I thought he would, rearing up on me. I dropped the rifle to my chest on its sling and put the spurs to Marathon at the same moment. He jumped forward headlong into the river as I let out the loudest whoop I could. The sound of the muzzle blast, us hitting the water, and my whoop would carry the fifty yards up the river and get Teddy's immediate attention. I thought it might also spook his horse. I was right.

As we barreled out of the river on the west side, I pulled my 44.40 revolver from the holster, aimed it up river in the general direction of Teddy, and let loose with three quick shots. Then, neck-reining Marathon up the west side of the river right at Teddy, I could see the effect of my noisy ambush. His horse was terrified. Teddy had jerked back on the reins, trying to control the horse, and had dropped his rifle in the process. But he still had his Colt, strapped in that military belt and holster he favored. I was close enough to see him trying to draw the pistol and control the spinning horse, at the same time.

Could I make it the last forty yards to him before he drew the Colt, I thought, in a small panic of my own. But as he didn't have spurs he had no way to get his horse's attention. He and the poor horse saw us thundering up the trail right at him. When I got twenty yards away, I let loose the last three rounds in his direction. I fired high and to the right because I didn't want to hit him. My aim was to rattle him so bad we could close the distance and I'd ram him with this giant Tennessee Walking horse. But I had not counted on how terrified his poor horse was or how unstable he was sitting the horse in his exhausted condition. His horse lunged to the right, hit the river bank, and somersaulted forward, throwing Teddy over his head. Then they tumbled down in a ball to the rocky shale on the river's edge.

I could not tell rider from horse at this distance, but both were down and the horse continued to thrash. The rider was motionless, face down in the water, with the rest of his body on the rocks rimming the river. By the time I got to him, he was dead of a broken neck and a crushed skull.

CHAPTER 28

"The Ride Home"

I T TOOK ME A DAY AND A HALF to work my way back
to the Maxwell Ranch, and what remained of the Bosque
Redondo. Sgt. Bell, riding his nearly exhausted ranch horse,
got here the night before. He'd brought the good news—I
was alive—to Jill. With that came the lingering question of
whether I'd found Teddy.

As I rode into the former parade ground in front of the
Maxwell ranch house, the answer to what happened to Teddy
was there for all to see. I was riding Marathon and leading the
horse Anderson had loaned to Teddy. He was wrapped in a
canvas tarp, draped over the cheap cowboy saddle.

As for what madness drove Teddy to try to kill J. Leonard
then Sgt. Bell and finally me was a matter of much discussion. Most of what we knew was relayed to Jill, Luci, Ora,
and Johnson Ortega before I got back, with Teddy Bridger

in tow. There was no consensus other than the madness of slavery, the lure of easy money, and the passion that family shame begets.

I went up to the porch of the Maxwell Ranch House where J. Leonard was waiting to talk to me. I gave him the details of how I found Teddy Bridger and how he died. He gave a longer, but not more illuminating version of what Bridger said just before trying to kill him.

Next day, just after breakfast, everybody was about the business of packing up and loading the coach for the trip back up the Pecos. J. Leonard got me aside and motioned for me to follow him out into the big yard. When we were out of earshot, and the others were doing the work getting ready to move out, he asked me a curious question.

"Marshal, I have to say, you've been a splendid addition to this adventure, but I have a feeling you're getting a little tired of riding with a crowd of people, am I right?"

"Mr. Leonard, you know I'm given to long rides by myself in high country. Before Jill came along, most of my talking was to my horse. But this ride has been the only one, in a group, I ever enjoyed. I am itching a bit, I guess, to get home, but that's true for all of us. Right?"

"It surely is, Angus, it surely is. But last evening, up there on that fine porch after dinner, your fellow travelers and I discussed a possible route change. The consensus view was that we take the Concord north from here, straight up to Fort Union. The railroad is there. They'll assist me in getting to the station, onto the train, and on my way back to Washington, D.C., via Chicago. Luci wants to visit that fort as well, for it figured in the Long Walk of many of her people. From there, she can take the westbound train back through Albuquerque and then on to Gallup. Sgt. Bell, who has proved to be a most independent man, has offered to personally escort me half way home. Turns out he has kin in Nebraska and he'll get off there. Of course, since he saved my life, I'm inclined to give him whatever he wants. I've even offered him a security position at the Smithsonian. He said we didn't have enough money to make him do that. That brings us to you, our intrepid leader and chief security officer. Given your penchant for riding high mountain passes, I thought I'd say it's perfectly alright with me if you consider your watchdog job done now. You and Jill could take your leave from this task right here. You can follow the Pecos all the way to its headwaters, or follow it south down to the Mexican border. What say you, Angus, my treasured and life-saving friend?"

"Well, sir, it's been a mighty fine trip, but I'm sure Jill and I would appreciate the chance to skedaddle, just the two of us, maybe straight home to Chama. Maybe not. I've seen more towns, hotels, and dining rooms in the last month than I have in the last two years. Let me just clear this with my wife and then we'll make our own way, somewhere. All right if we take the extra horse? We'll get it back to Perfecto's ranch soon enough."

"Splendid. Let's call it done. But, if you don't mind, I asked you to come out here in the middle of what was for nine thousand Navajo prisoners and hundreds of Union Army soldiers a truly desolate place. This ground has seen more pain than most battlefields. So it's a perfect place for me to leave you with a slightly different perspective about the Navajo wars than you might have gleaned from what I had to say about the 1868 Treaty. We didn't finish that conversation, but I can sum it up for you right here. "

"Sure, I'd like that."

"The Navajo wars are only explainable if you consider how the Navajo people lived in the fifteenth and sixteenth centuries. They were an acquisitive, adaptable people, with a keen propensity for raiding their neighbor's property. This badly thought-out, ill-conceived social experiment, perpetuated hostility and great depredations on both sides. There was no history of slavery or taking slaves as captives until the Spanish came here. Then, in the 1840s, when Americans came here in large numbers, the slavery problem increased, given the heritage of slavery in the Southern states of this country. Americans here in New Mexico participated as evidenced by the slave markets in Santa Fe. But still, there was much decrying the practice of slaving while doing nothing effective to end it. The agents of three governments entered many treaties with the Navajos. But the treaties became contributory to renewed and intensified hostilities. You'll remember that all the treaties we talked about had mutual promises of returning slaves and not taking new ones. The American treaties became progressively worse than those entertained under Spanish rule. And the central focus was on the American right to seize land or anything else owned by Indians. This was the case when the Civil War ended. The Navajos were given only one option: they could choose between unconditional surrender and extermination. That impossible choice demanded the ultimate solution—the Bosque Redondo."

"So, you're saying the American approach was much worse than the Spanish approach?"

"Yes, Marshal, that's exactly what I'm saying. But you see, my good man, there is a subtle point not understood or appreciated here in the New Mexico Territory. Because the Spanish did not encroach on Navajo land, they never tried to enslave the entire tribe. Only the Americans took that approach. We wanted their land. And the only way to get it was to exterminate them or enslave them in a poor place, like Bosque Redondo. Remember that as you and Mrs. Esperraza talk about this adventure on your way home to Chama."

We said goodbye to the Maxwell ranch foreman. Jill and I said our goodbyes to the rest of the group. Ora had announced she'd drive the Concord, making clear she didn't want to ride inside with the still recovering J. Leonard. Anderson Kipfer ponied his horse back of the Concord and rode up top with Ora.

That's the last I saw of Anderson, or Ora. Later, Jill and I learned that Ora moved to the Rocking K Ranch after she and Anderson got married in the little chapel on Perfecto Armijo's ranch.

Jill and I walked down from the house toward the mound of cottonwoods this place was named after. Can't say we spent another minute talking about J. Leonard's grand adventure. It only took us ten minutes to talk about our next adventure. I'd told Jill many times how I wanted to ride the Rio Pecos south to Del Rio Texas where it empties into the Rio Grande.

"Why?" she asked. "Why, pray tell, would you want to do that?"

"Because from there, the Rio Grande meanders its way all the way down to the Gulf of Mexico, which is part of the Atlantic Ocean, you know."

She was quiet for five minutes. Then she asked me a strange question.

"Do you even know how to swim?"

"What? What's that got to do with anything?"

"Well, Darlin', I think we ought to ride to Del Rio, follow the Rio Grande south, and then go swimming in the Gulf of Mexico."

So, we did.

THE END

Author's Note

THE BOOK YOU'VE JUST READ is the third in a series about a fictional New Mexico lawman named Angus Esperazza. It is a novel with an historical event as backstory. All of the speaking characters are fictional, as is all of the dialogue. The U.S. government's internment of a significant majority of the Navajo people at Fort Sumner, New Mexico between 1863 and 1868 is real. The Army records were not consistent with the starting date because the land at Bosque Redondo was commissioned as a military fort dedicated in 1862, the buildings were started in 1863, and the first mass of captured Navajo Indians came in 1864. However, there were a few hundred Mescalero Apache detained there in 1863.

The Navajo Long March fictionally reconstructed in this novel is the true story of a small part of the Navajo Nation's tragic history and the relationship between its people and the people and governments of what is now New Mexico.

There are several nonfiction, book-length treatments of the Navajo Long Walk. Many excellent exhibits are displayed at the Bosque Redondo Memorial in Fort Sumner, New Mexico and the Navajo Museum in Window Rock, Arizona. Well-written, comprehensive books that tell the story in much greater detail than is presented in this historical novel include Lynn R. Bailey's Bosque Redondo—The Navajo Interment at Fort Sumner, 1863–68, Volume 69 of the Great West and Indian Series, published by Westernlore Press in 1998 in Tucson, Arizona (ISBN 0-87026-100-2); Navajo Stories of the Long Walk Period, published by Dine College Bookstore/Press, Tsaile, Navajo Nation, Arizona 86556, ISBN 0-912586-16-8; and Frank McNitt's Navajo Wars—Military Campaigns, Slave Raids and Reprisals, published by the University of New Mexico Press, 1972 (Library of Congress Catalog Card N. 7286816). Many other articles and reference works detail one of America's most shameful events.

No single source, and certainly not this book, can tell the full story of the cultural, economic, and personal devastation forced on the interned Navajos, the ones the Army didn't capture, and their descendants. What is clear is that an entire tribe of people, who had lived for hundreds of years in relative peace, were brutally subdued by a war plan that laid waste to men, women, children, livestock, water supplies, corn fields, orchards, herds, flocks, granaries, corrals, hogans, wagons, and dignity. The attack was led by the U.S. Army and local militias from New Mexico. But the wars that led up to the scorched earth campaign by General James Carleton and Colonel Kit Carson were aided and abetted by Utes, New

Mexicans, Puebloans, and citizen volunteers. Every stratum of Navajo society was diminished exponentially by the war that either killed or captured the vast bulk of the Navajo people. As Lynn Bailey put it, "Nearly 9,000 Indians lived by Army doctrine, attempted to till alkali-impregnated soil, and died of pneumonia and dysentery induced by poor sanitation, and brackish water. They were also ravaged by mumps, smallpox, and syphilis. So traumatic was this event in Navajo life, that tribesmen would reckon all future events from the day of release, as if the tribe had been reborn and all earlier happenings were of little consequence."

Frank McNitt's scholarly treatment of the cycle of war, slave raids and reprisals faithfully chronicles three centuries during which the survival of the Navajo nation was constantly threatened by white aggressors. It started with Coronado's arrival on the plains of New Mexico in 1540, lasted through the Fort Fauntleroy massacre of 1861, and then moved westward to Bosque Redondo between 1863 and 1868. McNitt lays bare the tragic history of mistreatment and all-out war by early Spanish settlers, then Mexicans, then Americans. They all wanted what the Navajos had—land, pastures, water, and a peaceful pastoral existence. He posits in his book that all three cultures and their governments were "essentially alike in their mistreatment of the Navajos and that all attacks and depredations followed the pattern that visited on the Indians the ancient slaving practices of Mediterranean Europe." McNitt's preface to his 1972 book sums up the Navajo experience well, and seems particularly apt for what Angus, my fictional character, might have felt, had he been real. "The wonder of it is that the Navajos not only managed to survive but continued increasing in numbers until now [in 1972] they are the largest and most progressive tribe of Indians in the United States." The 2010 U.S. Census pegs the Navajo Tribe at 169,321. It is ten times larger than the second largest (the Pine Ridge Reservation in Nebraska).